NOW I HAVE A RAYGUN, HO HO HO!

An anthology of holiday-themed sci-fi stories—with recipes!

Edited by
JESSIE KWAK

EDITOR

Jessie Kwak

COVER ART AND DESIGN

Lena Semenkova

ORNAMENTAL BREAK

Elements by Freepik and Good Ware from www.flaticon.com.

PUBLISHER

Bad Intentions Press

Portland, OR, USA

For more information, please visit: jessiekwak.com/crooked

CONTENTS

THE STORIES MUST FLOW

For reasons forgotten to history, a few years ago I decided to throw a Dune-themed party around the holidays. It was primarily a reason to make a sandworm using my mom's famous cinnamon roll recipe, and to serve a Water of Life punch that was frankly terrible—I recall it being mainly vodka and blue curaçao, with a bunch of gummy worms "drowned" in it as a garnish.

I've never made the punch again, because I do actually have culinary standards, but the Spice Roll Shai-Hulud has become a regular part of our holiday celebrations each year.

What can I say? The spice must flow. And it must especially flow around the winter solstice celebrations.

I will never pass up an opportunity to make a themed party meal—particularly if it's nerdy. And, apparently, I also won't pass up an opportunity to edit a holiday- and recipe-themed sci-fi anthology.

When I was ~~blackmailed into editing~~ invited to

edit this collection, I knew it would be a good time. I've featured several of these incredible authors in my *CROOKED* sci-fi crime anthologies in the past, and I was excited to return to their delightful worlds and spend more time with their beloved characters.

While the *CROOKED* sci-fi crime anthologies sometimes got a little dark (they're shelved in the seedy underbelly of the sci-fi shelf for a reason), *Now I Have a Raygun, Ho-Ho-Ho* is (mostly) anything but.

You'll find cookie capers, jolly toy thieves, and latkes that save the universe. People will go to great lengths to rescue each other from pirates, help each other out of tight spots, and feed each other delicious meals—even when times are tough.

Especially when times are tough.

It's the holiday spirit, stretching into the farthest reaches of the universe.

Each of these stories involves a holiday dish of some sort—some inspired by the world itself, some inspired by the author and their own traditions. All of them look amazing.

Please enjoy the adventure! Both in reading the stories themselves, and in making the delightful recipes that accompany them.

And remember: life's hard out here in the black. It's up to us to take care of each other.

Cheers,
Jessie Kwak

SPICE ROLL SHAI-HULUD

Ingredients:

Dough

- 1 T yeast
- 1 c warm water
- 1/3 c sugar
- 1/2 c melted butter
- 1 t salt
- 2 eggs
- 4 c flour

Spread & Teeth

- 1/4 c butter (room temp)
- 1 c brown sugar
- 2 T cinnamon
- 1 T nutmeg
- 1/2 T ground cloves
- 1/2 T allspice
- 1/4 c slivered almonds

Icing:

- 1 c powdered sugar
- 1-2 t water or milk

Instructions:

1. Mix together dough ingredients to form a soft dough. Let rise until doubled. (About 1 hour.) Then, preheat the oven to 400°.

2. Once doubled, punch down and roll into a 1/2" thick rectangle that's about 18" long by 12" wide.

3. Spread dough with butter, then mix brown sugar and spices together and sprinkle over the top of the butter. Feel free to adjust spice combination to taste. Do not be afraid to add more spice, if you so desire. The spice must flow.

4. Roll dough into a log. (A worm-shape, if you will.) Gently taper one end into a tail, while leaving the other end fairly flat.

5. Coil Shai-Hulud carefully on a baking sheet, then decorate the flatter of the two ends by sticking rows of almond slivers into the dough to form a horrific maw. Try to angle them inward, but be warned that as Shai-Hulud bakes its teeth will splay maniacally in all directions. This cannot be helped.

6. Using a sharp crysknife or razor, slash segments across Shai-Hulud's back, about 1/4" deep, every 2" or so.

7. Bake at 400° for 15-20 minutes, checking after 15 minutes to make sure it's not getting burned. Your Shai-Hulud is finished when it's a nice dark golden brown. Don't be afraid to let it get a little darker than you think of cinnamon rolls as being. Too pale, and it won't have cooked through.

8. Meanwhile, mix the icing. Add enough milk (or water) to the powdered sugar to make it spread-able but not runny. While Shai-Hulud is still pretty hot, spread the icing over the top to make a yummy glaze.

9. Once cooled, share your Spice Roll Shai-Hulud with the rest of your sietch in a celebration of friendship and nerdy community.

COOKIES FOR MISKO

by R.M. Olson

THE THING ABOUT PRASVISHONI IN THE WINTER, Jez reflected, was that it was basically crap. Prasvishoni was always a little cold and a little damp and a little miserable, but in the winter, the sharp bite of the air turned vicious, the wind seeking out the cracks in your scarf or between your mittens and your sleeves, driving the icy sleet against your skin, the sky overcast and claustrophobic with clouds. And this part of winter was always the worst—she remembered it from when she was a kid.

Well, she thought philosophically, at least running for her life kept her a little warmer.

She skidded around the corner of a building, heat blasts pursuing her from the alley she'd just exited, and grabbed for a hold to keep her boots from sliding out from under her on the slick cobblestones. She flattened herself against the wall, gasping. Her pursuers' footsteps pounded after her, and she grinned to herself.

The first of her pursuers appeared in the mouth

of the alley. He'd probably meant to slow, check up and down the street for her. Instead, he skidded across the long stretch of black ice and slammed into the corner of a building on the other side of the street before landing hard. He was followed momentarily by another man, then two women, then a handful of others who, honestly, Jez hadn't really had time to figure out much more about them than that they were trying to kill her. Seemed like the most important detail at that point, to be honest.

The second and third of her pursuers slammed into the first, who'd been trying to get to his feet, causing all three of them to go down in a heap. The fourth didn't make it all the way across the street before executing an impressive fall that had left her momentarily with no point of contact with the ground, and the others had tangled up at the mouth of the alley and gone down in a cursing pile.

"Hey, you plaguers!" she called cheerily. "Not supposed to run on ice, you know. Might fall and hurt yourself or whatever."

The first man, who'd managed to struggle to his hands and knees, grabbed for his heat gun and fired. She yelped and ducked back into the alley as the air above her head sizzled, then snapped off a shot of her own. He tried to dive out of the way, lost his footing entirely, and landed spread-eagle on the ice. She grinned and started off, the sound of their furious cursing following her down the alley like holiday music.

Prasvishoni in the winter was basically crap, but it did have its advantages.

"Jez? Are you alright?" Tae's voice through her earpiece was worried, like always.

"I'm good, tech-head," she said, tapping her com. "Hey, remember that stupid street corner on Rybochka Street that was always covered in black ice because the bastards in government never paid for it to be cleared? Apparently they still don't."

"Jez, what the hell—" He didn't sound noticeably less worried.

"Also, you can tell Lev that he was right about those plaguers from the outer-rim planet having friends here."

"What happened?" He sounded like he was speaking through his teeth.

"To me, or to them?"

"Jez..."

She grinned. "Told you, I'm good. I'll tell you everything when I get back."

She reached the hangar bay where she'd left the *Ungovernable* and ducked inside, blinking as her eyes adjusted to the dim light. Then she paused a moment, just like always, and let her eyes run over her perfect ship.

She'd never get used to this. She'd never see her beautiful ship, its elegant curves gleaming in the low light, its entire graceful shape whispering of speed and flight and deep space and everything she loved, and not have a spark of utter wonder light in her chest and a thick knot start in her throat.

"Hey, beautiful, I'm back," she whispered. A soft

smile had spread across her face all by itself, and happiness suffused her chest, light and warm and perfect.

"Well, I suppose we know she's alive, anyways." Ysbel's heavy outer-rim accent was unmistakable. Jez tore her attention off her perfect angel ship with an effort.

Lev and Ysbel waited for her at the base of the gangplank. Ysbel looked as intimidating as always, with her shaved head and pale skin and visible weaponry and the bulk of her muscles apparent even under heavy winter clothes.

"Hey, you bastards," Jez said cheerfully. "'Course I'm alive. You think a few plaguers with heat-guns would be able to take me out?"

Sudden sharp concern crossed Lev's face. "Heat guns? Who was..." He stopped himself with an effort and took a deep breath. "I'm glad you're alright, Jez."

She loved her ship. Hell, she wasn't sure what she felt for the *Ungovernable* could be called something as simple as love. The ship was basically a part of her, and she loved it the way you loved the air in your lungs and the blood in your veins. But honestly...there was something about Lev, with his disheveled dark hair and rumpled clothing and scholarly air and the softness in his eyes when he looked at her that felt a hell of a lot like home.

"Hey, genius." She leaned in to kiss him, and he slid his arms around her and kissed her back, and OK, so this was another thing she could definitely get used to. His mouth was warm on hers, the shape of his body familiar and comfortable, and his hands tightening around her back were sending pleasant shivers through her entire body...

Ysbel cleared her throat pointedly.

Jez ignored her.

She cleared her throat again.

Finally, reluctantly, Jez broke off the kiss and turned, shooting Ysbel a mild glare.

Ysbel raised an eyebrow. "I am very glad you two are so happy to see each other. But there are private rooms on the *Ungovernable*. And also, I believe the others are waiting to hear why there were people with heat guns chasing you through the streets of Prasvishoni." She shook her head. "With anyone else, I'd be surprised they were being shot at under two hours after arriving in the city. But since it's you..."

Jez gave her a jaunty grin. "I know, I know, not many people as hot as me around here."

"That wasn't exactly what I meant," Ysbel muttered. "Come on, our tech-head is probably worrying."

"Tech-head wouldn't know what to do with himself if he wasn't worrying about something." She slipped an arm around Lev and they started up the gangplank.

Ysbel had been right—when they reached the main deck, the entire crew was waiting for them. Tae looked worried, as always, the scowl on his dark face half-obscured by the tangle of wavy hair he'd shoved impatiently back, which always made him look a little younger than his twenty-odd years. Ivan, beside him, tall and elegant, looked concerned, and Masha managed that pleasant, mild expression that was basically her damn trademark. Even after how long Jez had known her, she couldn't quite help a little jolt of surprise sometimes at how damn...ordinary Masha looked, with her average brown skin and her average dark hair pulled back in a businesslike rat's tail, her clothing neat but just rumpled enough not to draw attention. Unless you knew her, that was, and could see the sharp, dangerous intelligence under her pleasant expression.

Tanya stood with the children. She had long brown hair and skin as pale as Ysbel's, and her slender build and wistful look made it easy to forget she could kill people with her bare damn hands. Six-year-old Misko was holding her hand and bouncing up and down in excitement. Olya, who was eight, stood beside him. She was clearly trying to look more mature than her little brother, but there was excitement on her face as well.

"Aunty Jez!" Misko shouted the moment she stepped through the door. "Aunty Jez Aunty Jez Aunty Jez! Did you bring me the cookies?" He let go of Tanya's hand and pelted across the floor, grabbing Jez's legs hard enough that she almost lost her balance.

"Misko, wait to see if your Aunty is hurt first!" Tanya called.

"Ah, Misko knows the bad guys couldn't hurt me if they tried," said Jez, reaching down to ruffle the kid's hair.

Olya, who'd followed her brother at a more sedate pace, glanced up at her and raised a skeptical eyebrow. "Really, Aunty Jez? Because do you remember that time when my mamochka had to put like three heat-blast bandages on your leg after you'd gotten shot? And the time when you broke your arm? And the time..."

Jez shook her head, still grinning. "Ah, that was only because I let them."

Olya was still giving her a skeptical look, and Ysbel was hiding a grin. Jez gave a mock sigh. "Alright, fine, gang up on me, why don't you?"

"May I ask what exactly happened out there?" Masha's tone was as pleasantly polite as usual.

"Well," Jez drawled, "I figure genius here was right—the damn bastards who were mad at us for basically no reason back on that zestava have friends in Prasvishoni."

"When you say, 'basically no reason,' I assume you are referring to the fact that you robbed them blind and Tae hacked through and deleted all the data from their systems?" Masha asked dryly.

Jez shrugged. "Like I said."

Tae blew out a breath. "Look. They were weapons dealers, and for once in my damn life, probably, I agree with Jez—they deserved everything they got. But..." He shook his head. "I was hoping they were just local weapons dealers. I was really, really hoping they weren't connected to organized crime in Prasvishoni."

"What does this mean, then?" asked Ivan, his forehead creased in a frown.

Lev sighed. "It means, most likely, that we need to stay away from the city until we can come up with a plan to take care of this. I'm not sure we're currently in a place to take on the organized crime infrastructure in Prasvishoni without knowing more than we do."

"Lev is right," said Masha. "We aren't equipped to deal with this at the moment. And considering tomorrow night is Zimniye Prazdnik, it's hardly a good time to get into a heat-gun fight in the streets. Our best option, I think, is to head off-planet and take stock."

"The cookies?" Misko demanded, clearly too excited to wait.

Jez sighed. "Hey Misko, I'm sorry. I didn't get to the cookies before the bastards started shooting at me. I got you this, though." She rummaged in her bag and pulled out some slightly crumbled honey cake.

Misko looked it, then back up at her, his face falling. "You said you were going to get us gribochky cookies," he said in a small voice. It made something in Jez's chest hurt a little.

Dammit, she kind of hated being reminded of what it felt like to be a kid and to be disappointed.

"Yeah," she said, crouching down to his level. "I know. I tried, I promise. But they were all out by the time I got there and there won't be more until tomorrow."

His lip trembled a little.

"It's just cookies, Misko," said Olya, stepping forward. She took her brother's hand. "It's not a big deal. We can always have them another time." She was clearly putting on a brave face.

Misko's lip was still trembling. "But I've never had them before, and tomorrow is Zimniye Prazdnik night. And Uncle Lev said how good they were, and Aunty Masha, and Mamochka..."

"Well, sometimes we can't always get what we want," said Olya. "Anyways, last time it was Zimniye Prazdnik, we were living in the prison, remember?"

Misko shivered. "I didn't like it there," he said softly.

"Yeah," said Olya. "Neither did I. So we don't have to complain about cookies, right?"

Misko nodded dejectedly.

Tanya looked up at the rest of them ruefully. "Come on, Ysi," she said to her wife, "I think it's bedtime for the children."

"Mama, I want the bedtime story about the time you blew up a whole spaceship," said Misko, perking up a little.

"Well..." Ysbel began, casting a quick look at Tanya, "I'm not sure..."

"Or how about the time when you told that bad guy that if he didn't leave our Aunty Jez alone, you would..."

"Perhaps we can discuss this with your mamochka," said Ysbel.

"Or the time that Mamochka took out an entire squadron of police officer bastards..."

Ysbel glanced at the expression on Tanya's face and shooed the children ahead of her out of the room. "Go on, you two. And you know you're not supposed to say that word until you're older, Misko."

"Bastard? But Aunty Jez always..."

"Go!"

"Yes, go on, please," said Tanya. Her tone said

she was planning to have a serious talk with Jez in the very near future.

Jez grinned as the kids allowed themselves to be herded down the corridor towards their bedroom. Then she sighed. "There weren't any gribochky cookies, I checked. Apparently they basically sell out first thing in the morning this close to Zimniye Prazdnik. We'd have to wait for tomorrow to get any."

"I know," said Lev, sliding his arm around her and leaning in to kiss her temple. "And the kids know it too. They might be a little disappointed, but they know you tried."

"I'm certain we'll make it back here on Zimniye Prazdnik another year," Masha murmured. "The important thing is that we're all safe."

"Yeah," said Jez. "I mean, I don't actually remember ever getting gribochky cookies during Prazdnik when I was a kid. And hell, I left home when I was fourteen. Usually was doing smuggler runs during the holidays, that was our busy season."

"It's not like there won't be other Zimniye Prazdniki, right?" said Tae.

It was quiet for a moment.

"Dammit, it's not fair!" Jez burst out at last. "They're just kids. And they spent their whole damn lives in prison, basically, and they've never had gribochky cookies, and tomorrow is Zimniye Prazdnik night, and..." She gestured helplessly.

Lev tightened his arm around her briefly. "I know," he said in a low voice. "I know."

The silence stretched for a few moments more. Still, no one turned to leave.

"You're going to stay to get the cookies, aren't you?" Ivan said at last. There was a small smile on his face.

Tae blew out a breath and shook his head ruefully.

"I mean, getting some cookies for two children hardly seems like the most complicated plan we've carried out in the past...however the hell many months it's been," said Lev, a trace of resigned amusement in his voice.

"Getting cookies for two children while the entirety of the organized crime infrastructure of Prasvishoni is trying to kill us, you mean?" Masha's voice was also wry.

Lev turned to her, raising his eyebrows. "Are you saying you don't think we should do this?"

Masha sighed. "No. I am saying it's rather foolish. But I'm also saying that never seems to have stopped us in the past, and had I thought about it for five minutes, I would have realized this outcome was more or less inevitable. And..." She paused. "And, I suppose, children should be allowed their gribochky cookies, organized crime notwithstanding."

Ysbel and Tanya found them in the conference room a few minutes later. Ysbel stepped inside, stopped, and raised her eyebrows. "I thought we were getting ready to go."

Jez winked at her. "Yep, we are. We just figured we'd get Misko and Olya some cookies first."

Tanya stepped in after Ysbel. "What..." she began. Then she must have realized what Jez had said.

She looked around the conference room at the five of them, then at Ysbel. Then she looked down, blinking hard. After a moment, she cleared her throat. "I'm sorry," she said, her voice a little thick. "It's only that I was never able to give them that while we were in prison. This is their first Zimniye Prazdnik outside of prison, and I wanted so badly..." She stopped. "Thank you," she finished softly.

Ysbel leaned in and kissed her wife gently.

"Hey Ysbel, there are private damn rooms on the *Ungovernable*," Jez said, grinning.

Ysbel shot her a flat look, sighed heavily, and turned to Tanya. "Alright, my Tanya, I suppose we'd best find out what these lunatics have come up with so far."

Tanya smiled, the expression still a little watery, and nodded, and for some reason Jez had to swallow down a sudden lump in her throat.

She'd basically always been a little afraid of her parents, growing up. She'd thought that was normal. But...well, dammit, she was glad that Olya and Misko had parents like Ysbel and Tanya. Who, in fairness, were incredibly damn scary, but only to people who weren't Olya and Misko.

"So," said Ysbel, dropping into her seat. "What do you have for us, Lev?"

He looked up with a wry smile. "As plans go, it's not particularly sophisticated. However, it should be sufficient, I think." He pulled up his holoscreen with a map of Prasvishoni. "The local organized crime syndicate clearly already know we're here. I suspect it won't take them long to guess where the *Ungovernable* is. So Tae is going to put up blockers that will scramble their weapons and equipment if they get within a five-block radius of the ship, and Jez has volunteered to, and I quote, 'make the plaguers regret the fact that they ever heard about my damn ship' if they get too close; I presume she intends to booby-trap the entrance, but I am leaving that to her discretion." He paused. "And also, I'm not entirely sure my nerves would stand up to knowing the details. So. That's phase one."

Ysbel nodded slowly. "Alright. So that keeps us alive during the night, yes? But that doesn't get us the cookies."

"That's phase two," said Lev, enlarging a section of the map. "Here, if I recall correctly, is the largest Prazdnichnyy market. From all the information I have, and I will remind you that is substantial, there's a cookie seller here whose cookies are widely considered to be the best in the city."

Tanya was biting back a smile. "You researched this?"

Lev raised his eyebrows. "If we're going to risk our lives for gribochky cookies, we may as well make sure they're good ones."

"He does have a point," murmured Ysbel.

Lev turned back to his map. "By tomorrow morning, we'll have to assume our friends will be waiting for any of us to step outside Tae's blocker zone. Tanya, between you and Jez, I think you have the best chance of getting past them and getting to the market. Ivan has volunteered to stay with the children, and the rest of us will provide you with a distraction to give you a chance to get out."

Jez grinned and winked at Tanya. "And you're very damn lucky I'm coming with, because I'll be the one getting us a ride there."

Lev glanced at her in mild concern. "A ride?"

Jez gave him her most innocent look. "Hey, I'll bet there are plenty of police officers in Prasvishoni who'd be happy to lend their skybikes to help get gribochky cookies for a couple of kids." She paused. "By which I mean—"

"We all know what you mean, Jez," Tae said, his expression grim. "Look, I'd really like to not have to break you out of prison. Again."

Jez shrugged easily, still grinning. "Hell, I figure giving the police bastards a chance to actually do something decent for once in their damn lives is basically like a Prazdnichnyy gift, right?"

Tae sighed again and pinched the bridge of his nose like he was fighting a headache. Ivan looked like he was fighting a grin, and Lev's expression was something between worry and amusement.

"Alright, then." Lev shut down his holoscreen. "Does anyone have questions?"

"For a shopping trip, I believe your plan is sufficient," said Masha. "I'd say I'm very confident in our success except that I've flown with this crew for a while now. So I'll only say that, with a great deal of luck, I believe we may be able to purchase holiday cookies without anyone suffering severe bodily injury."

"Without any of *us* suffering severe bodily injury," said Ysbel. "Because I'm not going to make any promises about the people who are trying to kill us."

"Without anyone who is not trying to kill us suffering serious bodily injury," Masha amended.

"Alright," said Tae, shoving back his chair. "I'll put up the block around the hangar bay."

"And I'll go make sure that if the bastards try to come in anyways, they'll damn well start questioning their life choices," said Jez cheerfully. "Ysbel, you coming?"

By the time she and Ysbel returned to the hangar bay, Tae's blocker was already set. Which she knew, because a squadron of damn police officers who'd been walking down the street had stopped abruptly, frowning, shaking their coms and tapping their helmets as if trying to figure out why their earpieces weren't working, and then, to her absolute delight, trying with exactly zero success to restart their skybikes. The sight of half a dozen police officers dragging their skybikes after them as they trudged through the frozen streets was a pleasant ending to an altogether enjoyable day.

As it happened, there were only four explosions between the time Jez dropped into the cot she shared with Lev and the time the black darkness of night had turned to the black darkness of a morning in wintertime Prasvishoni. At the first, she sighed and snuggled deeper into the warmth of Lev's arms.

He kissed her forehead and murmured sleepily, "Do we need to get up to check on that?"

"Nope," she whispered back. "Didn't want to have to get up in this damn cold, so Ysbel and I made sure we wouldn't have to."

It was still dark outside when they finally got up, but hell, it was always dark in Prasvishoni in the winter—it would be late in the morning before the first reluctant rays of sun oozed over the horizon. They ate a quick breakfast, and then the six of them stepped outside to check on the explosions.

"Well, it looks like you were right, pilot-girl," said Ysbel, glancing at Jez. "This did keep them back. Considering if it hadn't, we'd see pieces of the ones who tried to get through splattered across the buildings on the other side of the street. But I'm very, very certain there will be plenty of them waiting for the first one of us to set foot outside Tae's blocker radius."

Jez sighed happily. This was actually looking to be a pretty damn good day, all things considered. "Alright, tell me when you plaguers are ready and I'll go find a ride for Tanya and me."

Lev's voice came through her com a few minutes later. "Ysbel's about to get their attention. You ready?"

Jez glanced at Tanya, who nodded.

"Heading out now," she said, tapping her com. "I'll be there in ten minutes or so."

Fetching the skybikes, it turned out, was a simple enough exercise. When she pulled up in front of where Tanya waited just outside the range of Tae's blocker, Tanya raised her eyebrows. "No heat-gun blasts? I'm impressed."

Jez grinned. "Don't know why you'd think there

would be." She paused, glancing over her shoulder. "But we should probably get going."

Tanya gave her a look. She shrugged. "I mean, apparently there were like three squadrons of police officers who weren't really feeling the holiday spirit and whatever. I lost them back there, but I'm pretty sure they're going to catch up in a minute here. So..."

Tanya heaved a sigh and swung onto her skybike, muttering something under her breath as sirens wailed in the distance.

Jez glanced over her shoulder again, then turned and gave Tanya a wink. "OK, new plan—I'll catch you up at the market. Got to give those plaguers some morning exercise."

It was five squadrons of police by the time they reached the place Jez waited for them, and she smiled to herself nostalgically as she took off, leaning low over her bike, the freezing Prasvishoni air burning her cheeks and making her eyes water and her teeth ache even through her thick scarf as heat blasts crackled around her. It had been a while since she'd been in a damn police chase.

She led them down a street, through a couple alleys, popped up over a building, and then turned and headed back in the direction she'd come.

"Give yourself up and we'll take you in peaceful-ly," one of them shouted through their voice amp.

"Well, I would, but honestly, how slow you're flying, probably don't have time for how damn long it'd take you to catch up to me," she called back, activating the voice amp on her com. "But if you need some flying lessons, I probably could..."

Heat blasts scorched the air above her, and she grinned and leaned forward, sending the bike careening down the narrow alley. "Hey Lev," she said into her com. "You ready for us? Because we're heading your way."

"Just give me a second..." he said. There was a muffled explosion in the background and the confused sound of several people cursing loudly. "Alright, we're ready," he finished.

She flipped up the map Tae had sent through to her com with one hand, steering with the other, and took a sharp turn. The police were close on her tail now, and she held back, letting them get even closer. She burst out of the alley and up into the shipping lanes over the street, and the police followed. Then, when she was right above where Lev had indicated on the map, she hit the controls on her bike, letting herself go into temporary free-fall. A patchwork of heat blasts turned the air momentarily visible in the place she'd been a moment before. She hit the controls again when she was close enough to the icy cobblestones below that her boots almost scraped the ground, and the bike coughed and shot forwards. She whooped in delight as the police dove after her and sent her bike straight for Tae's blocker.

She pulled up at the last instant, sending her bike shooting skyward.

The police didn't.

From high overhead, she smiled to herself in pleasant satisfaction at the sound of several dozen police officers abruptly and simultaneously losing power to their skybikes.

A moment later, there was a shout as the local

Prasvishoni organized crime syndicate came around a corner and discovered the police.

Normally, she would have expected heat blasts. Since both parties' weapons had been completely disabled by the blocker, she wasn't sure what they'd do next—fistfight, maybe? She grinned.

"Never mind about the flying lessons," she called down to the police. "Looks like you haven't got any bikes to practice on anyways. And also, looks like you might be a little busy there for a bit."

She flipped her bike around and started after Tanya.

They left their bikes in an alley just outside the market and walked up the small street towards it, their boots crunching in the dirty skiff of snow that lay like soot over the cobblestones. Even from here, the rich smells of sugar and butter and baking and the delightfully sharp scent of alcohol hung heavy in the air. The sounds of people bartering and laughing and the bright colours from the awnings over the stalls made the whole scene look like something she'd expect to see on a small off-world zestava rather than the dreary, cheerless streets of Prasvishoni.

The sight brought back a sudden flood of unwelcome memories from a long damn time ago, when she was just a stupid kid and still thought the world was basically supposed to be fair.

She stopped a moment and had to swallow hard. Dammit, they were here to get gribochky cookies for the kids; this was a stupid time to get all sad and crap about things that had happened a long damn time ago, and anyways, didn't even really matter.

"Jez? Are you alright?" Tanya's voice was gentler than usual. Jez blinked hard and pasted on a grin.

"Yep, I'm good. Just...thinking."

Tanya's gaze was far too perceptive, but she only nodded. "Alright, then. Come on."

It only took a few moments to locate the stall of the man selling the little mushroom-shaped cookies, with caps decorated in multiple colours and sprinkled with sugar. There was already a lineup, even this early in the morning. Tanya bought a box full, and then they browsed through the stalls for a bit. Tanya picked out a few small gifts for the children and Jez grabbed a scarf that Lev would probably like, and some crap for Masha and Tae and Ivan and Ysbel, and something for Tanya, too, when she wasn't looking. She looked at the gifts dubiously, but hell, she'd never really done this before and she honestly didn't know what sort of things people gave each other for gifts.

"Are you finished?"

Jez turned to find Tanya standing at her elbow. She forgot sometimes how quiet Tanya could be when she wanted to be.

"Yep." She grinned jauntily.

Tanya glanced at the bag and narrowed her eyes. "You paid for those things, right?"

Jez gave her an offended look. "'Course I did."

Tanya raised her eyebrows.

"Well, I mean, I paid for most of them." She reached into the bag and extracted a bottle of alcohol. "Didn't pay for this because I saw the damn bastard selling it throw a rock at a street kid. So I thought..." She shrugged.

"Ah," said Tanya, amusement in her voice. "And all you did was take that?"

"Well, OK, maybe I took two of them. And maybe I dumped the other one over the electronics on his damn skybike," Jez conceded.

"Good," said Tanya. "Let's go, then, before our friends stop fighting and decide to come find us instead."

The ride back to the *Ungovernable* was uneventful. Tanya radioed ahead to Tae, who took the blocker down as they approached, and Lev, Ysbel, Tae, and Masha waited for them a couple blocks out from the ship.

"Well?" asked Ysbel as they came up. "Did you get them?"

Jez and Tanya pulled up on their bikes at the corner and slid off. Tanya took the bag of gifts she'd bought the children to show Ysbel, and Jez sauntered over to Lev. He was waiting for her, smiling that soft smile that always turned her insides to mush, and he pulled her in for a quick kiss. She kissed him back, and maybe she didn't exactly hurry about it because hell, it had been basically forever since she'd last kissed him. Three hours or so at the very least.

When she pulled back, he was watching her with that mix of affection and hunger that made her entire body feel warm.

"Hey, genius," she whispered in his ear. "Ysbel

keeps telling me there are private rooms on the *Ungovernable*. You want to..."

The explosion shook the street.

All six of them looked at each other. Then they sprinted around the corner to the bikes.

There was nothing left of the place where the bikes had been but a large crater in the street. A handful of rough-looking people stood around the scene of the explosion, grim satisfaction on their faces, and one of them pulled out a heat gun as they rounded the corner. He was smiling, but it wasn't a nice smile.

"Unfortunately for you, we happen to know all the police around here. You might say we have a bit of a partnership. They gave us the tracking on your bikes, and then it was just a matter of waiting for you here until the blocker came down."

Tanya's already pale face had gone a shade paler. Now, she looked up, meeting the man's gaze. "Those were gribochky cookies for my children," she said.

There was something in her voice that, if Jez was on the other side of it, would have made her suddenly very uncertain about her prospects of surviving the next five minutes.

The man frowned. "I think your bigger concern should be the fact I'm about to kill you," he snapped. "Now..."

Tae was scowling down at his com, tapping something quickly. Now he glanced up, face grim. "No," he said. "I don't think you're going to kill anyone. Because I just put the blocker back up."

The man made as if to fire the pistol.

Nothing happened.

His face went suddenly very pale.

Ysbel looked at the assembled group of criminals, her expression even flatter than usual. "Do you know how much time my wife spent getting those cookies?" she asked. Her tone was conversational, if the conversation had been about dismembering someone with a dull gutting knife.

"Um," said the man who'd been holding the heat gun, his voice suddenly much less certain. "I'm certain you can buy some more."

"They'll be out by now." Tanya's voice was solid ice. "My children are waiting for me to get back with gribochky cookies for tonight, and I will have to disappoint them."

The man swallowed visibly.

"I don't like people who upset my children," said Ysbel. "And I don't like people who upset my wife. And you have done both just now."

The man seemed to be trying to shrink down into his coat. The people standing behind him were now huddled together into a tight mass of regret.

Lev turned to Masha. "Well," he said pleasantly, "I suppose if we have to go back and tell the children we don't have gribochky cookies for them, at least we can tell them a funny story about what happened to the people who blew their cookies up."

"Wait!" the man said desperately.

"Yes?" asked Tanya. Jez hadn't honestly realized someone could put that much menace into one word.

The man swallowed again. "My...my father taught me how to make gribochky cookies. I...I could probably..."

"How long will it take?"

Honestly, Tanya could basically teach classes about how to make death threats out of phrases that really shouldn't sound threatening at all.

"I have a stove in my apartment," one of the men in the back volunteered nervously.

"We have people all over the city," said a woman. "If I call in an emergency, we could probably get the ingredients in under ten minutes."

"They take less than fifteen minutes to bake," the first man said, his expression pleading. "And if I had help with putting them together..."

"Tanya?" asked Lev, still in that pleasant tone.

She cocked her head to one side, considering. "The place I got those cookies was a very good place," she said at last. "The cookies were supposed to be delicious."

"These are very delicious, too. I swear it." There was sweat standing out on the man's forehead. "It's an old family recipe. People were always asking my father for it, but he wouldn't give it out to anyone but family."

Tanya glanced at Ysbel. At last, she turned back to the man. "Half a standard hour," she said, her tone pure steel.

The man nodded so hard his toque almost fell off his head. "Half an hour."

Tae had a screen pulled up over his com. He glanced up. "I've got tracking on them," he said. "We'll know if they decide to try to take off."

"We won't," said the man fervently. "I swear, we'll bake the cookies and come back."

"Good," said Ysbel. Her smile was more a threat

than a smile. "Because if you do, it won't be hard to find you."

The man closed his eyes, as if either sending up a prayer to the Lady or briefly contemplating his demise.

"It's been a minute and a half already," Lev observed to no one in particular.

Their erstwhile attackers looked at each other, then started off down the street at a pace just short of a run.

The newly minted bakers returned to the square with two minutes to spare and a large, gaudily wrapped box.

Tanya inspected the cookies narrowly, and Masha tasted one. She raised her eyebrows. "My complements to your father," she said, turning to the man.

He gave her a wan, terrified smile.

"I suppose I will refrain from killing you this time," said Ysbel. "Think of it as an early Prazdnichnyy gift."

The man nodded nervously and began to back away. Within a moment, the entire group had scattered.

The walk back to the *Ungovernable* was pleasant, despite the icy air. Generally, Jez figured walking was wasting time you could have been flying, but with all of them walking together in companionable silence, snow drifting down in fat flakes that clung to her eyelashes and the edge of her toque and the warm, sweet smell of freshly baked cookies wafting from the box, Lev's mittened hand in hers...honestly, she could get used to this.

Tanya had called ahead to Ivan to let him know they were on their way, and by the time they stepped into the hangar bay, Olya and Misko were waiting at the bottom of the gangplank. Ivan smiled ruefully. "I told them to wait in the ship, but they were too excited."

Olya was clasping her brother's hand to hold him back, the look on her face wavering between excitement and the caution of someone who'd been disappointed too many times in the past.

"Hey, Olya," said Lev, and there was something in his voice that made Jez think he'd noticed too. "Your mamochka has something for you for when we're back in space, I think."

Tanya smiled. "I do. I'll let you see when the *Ungovernable's* taken off again, alright?"

The children's eyes went wide, and Olya's hand tightened on her brother's.

"Ow! Olya let go!" Misko grumbled.

"Well, I was just holding your hand because you always go running off when you're not supposed to," said Olya in a superior tone.

"I do not!" Misko shouted, his face lit with righteous indignation.

"Alright, you two, up you go," said Ysbel, turning them gently and shoeing them up the ramp. "You can't see what Mamochka brought until we're up in space, so we may as well get going."

The rest of them followed the children up the ramp. Tanya and Ysbel got the children settled, and finally, Jez stepped back into the cockpit of the *Ungovernable*.

She sat down in the pilot seat and closed her eyes a moment, basking in the feeling of it. Even after all this time, just being in the cockpit of her perfect, perfect ship still made a lump form in her throat.

"Hey, beautiful," she whispered, running her hands gently over the controls. "You miss me?" She pulled up the power and the ship hummed to life under her feet, the steady vibration soothing and comfortable and as much a part of her as the blood pumping through her veins. "Strap in, you plaguers, we're heading out," she called, and listened contentedly over the com to the panicked scrambling from the main deck.

Lev slipped into the cockpit a moment later and took his place in the copilot seat, tapping the control to open the hangar bay. Jez hit the throttle on the *Ungovernable*. They shot forward, and she smiled in absolute bliss as she maneuvered her beautiful angel ship through the narrow streets of Prasvishoni. By the time they were through the city gates and outside of the forcefield and she'd pointed the *Ungovernable's* nose for the sky, Lev's face was a little pale.

The ship trembled ever-so-slightly as they shot up through the atmosphere, and then, finally, shallow space stretched out around them, black and beautiful and perfect. She set the controls, then leaned back in her seat, letting the peace of it wash over her like a warm bath.

When she opened her eyes at last, Lev was watching her, his expression fond. "You ready?" he asked. "Ysbel just called and said she and Tanya had finished hiding the presents, and I'd hate to keep Misko waiting any longer than I have to. For Ysbel's and Tanya's sake as much as anything."

She laughed and jumped up, holding out her hand. He took it and pulled himself up as well, and OK, so maybe when he was standing there so close to her, the vast expanse of space spreading out around them through the plex windows of the cockpit like a pool of ink, she might have pulled him in for a kiss. And he might have kissed her back, and maybe there was something about his kiss, just like always, that made her whole damn body go shaky in a warm, pleasant way—but hell, no one could really blame her for that, probably.

When they wandered back onto the main deck, the others were already there.

"Aunty Jez! Uncle Lev! We were waiting for you!" Misko's voice was a mix of excitement and impatience.

"They were probably kissing," Olya whispered to him loudly. "They always kiss when they think people aren't looking."

Ysbel shot Jez a pointed look and Jez grinned. "I mean, if you wanted a demonstration..."

"Jez, believe me, none of us needs any more demonstrations from you two," Tae muttered.

"Alright," said Tanya. "Who wants presents and gribochky cookies?"

The children squealed with delight and took off down the *Ungovernable's* corridors.

"I hid the presents in places you can reach, no need to climb up on anything!" Tanya called after them. Ysbel pulled her in and kissed her hair, and the two of them watched after the children, soft smiles on their faces.

Lev slipped his arm around Jez's waist, and she leaned her head on his shoulder.

It didn't take long for the kids to find the gifts and bring them out onto the main deck. They unwrapped them noisily, shouting and laughing, and finally, Tanya brought down the box of cookies.

The children watched wide-eyed as she opened it, and then they just stared.

"Olya! Look! They look like little mushrooms!" Misko whispered in a tone just below a shout. "I want the yellow one!"

"Well, I want the red one," said Olya, reaching in to take it.

"These are my favourite food in the entire system!" Misko said through a mouthful of crumbs. "When I grow up I'm going to eat them for dinner every single day!"

"Don't talk with your mouth full, Misko," said Tanya, but she was smiling softly.

Olya had finished her first cookie, and she took a second, turning it over in her fingers to study it. "How did they make it like this, Uncle Lev?" she asked, looking up.

Lev shook his head ruefully. "I'm not actually certain." He glanced at Masha. "It occurs to me that if any of us had been a competent baker, it's possible we could have avoided this entire adventure."

Jez bumped him with her shoulder. "What's the

fun in that? We got to harass a few police officers, check out a Prazdnichnyy market, blow some crap up..."

He smiled at her. She grinned back, then sobered a bit. "Um. Anyways. I got you a present too, because, like, Zimniye Prazdnik and whatever, but it was still on the bike when the bastards blew it up. Sorry." She paused, and cleared her throat. "Um. I didn't...OK, so holidays weren't really a good thing when I was a kid. You know. So I guess I'm not really actually the best at them."

He leaned in to kiss her. "I think you're perfect at them," he whispered. "Who else could have taken down five squadrons of police on their way to go shopping for cookies?" He grinned a little. "And I have something for you." He rummaged in his pocket. "I got it a little while back, but I thought I'd save it, since I know holidays weren't always the best for you. I thought maybe this might make it a little better."

She stared at him for a moment, and actually she was pretty sure there was something in her eyes, because suddenly she was blinking back absolutely ridiculous tears.

"Go on, open it," he said, and she pulled off the wrapping. Then she gasped, running her fingers over the smooth surface of the gorgeous thing inside.

"I figured since you didn't really need speed capacitors for the *Ungovernable* anymore, you might want one you could hook up to a skybike," he said.

She was still staring at it, except the tears were a little bit blurring her vision now and she had to squeeze her eyes shut for a moment.

"Aunty Jez! Aunty Jez!" Misko was shouting, tugging on her arm, and she blinked her eyes open.

He held out a cookie for her, the chocolate top on it a little melted from his warm hand. "I saved it for you because you said you didn't used to have them when you were little."

"We both saved it for you," said Olya importantly.

She couldn't really speak, and she actually wasn't even sure what she would have said anyways. She brushed her sleeve across her eyes and took the cookie and bit into it. It was soft and sweet and tasted of chocolate, the crumbs melting on her tongue.

"This is the best holiday ever," Misko declared jubilantly, his mouth once more full of cookie.

And looking around the cozy deck of her ship, full of people who she cared about a whole hell of a lot more than she'd ever thought she'd care about anyone and who, for some ridiculous reason, cared about her back...Jez couldn't honestly disagree.

"Cookies for Misko" features the crew of the Ungovernable series, by R.M. Olson. To read more about their adventures and misadventures, or to read more by R.M. Olson, check out rmolson.com.

RECIPE: GRIBOCHKY COOKIES

from R.M. Olson's "Cookies for Misko"

MAKES 30-35 COOKIES

Ingredients:

- 2 1/4 cups all purpose flour
- 1/2 cup corn starch
- 1/4 tsp sea salt
- 1/2 tsp baking powder
- 1 1/4 cups sugar
- 1/2 cup unsalted butter at room temperature
- 1 egg at room temperature
- 1/2 cup sour cream Let this sit out about an hour before hand.
- 1 tbsp vanilla extract
- Additional flour for your hands and rolling the dough.

For assembling/decorating:

- semisweet baking chocolate or chocolate chips
- icing sugar for dusting the tops of the cookies
- Oreo crumbs or green-dyed coconut flakes (optional)

If using white chocolate topping:

- red food colouring paste
- white chocolate baking squares or chocolate chips

If using glaze:

- red food colouring paste
- 1 cup icing sugar
- 1-2 tbsp milk

Mix together with a whisk or a fork until you have the colour and consistency you want and then dip the mushroom caps into it.

If using icing:

- red food colouring paste

- 1 cup icing sugar
- 1/3 cup butter
- 1/2 tsp vanilla
- pinch of salt

Mix together well with a bowl mixer or a hand-mixer until it's the colour and consistency you want. Use it to ice the mushroom caps.

Instructions:
Preheat the oven to 350 degrees.
Mix the dough:

- Sift or combine the flour, corn starch, sea salt and baking powder in a bowl and whisk.
- Cream together the butter and sugar. Then add in the egg, sour cream and vanilla and mix well.
- Add the flour mix to the butter mix little by little, about 1/2 cup at a time.

When the dough is thoroughly mixed, line a pan with parchment paper, dip your fingers in flour, and shape the cookies: for the mushroom tops, roll some dough (maybe a rounded half-tablespoon or so) into a ball and flatten it against your curved palm, so it's shaped like a mushroom cap. For the stems, take a bit of dough and roll it until it's about the width of your little finger and about half an inch long, and shape it into a cone with the bottom wider than the top (make the base nice and wide and flat, it's going to be supporting the whole cookie).

Place the pieces separately on the baking sheet (don't try to attach the tops to the bases just yet--we'll do that after they're cooked).

Bake for about 12 minutes. It's ok if they haven't browned when you pull them out.

While they're still warm, use the end of a spoon to make an indent into the bottom of the mushroom caps for a place to fit the stems. Let cool for about an hour. When the cookies are cooled, ice the top of the mushroom caps with red or other coloured icing/glaze or dip in dyed white chocolate. Then dip the narrow end of the stem in melted chocolate as "glue" and place the mushroom caps on top. Once the chocolate has dried and is holding the cookies together, sprinkle the top with powdered sugar to finish.

If you are feeling especially ambitious, you can dip the bottom of the stem into dark chocolate and then Oreo crumbs or green-dyed coconut flakes for grass/dirt.

FREEZER BURN

by K. Gorman

SHE CAME FOR HOLOSCREEN PARTS…AND GOT BURNED.

1

"A *week?*" Soo-jin emphasized, aghast. "We're here for a *week?*"

Cold blew in like from a broken cryopod. The first gust had chilled her to the bone. All the ones after were just…unnecessary. And *rude.*

Her first officer stood framed by the dirty shine of aged metal and *Huli Jing*'s tired security lighting. Beyond, draped in the frigid blue of the mountain's high-altitude twilight, the snowy wilderness they'd parked in resembled something straight from a winter postcard.

Which was *precisely* where she'd rather it had remained: in a picture. Not touching icy fingers all over her through the *open fucking door*.

And Zan wanted to go *out* in it? Without *Huli Jing*'s climate control? For a *week?*

Were they insane?

Yes. Probably. And also wearing more than her.

A *lot* more than her.

Definitely dressed for winter.

Shit. She'd thought they'd come here for parts. A simple one and done, bye and gone.

Had she missed something?

Probably.

"Yes." Zan's expression mottled in confusion, concerned brows furrowing as they perused her more carefully. "You *did* read my message, right?"

Message?

Hells.

She winced, guilty. "Refresh my memory?"

Zan blew out a breath, annoyance taking the place of confusion. The fresh winter breeze gusted around them, licking Soo-jin's bare arms with another admonishment. "I have a weeklong reservation with a friend at a Heian-style hot spring resort on the north side of the mountain, which I plan to greatly enjoy."

Ah.

"But why is there snow?"

"Because it provides an exquisite contrast to the heat, and snowy, broody nights at a candlelit hot spring, surrounded by Old World comforts, are what my heart aches for."

Okay, that did sound nice.

Really nice.

If she remembered correctly, the old Japanese-styled resorts here did amazing things with warmed liquor, too.

Hmm...

"Is there room for—"

"No." Zan huffed. "You need to find somewhere else to be."

Oh.

"I am also planning to greatly enjoy the company of an old friend. We're not interested in a third."

Understanding clicked—and she was suddenly *very glad* for the cold blowing through the door.

"Got it. Anything you need from me, other than a wide berth?"

"No. But I *did* park us next to Eisvel, and it's midwinter."

Wasn't midwinter the literal *coldest* part of the season?

Great.

But something in Zan's tone made her think she was missing something. *Again.*

"And that means...?"

Zan gave her a look. "Midwinter festival? In *Eisvel?* Come on. It's about as awesome as you can get. We're a week ahead of it, so we get the quiet, local version of the festival instead." Their eyes sparked. "Should be fun."

"I prefer my winter vacations closer to a planet's equator. Beachside, and above room temperature."

"That's not *winter*. You need snow! And ice!"

"I absolutely do *not*." And that hatch had stayed open *far* too long. She'd need to stoke the reactor just to warm the place up again. She waved them off. "Go. Have fun. I'll be fine. Got *lots* to occupy my time with."

Just because Zan took a holiday didn't mean she had to. She lived, and worked, on a spaceship. It didn't matter where she parked it, right? She had lots to do, her workshop was comfortable and familiar—and, best of all, *Huli Jing* had climate control.

She'd be fine.

Besides, *someone* had to install these new parts—and apparently, that someone would not be involving Zan.

It was the perfect downtime, really.

She totally wasn't jealous of Zan's hot spring plans at all.

Zan must have read something in her expression, because they hesitated.

"Soo-jin—"

She shooed them out. "Go. I'll be fine. I'm an adult."

Zan snorted. "Debatable."

"Ha *ha*."

Zan hesitated again. "Are you sure—"

"Oh my *gods*," she said, cutting them off with an eyeroll and a flourishingly dramatic wave of her hands. "*Go*. You're letting *all* the heat out. I'll be fine. Besides, Bob is here. It's not like I'll be alone."

Bob, the unofficial third member of their crew, was a multidimensional being known as a Shadow. He spent most of his time in a subdimension, but popped out to lurk in hallways, develop his speech center, and eavesdrop.

He also had a bad habit of stealing people's chocolate.

"You seen him lately?" Zan asked, curious.

"No, but you know him." She gestured around her. "Now that we've landed somewhere, he'll pop out to investigate."

For an entity allegedly linked to primordial chaos, he could be exceedingly predictable.

"Now *go*," she said, shooing them again. "I'll be fine!"

"Fine, fine. I'll go. But you should definitely check out the town. It'd do you good to get out."

"I'll think about it," she promised. "Now go have fun. You deserve it."

2

Two hours later, she was less confident in her decision to hole up in the ship and work.

The new parts—node replacements for one of *Huli Jing*'s vintage holoscreens—had taken less than an hour to install. Even a full test had barely pushed it over the hump of the clock. An old episode of Moon Sailor had killed another hour but not her ever-growing boredom.

And all her 'honey do' projects, though numerous, just...weren't catching her attention.

She forced herself to pick one up, anyway. Sometimes, you just had to *start* a project. It'd feel so much better once she'd finished. That's how brains were supposed to work, right? You did the good deeds, your neurons squirted some dopamine into the party, and the neurochemistry did a happy dance?

So, she put on music, sat at her workbench, and started cleaning a set of steering arms for an old groundcar she'd scrounged last year.

Thirty minutes later, when they looked exactly

the same except wetter, she sat back in disgust, muttered a swear, and rooted around for the heavy-duty cleaner she kept around for grunge that was being a persistent asshole.

Forty minutes later, after rediscovering the fault in her fume dispersal unit and nearly becoming another workplace safety statistic when it recirculated the fume-air right back into her workshop, she staggered to *Huli Jing's* exit and smashed the hatch release.

Ice-cold air blew over her, soothing the burning in her eyes and the shake of her body. Her throat took longer to recover, but the cold helped there, too.

Gods.

There'd been a reason she hadn't cleaned the steering arms yet, and that reason was 'faulty fume hood' and 'I live in space and can't just open the door.'

Grimacing at her own idiocy, she massaged the shoulder she'd smacked in her panicked exit and took a moment to appreciate the view.

Only a faint streak of twilight remained, confined to the far horizon. The rest of the sky had turned into a deep, achingly-beautiful cobalt, speckled with shimmering stars. The mountain's rocky, snow-crested peak stood silent, still, untouched—a bridge to the stars as rugged and sincere as an uncut gem. A smudge of clouds to the east promised snow.

And below...

Eisvel nestled in its valley, lights glowing in cozy defiance of the harsh landscape. Smoke lifted from old-fashioned chimneys, promising warmth. People laughed somewhere in the distance. Faint strains of music drifted up like a fairy-tale.

Why was she staying in the ship, again? Money?

Psh. She could afford a few beers. Even tourist-priced ones.

And the steering arms *clearly* needed something stronger. Like an overnight soak in some different fume-producing chemicals.

It did seem like a long hike, though. Uphill on the way back. And gods *damn* it was cold.

She shivered—violently—as if her body had only just noticed.

She almost slammed the hatch closed, but the fumes were still an issue. Muttering, she turned for the stairwell—

And walked straight into a tingling, fizzing mass of sentient void.

"Argh!"

She flailed her way out, arms pinwheeling like she was fighting spiderwebs—gods, it felt like a thousand ants had crawled under her skin—and stumbled out the other side.

"For *fuck's* sakes, Bob, you gotta stop doing that!"

The Shadow didn't answer. Didn't move, either. Just stood there, six feet of roiling void cut in the shape of a person, his edges blurred where the knife had pressed in.

Hard to look at.

Was he taller than usual? And... was his *back* to her? And if it was—how did she *know* that? No matter which way you looked at a Shadow, they looked *two-dimensional*. All that depthless void matter really took away from the third dimension. Some theorized they bit into the fourth dimension, too.

Shadows were weird.

He still hadn't moved.

She frowned, stepped around him, and peered up where his face should be. "Bob? You okay?"

The response was immediate.

"You—you—you—okay, okay—you—you—you?"

Yep. Shadows were *really* weird.

And she was even weirder for actually *understanding* that.

"Yeah, I'm okay. Just trying to fumigate myself, apparently."

Shadows, despite appearing in the rough shape of fully-formed adult humans, didn't start off with verbal speech. They had to learn it, usually by skimming nearby brains and matching thoughts to speech.

Or something like that.

She wasn't a Shadow Scientist. She didn't know how it worked, just seen it happen a time or two—and they *always* started with the creepy-weird speech mimicry.

Bob's void-head tilted.

"Fumigate?"

"Yes. It's when a person fills up a space with toxic fumes in order to kill pests."

The Shadow paused, processing.

"Are you... pest?"

That speech center was sorting itself out in a right hurry, wasn't it?

She sighed. "You know what, Bob? Yes. I am the

worst pest. Now, if you'll excuse me, I need to find something warmer to wear."

3

Soo-jin gaped.

Eisvel looked like a gods damned *movie set*. Hells, it probably was—no way local government wasn't renting out *these* looks. The 'town square' wasn't so much a square as a square, a park, a promenade, a frozen-over canal for skating, a midwinter-themed market, and every single inch fully committed to the 'cozy fantasy European village in winter' vibe.

Even more, it looked *real*. Like someone had lifted it from Old Earth and ported it brick by brick across two star systems—so much so, she pulled her tender, ungloved fingers from her pockets and checked her netlink to see if they had.

You never knew with rich people. Money made anything possible, and people in Sirius *loved* Old Earth nostalgia. Even if they hadn't lifted it, she'd bet the buildings were copies of real places, stitched together and decorated into a fairy-tale fantasy.

This place felt more like a dream than reality ever had.

Sugar-coated. Or, in this case, *snow*-coated.

Both?

That's what vacationers wanted, wasn't it? To live a dream?

Zan was certainly living one. Gods, she was jealous. LARPing at a pseudo-ancient Japanese hot spring resort sounded like a killer way to spend a week, even without the 'company enjoyment' they'd also arranged.

Aaaand according to the town's netsite, someone *had* brought buildings from Old Earth. A church, a house, and a...

An honest-to-gods *castle?*

Her head whipped up, scanning the rooftops for a medieval fortress.

Nothing.

Damn.

She kept reading.

Oh. Outside town. And the shuttle buses had already stopped for the day.

Tomorrow, then. If she hadn't frozen into a Soojin-cicle by then.

She shivered and burrowed deeper into her jacket. The cold sliced through, but at least it kept the snow out, the thermal bodysuit underneath doing the heavy lifting. Meant for exosuits, its programming adjusted to counter environmental temperatures and was keeping her body...well, not *toasty*, but lukewarm with occasional toasty spikes whenever the draft poked through her collar enough to set it off.

Mostly, it felt clammy.

Heat was more of a problem in an exosuit, so the suit was designed to cool more than to warm—and definitely *not* designed for treks through a snowy forest without the exosuit. But wearing the exosuit would have been fucking weird, so she'd put normal clothes on top.

And she'd left the damn gloves back in the ship.

Too expensive to risk losing. The whole suit was

too expensive to lose, but she trusted herself not to misplace a full-body outfit. Gloves? Less so.

With a sigh, she shoved her hands—and the netlink—back into her pockets.

Too cold for reading. She needed warmth before answers.

Bob, meanwhile, was naked.

As usual.

He stood next to her, dwarfing most doors and making her feel like a midget. On the way down, he'd zipped around the forest like some happy, human-shaped ghost dog—darting ahead, sniffing trails, circling back, then vanishing again.

Being selectively corporeal, the snow and ice didn't touch him. Unlike her, who'd been muttering swears and slogging through unmarked snow most of the way here.

To add insult to injury, the clouds had moved close enough to start adding new snow to the mix.

Bob stared down at his void-abdomen, watching snowflakes fall right through it.

She stared, too, several unkind phrases coming to mind.

She wished *she* could just stand there with snow falling through her, feeling nothing.

The jealousy, at least, helped warm her blood.

Unless...

"Can you feel that?" she asked, curiosity edging out the grudge.

His void-form rippled as he considered her question, and she felt his mind skim hers, like a brush of a feather.

"Yes... Feels like... cold butterflies."

She shivered.

Weren't cold butterflies *dead* butterflies?

Bob's head lifted with another ripple, like a balloon hit by an anti-grav charge.

"Here... why?"

Yeah... She was asking herself that, just now.

"Because I'm cold and lonely, and Zan said this would be a *'magical winter festival experience.'*" She rolled her eyes and made sarcastic air quotes—and immediately regretted exposing her hands. She shoved them back in and stamped some feeling back into her feet. "I dunno. I was bored."

The Shadow paused, void swirling dizzyingly.

"Chocolate?" he asked hopefully.

"Probably," she said, scanning the market.

"Love," he said, and sped away.

Blotches of darkness pulsed in his wake like void-shaped retinal burn.

She sighed.

If there was one thing she could count on, it was Bob's love of chocolate.

Good thing no one was around to see him go.

Actually...where *was* everyone?

She frowned, re-examining the square.

Okay, there *were* people. Here and there, a couple walking hand in hand, a family exploring the ice sculptures, some skaters on the canal, vendors manning their stands...

But not many. Certainly not enough to fuel a local economy. Unless the drinks were, like, three hundred credits a cup.

What the hells?

Maybe everyone's at dinner.

Possible. But not enough to shake the creeping unease now gripping her. Especially not with the fairy-tale *magic town* vibe. Fairy-tales weren't often friendly. Too many of them skewed toward the horror genre.

Sol. Maybe they were serving *people* for dinner. Luring them in with lights and cocoa, then trapping them in a cannibalistic hellscape.

A cheery voice sprouted behind her.

"Hi! Are you new here?"

She spun—panic flaring—and came face-to-face with...

...an elf?

No. Just a short, pretty woman. Soo-jin stared, brain sluggishly picking up the pieces and connecting them for an explanation. The woman was shorter than her, and prettier. Pale skin, blue eyes, delicate build. She wore a parka trimmed in white faux-fur, dark blue leggings, and a matching knit hat. The parka's pale blue matched her eyes, and she'd donned ice-white make-up that high-lighted her features and mimicked frost patterns. With *glitter*.

Pretty.

Soo-jin forced her frozen tongue to work.

"Uh. Yeah?"

Smooth.

The woman smiled and spread her arms wide. "Welcome! I'm Claire, your festival guide!"

Er. What?

They needed to pay for *guides* here?

She shifted the town's label from 'cannibalistic hellscape' to '*capitalistic* hellscape.'

"Sorry. I don't have cash for a guide. Just wanted to poke around a bit."

"Oh, don't worry—I'm paid by the town!" Claire said cheerily. "They bribe us locals to get involved instead of loitering smugly, complaining about tourists."

Soo-jin's eyebrows arched into her forehead. "Seriously?"

How much money did this place *have?*

"Yep!" Claire winked and waved her forward. "Come on! I'll show you around!"

Huh.

Okay, then.

She *did* have questions about the architecture— and Claire probably knew where to find a nice hot beverage to keep her hands warm.

She let the government-sponsored elf lead her along.

4

"—And that's why they built this place. One small grain winter festival magic—and a *lot* of money," Claire finished, gesturing grandly before leaning on the drinks stall and beaming a grin at her

Soo-jin grinned back. Claire's enthusiasm was contagious. She'd forgotten all about cannibalism, instead finding a cozy contentment as she listened to Claire talk about her town. So far, she'd learned a crapload about the town's architecture and history, including what dramas had filmed here and which studios still held licensing, and her hands were *warm* again, cupped around a local hot chocolate mix—

Which was *green,* for some reason.

She'd been skeptical. Then she took a sip.

Holy *shitballs.*

Fucking chocolate *crack.*

A void ripped open beside her.

Claire yelped in surprise, but Soo-jin was already hunching over her mug—like a predator guarding a fresh kill.

"No. Find your own chocolate."

Bob grumbled—a static-brushed echo in her mind—and vanished.

Damn Shadow.

Claire stared, stunned.

"You...*know* that Shadow?"

"Yes. He's part of my crew."

"Crew?" Claire gaped. "You have a ship?"

"Yep." She tucked a thumb in a direction she hoped was accurate. "Parked it outside of town."

Claire looked even more astonished. "You *flew* here?"

"Yes?"

How the fuck else did people get here? *Climb?*

"How'd you get through the no-fly zone?"

There's a no-fly zone?

Huh. Now that Claire mentioned it, she vaguely remembered something about airspace restrictions on the way in. Then it had gone away, and she'd dismissed it from her mind.

Zan must have taken care of it.

Zan, who'd insisted on spending a week here.

Zan, who'd wandered off into the snow to have a *fantastic fucking time* with some undisclosed person at a fancy-dancy hot spring resort.

Zan, who she wasn't jealous of *at all*.

"Why is there a no-fly zone?"

Claire quirked a brow. "For the visiting royals?"

"*What?*" Okay, *not* the answer she was expecting. "Which royals?"

"The Biostrat Stirling-Ross clan. You seriously didn't know?" Claire had both brows up now. "What *are* you in town for?"

"Vintage holoscreen nodes," Soo-jin said weakly.

Actually...hadn't Biostrat *made* those nodes? They mostly manufactured weapons now, but back in the day, when *Huli Jing* had been serving her military days, they'd definitely had a bigger reach.

And if a member of Biostrat corporate royalty were supplying those nodes...

Just whose company was Zan 'greatly enjoying' this week?

Totally not jealous. Not even a little.

Claire grabbed her elbow. "Oh my gods! Don't be obvious, but I think that's one of them!"

Soo-jin followed her gaze. Two men, one bundled in cushy-looking furs and the other obviously a bodyguard, stood at a nearby stall. Both turned at the sound of Claire's squeal.

Soo-jin gave her a flat stare. "Smooth."

Claire shrank.

Gods, she was cute.

"Do royals visit often?"

"These ones do. Every year."

"Then shouldn't you be more used to them?"

"Probably." Claire stared at her drink with a pinched expression. "Is that Shadow really part of your crew?"

Soo-jin snorted. "Changing the subject?"

Claire blushed.

"You know royals are just people, right?" She grinned. "I bet they'll have a drink with us if we asked."

"What? No, don't—!"

Too late. She was already beaming a broad grin at the two men up the row, lifting her mug in salute. "Hey, hotties! Grab a drink with us?"

5

To her surprise, the royal and his guard *did* join them.

Claire remained stiff, eyes flicking toward a clock tower at the end of the square like she couldn't wait to leave. But when Soo-jin got one little detail about Eisvel wrong...

"No, no, no, *that* one was a local build. *St. Barnabas* was the import!"

Soo-jin hid a smile.

She might have gotten that fact wrong on purpose.

The royal—Osgood Barfield, a minor duke on the Ross side of the Stirling-Ross clan—was peppy, polite, and a bit too refined for her tastes. But she could work with that. Hells, she could work with *anything* now that her hands were warm.

"So," she said, toying with her mug. "You guys buy this place out for a week?"

Ah, to have that kind of money. She used to, but hadn't liked the strings it came with.

"Yes. It's a long-standing agreement. This is the

only way to keep the paparazzi away—and one of the few times the whole family can get together." Osgood tilted his head. "What brings *you* here?"

As in...how'd she slip past the no-fly zone?

She gave a sly smile. "My first officer has more connections than I thought."

And I'm pretty sure they're shacking up with one of your relatives right now.

His brows pinched slightly.

"Disappointed? *Sorry*. If it's any consolation, *I'd* been hoping for a beachfront vacation." She grinned. "You know—somewhere warm enough to eat ice cream."

"*We* have ice cream!" Claire butted in. "All flavors of fir tip, just like the hot chocolate."

Soo-jin glanced at the green in her mug.

Just how many fir tip variations *were* there?

Osgood grinned. "It's the local delicacy. They work it into *everything*."

"Of course we do," Claire said brightly. "It's *delicious*."

It *was*. And very green.

But she could deal with green. So long as her hands and butt stayed warm.

She took a sip and looked out at the town again.

Gods, it was pretty. Quaint, snowy beauty, all decked out for the festival. Boughs of evergreens adorned every building, stall, and light fixture, strung through with ribbons and glittering lights. The drink vendor overlooked the iced-over canal. Elegant designs lit up under the weight of passing skaters, turning the ice magical. Beyond, a forest of ice and snow sculptures turned the adjoining park into a glittering wonderland. Holiday music drifted through the square, mixing with the clop and jingle of a returning horse and carriage.

She spotted Bob to the left. A prescient tingle lifted the hairs on her neck at the sight of his cut-void silhouette.

Something was off.

She frowned, zeroing in. The Shadow stood tall and amorphous, void-form dizzying and incongruent against the cozy holiday cheer, the rest of the market-goers giving him a wide berth. Fairly normal for a Shadow, but he was *fixated* on something.

She followed his line of attention—and her stomach dropped clean away.

Eisvel's finest chocolatier had a stand near the center of the market. Smack dab in front of it was a chocolate *fountain*.

Bob stared at it with a hyperactive energy—like a border collie sighting a dancing stick.

Oh, no. No, no, no—

She launched to her feet, voice snapping out. "Bob! *No!*"

The Shadow jolted, rippling like she'd chucked a rock into the pool of his being.

But he didn't stop staring.

She pointed a finger and sharpened her tone. "*No!*"

He finally looked away, head retracting with obvious reluctance. Even without a face, he managed to shoot her a reproachful look.

Then he stalked off, sullen as a child denied candy.

Sol. She'd have to watch him.

When she turned back around, everyone was staring.

She sighed. "He is *obsessed* with chocolate."

Osgood blinked. "Chocolate?"

"Chocolate." She rolled her eyes. "Now, where were we?"

If she played her cards right, maybe *she* could 'greatly enjoy' some royal company, too. After all, he seemed single, and like he said, the paps weren't in town. Plus, he'd already ditched the reunion to wander the market alone.

He smiled. "You were telling me why you came here, then we got sidetracked by ice cream."

"Ah, yes. Unfortunately, ice cream is more exciting than me. I just came here for ship parts."

"Ship parts?"

"Vintage ship parts. You said this was a yearly reunion? What do you guys do? Any special traditions?"

"Well, there is one thing..." He leaned in, eyes gleaming. "Promise you won't tell the paps?"

She crossed her heart. "They'll have to dig it out of my grave."

"We have a pajama party at the castle."

"What?! That sounds *awesome!*"

"It is. Everyone gets new PJs, then we hang out in a big cozy great room."

Yeah... That was definitely awesome.

"How about you? Any family traditions?"

Ice flooded her spine. She keeled back with a grimace. "My family is...a depressing topic."

"Oh." His smile faltered. "Sorry."

Her family was a brainwashed, cultist mess. Any cozy family 'traditions' wore scars of abuse.

Silence fell between them. She exhaled, forcing the memories down. Over Osgood's shoulder, Claire watched her with a guarded look. Then, she turned to the clock tower again.

Maybe her shift was ending.

Claire's netlink buzzed with a notification. She stared at the screen, then slid off the stool and bent to retrieve something on the ground.

The sky flashed with light—and everything exploded.

Snaps and crackles hit her ears. The lights above blew, showering her in sparks. Bright, burning agony zapped her body. She yelled, convulsed, slammed into the bar. The stench of burnt electronics filled her nose as she slid down. Someone—Osgood?— tried to catch her.

Then, she was being grabbed.

"Don't move," Claire spoke in her ear. "We don't want to hurt you."

Sure. That made sense. She was clearly being injured by *something*, so medical attention was a logical next step. She was glad someone *else* was organizing it, because right now, all she could do was—

"I said don't *move!*"

Someone hit her. Hard.

Everything went dark.

6

Everything hurt, it was cold, and the floor was vibrating.

She pondered that last one for several confused, painful moments before a bump smacked her head and she recognized the rumble of an engine.

A truck?

...Why was she in a truck?

"Welcome back."

Her gaze flitted down. Osgood lay nearby, his puffy fur coat lumpy around the ropes he was tied with. Blood smeared his mouth and cheek, and his eyes met hers with tired wariness.

Eyeing his ropes, she tried an experimental wiggle.

Yep. She was tied, too. And moving felt like chafing against raw diamonds.

Her brain scraped a conclusion together.

"We've been kidnapped?"

Or, rather, *tried* to ask. What actually came from her numb and prickling lips was a slurred, *'Kitmmraaa?'*

His brows pulled together in concern.

Okay. Articulation was down the shitter.

She tried again.

"K-kidnapped?"

Better.

"Yes." Osgood winced. "Sorry, this is probably my fault."

No kidding. He was a royal. Killer ransom prize.

But why was *she* here? And why did everything hurt?

Memory flickered. The flash in the sky. Lights exploding. The smell of burnt electronics. Her suit fucking frying. "Did they use a fffucking *EMP?!*"

"I think so. Whatever it was took out every light at once. My netlink, too."

And her suit. Her *expensive-ass* suit.

Fuck.

The blood in her mouth tasted like derision. Anger roiled like a gods-damned volcano, but she forced it back, banking it for later. She needed to keep her head clear.

"Seems o-overkill for a k-kidnapping. Too flashy."

"They had to disable our SOS alerts."

What?

At her raised brow, he closed his eyes and sighed. "Every family member has an augment that sends a distress signal if we're under duress. If we— or our guards—don't cancel it, it pings local authorities."

Ah.

"Where is it?"

He frowned. "I can't tell you that."

She rolled her eyes. "Fine. But unless you have a fresh burn where it's implanted, it's probably fine. Those things are built to withstand EMPs—like those...metronome things they put in hearts—"

"Pacemakers?"

"Yeah, those. So, if there's no new burn, I'd wager it's working." She had something similar—a tracker embedded deep in her thigh. Not that anyone would think to activate it. She groaned as her mind wandered to another conclusion. "The

EMP will definitely have knocked out the local comms station, though."

Which was probably what they wanted. Everyone in the dark, scrambling, with no easy way to call for help.

She wiggled around, searching the dim recesses of the truck's cargo area...which was unhelpfully empty.

How had they kept the components sheltered from the EMP? Foil? No, probably just kept it underground. That'd be easier.

The truck hit another bump, rattling her shoulder.

"I'm sorry you got caught up in this," Osgood said.

"Buy me a drink—and a new replacement suit—and I'll call it even."

He snorted. "Really?"

"I'm a cheap date."

Good. He was smiling again.

Before she could open her mouth for another rousing burst of flirty humor, the truck's cab door opened with a squeak and a burst of warm air.

A familiar pair of snow boots with elf-blue leggings thumped through.

Claire?

Oh. Oh, shit.

Suddenly, a few things made more sense.

But only a few.

The woman beamed, a delighted smile splitting her pretty face. "Good. You're awake!"

Soo-jin wished she wasn't.

"Imagine my surprise—here I was, already planning this heist, and a prize like *you* wanders into my lap!" Claire knelt beside her and traced a cold finger along her jaw. "Him, I need for the weapon codes—but you? Pure, hard cash." Her grin sharpened. "You're a holiday bonus!"

Oh. Great.

Guess her father still had the black-market bounty out on her.

She licked her lips, tasting blood where one had split. "You're not even gonna buy me a drink first?"

Claire laughed. "You're right! I should. But for now..." She tapped Soo-jin's cheek lovingly and rose. "Just sit tight. We'll unload you shortly."

She left, slamming the door.

Silence fell.

Her gaze drifted to Osgood. "So...shall we split the blame on this one?"

His lips cracked a smile.

She sighed. "Remember how I said my family was a depressing topic?"

"Yes?"

"This is why. That...and I clearly have *terrible* taste in women."

7

When they dropped her, pain shrieked across her body, each burn point flaring like she'd rolled in hot sauce.

"Ffffuck me, that *hurts*," she hissed. "*Fuck!*"

The guy who'd dropped her clicked his tongue. "Don't be a baby. You didn't hit *that* hard."

"Yeah? Well *excuse me*, but your EMP *fried my*

fucking suit while it was on my fucking body, so why don't you cram that attitude and floss your ass with rusty piano wire!"

The man snarled a slur, spat on her jacket, and left. The door thumped shut.

Silence reigned.

"Rusty piano wire?" Osgood asked.

"My mouth gets smart when I'm hurt." She groaned and twisted enough to see the room—and swore. "Are we in a fucking *refrigerator?*"

"A freezer, actually."

A freezer? On a literal *ice mountain?*

"Why even bother," she muttered. "Couldn't they just shove everything into the nearest snow drift?"

"Nope. Snow's too cold." Osgood grinned. "Besides, this place isn't covered in snow all year. It does get summer."

"Right. And that's when you cut down trees and make ice cream."

"Just the tips. It's actually quite good."

"Great. You can get me some when I get us out of this."

A thump hit the door, and it opened again. A now too-familiar pair of boots and leggings strutted in.

"Room service!" Claire set a steaming mug in front of Soo-jin. "See? Now I *have* bought you a drink! Specialty hot chocolate!"

She lifted an unimpressed eyebrow. "No whipping cream?"

"Alas, no. But it's better than what you'll get on your upcoming trip, so enjoy it while it lasts!"

"You're going on a special section of my shitlist. You know that, right?"

"Sure thing, sugar! But you'll have to find me first!" Claire winked and gave a cheery wave as she left. "Better drink it before it gets cold!"

The door shut.

Soo-jin snarled at the mug. "Drink it *how?* My hands are tied!"

"Piss-poor room service," Osgood commented. "You should file a complaint."

"Oh, yes. I will. With very stern wording and a lot of expletives." And a blaster, if she could swing it. She rolled onto her side to face him. "So...any escape plans yet?"

"Not unless you have a working netlink."

"I do. On my ship." She sighed. "Of course, if we were there, we wouldn't need it. We'd just close the door and call the authorities. *It* has EMP safeties."

Osgood grunted. "I expect they'll move us soon."

"I expect you're right. They flashed an EMP. Someone will have noticed. They'll have to move quick." She grimaced at the mug. "Gods. She could have at least left a straw."

"Truly." Osgood eyed it. "Is that ceramic?"

"Maybe?"

"Think you could break it? Use the shards to cut your ties?"

"That only works in dramas."

"You sure? The physics are sound."

"Those physics are *bullshit*. I—*argh!*"

Pins and needles exploded through her body, and the freezer blinked out in an eruption of darkness.

When her vision cleared, a different pair of familiar legs crouched next to her.

"*Bob?*"

No response.

Then, his void-form hand reached for her mug.

"Hey! That's mine!"

The hand stopped.

"*Chocolate.*"

"Yes."

"*Not mine.*"

"Also yes." She thought fast. "Do you...want it?"

"*Yes!*"

"Awesome! I need you to go to *Huli Jing* and bring me a bunch of guns. And knives."

Bob rippled, eerily quiet. Darkness swirled with dizzying excitement, taking over half her vision as he leaned over.

"*Guns?*"

"Yes!"

"*Hmm...*"

Osgood cleared his throat. "Help us, and I'll buy you *fifty* of those."

Bob turned on him with a terrifying intensity. A high-pitched whine hit the air, like a microwave burning its last fuse.

"Wait! No!"

"*Yes,*" Bob said, and vanished.

Shit!

"Guns and knives, Bob!" she shouted after him. "Get guns and knives!"

No answer.

Sol.

She groaned and slumped back.

"I...messed that up, didn't I?" Osgood said.

"Maybe. Maybe not. Bob can be...*creative* in his interpretation."

Just how would he interpret 'help us'?

Silence crept in again.

"How long do you think he'll take?" Osgood asked.

"No idea." She closed her eyes. "But unless you've got any better plans... all we can do is wait."

8

Time passed. She didn't know how much. There was nothing to track it except the growing cold and her rising panic.

The quiet pressed in. Sound filtered occasionally from outside, but it felt like it came from another world—like they'd been boxed into some subdimensional oubliette, cut off from everyone and everything. Like they'd never be free again.

...Yeah. That was her PTSD talking.

PTSD was a bitch. The 'C' in front of hers deserved a stronger curse.

She focused on her breathing. Slow inhale, longer exhale. *Feel the air move. Count the seconds. Distract from the triggers.*

It helped.

But breathing exercises could only do so much.

She'd been imprisoned like this before.

This was, literally, her nightmare.

When Osgood broke the silence, she sagged with relief.

"How long do you think they'll keep us in here?"

"No idea, but they have more rope." She'd seen it on the way in. "They're probably trying for more of your family."

"Probably."

She focused on breathing again, trying to ignore the way the walls pressed in. Talking was helping. Forced her to think logically. "They mentioned weapon codes. Think someone here has them, or are they trying to put pressure on a relative?"

"Don't know."

Oh, well. She'd keep talking, anyway—even if it was just out loud thinking.

It helped.

"What codes are they even talking about? Do you think they *have* a weapon?" Possible. *Something* had caused that EMP. "Or is it some *other* weapons?"

"No idea. That's my cousins' territory. I'm just...marketing."

Ah. Damn.

She grabbed the new topic. "How *do* you market weapons?"

"Fancy videos and solid statistics, usually." He shrugged. "We do government contracts, mostly. Can't get too creative."

"Posh."

Silence crept back in. She'd lost feeling in two of her fingers—probably from compromised circulation, but the cold wasn't helping. The clammy warmth had leeched from her fried suit a while ago, leaving her as cold and dead as its circuits.

She felt like a corpse in a morgue.

A clunk sounded. Distant, muffled. Like it echoed through deep water.

She flinched and started counting breaths again.

"Why do they want you?" he asked. "Do *you* have weapon codes?"

She laughed. "Gods, I *wish*. That would be their worst nightmare." Emotions stuffed themselves up her closing throat. She swallowed hard. "No, they're just brainwashed assholes. My father's been gunning for leadership in a cult since before I was born—and I stuck a giant middle finger into his plans."

Another clunk. She jerked.

"I'm sorry," Osgood said.

"Thanks. They locked me up like this before." Her gaze skated the walls. "Different place, different box."

"That's awful."

"Yeah." She flinched again—at memories, this time. "Compared to that—this is a step *up.*"

He said something else, but she missed it. Memories pressed in fast and hard. She sucked in a breath and fought them off, desperately sliding her mind somewhere—*anywhere*—else.

For nearly half a minute, she was lost, the walls pressing in.

When she came out, Osgood's tone had shifted.

"—that blasterfire?"

"What?" She followed his gaze—which didn't help, with a *wall* in the way.

Blasterfire? Here?

It came again—a whole series of muffled pops, like someone had gone crazy with a case of champagne.

Holy shit.

A knife clattered beside her. She yelped and jerked back—and a set of void-form legs appeared.

"Bob?!"

A ragged hand plucked the hot chocolate from the ground.

"Mine."

He and the chocolate vanished.

"Hey! What about the guns?!"

More popping sounded. *Closer.*

Fuck!

She scrambled for the knife, cursing her numb fingers. One hand smacked the blade, but she caught the handle on the next try. Grunting, she carefully flipped it and sawed at her bonds.

The popping stopped, but the silence didn't return. An undercurrent of activity wavered outside. Shuffles. Voices. Movement.

Footsteps. *Coming for them.*

"Soo-jin!" Osgood hissed.

She swore and tucked the knife up her sleeve, wincing as it dug into one of the burns.

The door squeaked open. Elf-blue leggings reappeared—and Soo-jin snarled.

"Claire, you coal-battered *shitbag.* I'm going to shove those weapon codes so far up your ass, they see the fucking moonrise!"

Claire's blue eyes snapped to her with burning hatred.

Er...what?

The woman stumbled, hopping to regain her balance.

Belatedly, she realized Claire wasn't moving on

her own. Behind her, holding the woman like a kitten caught by the scruff, was—

"Soo-jin," a familiar voice admonished. "That is no way to speak to our *esteemed host.*"

"Zan!"

A thickset man squeezed past Zan. His eyes slid over her and locked on Osgood.

"Oz," he said with gruff relief. "You good?"

"Yes. Just a bit numb. They tied us pretty tight."

Soo-jin grunted. "I have a knife in my sleeve."

"Good girl." Zan handed Claire off to someone behind them, then knelt at Soo-jin's side to retrieve the knife.

"I actually ordered a bunch of guns, but I guess Bob got lost."

"Ah... That explains it."

"Explains what?"

"You see... Raul and I were in the middle of a relaxing, gorgeous, candlelit soak in the hot springs, gazing out at the mountain vista..." They finished cutting through her wrist bonds and moved to her legs. "...when Bob appears out of *nowhere*, says 'Captain Danger', and drops a fuckload of vintage firearms *into the pool.*"

So that's where the guns had gone.

Right on cue, Bob reappeared.

"I bring help."

"You dropped guns in my favorite hot spring! *Vintage* guns! You're lucky you didn't electrocute us!"

But Bob wasn't paying them any attention. He'd already drifted to Osgood, void-form leaving a broken afterglow in his wake. *"I bring help. Chocolate?"*

Ah. That was how he'd interpreted 'help us.'

Honestly? Not bad.

She hadn't even thought to send him for Zan. Figured they'd be too far—that fetching guns would be challenge enough.

She should have remembered—Shadows were *predatorily good* at finding people.

Zan sliced the last of her bonds and helped her pull free. She shook out the pins and needles, wincing as she flexed leaden muscles, then levered herself up against some shelves with a hand from them.

Osgood was standing, too. Raul had cut him loose.

Bob hovered next to them, radiating a need for chocolate.

Unfortunately, it came off as fixated, predatory *hunger.*

She called him off. "Bob, leave them alone for a bit. You'll get your chocolate, but it's not *here.*"

His head snapped to her, aghast. "*It isn't?*"

"No."

"*But—chocolate!*"

"Yeah, yeah, yeah. And *I* wanted a knife *and* a gun, which you didn't bring. Technically, you got paid for a job you only did halfway."

"*Oh. Forgot.*" Bob zipped forward at the speed of light, causing an instant death and resurrection of her heart. Tingles crawled through her skin as his arm overlapped hers and a cold weight pressed into her palm.

When his darkness retreated, a small blaster sat in her tingling palm.

Huh.

"Thanks," she said. "Job completed."

"You are welcome. Captain."

The phrase came out disjointed, his form still looked like spiraling Chthonic madness—but at least he wasn't fixated on Raul and Osgood anymore.

Voices in the kitchen caught her attention. Voices and...radios?

Someone had working comms?

"We found Biostrat security on our way in," Zan explained. "The rest of the family is fine."

Good.

A familiar voice rose above the rest, loudly protesting her new situation.

Claire.

Soo-jin considered the blaster in her hands.

One little itty bitty shot couldn't hurt. Or maybe two. Somewhere non-vital. Just to cause a bit of harmless...pain.

"The electromagnetic pulse knocked out the local hospital," Zan said smoothly. "If you shoot her, she'll need to be fixed in *Huli Jing*'s med bay."

Damn it.

She sighed and dismissed the idea.

"Bob," she grumbled. "It's gonna take Osgood at least two hours to get that chocolate. Could you go...*stare* at her? Please? As creepily as possible?"

The Shadow turned to Claire like the cowl of the grim reaper, considering.

"The delay is technically her fault," she added.

Bob's darkness flowed forward.

"Biiiitch."

She shivered at his hiss. Something deep inside her flipped in unease at how gleeful he was to terrorize someone who'd wronged him. Then Osgood was at her side, and she decided to focus on something else.

"So," he said. "What are you doing after this?"

Her eyebrows rose at the classic line. Were they flirting, or joking?

"Probably finding something to warm my ass up. Why?"

His teeth flashed in the dim light.

"Want to join our pajama party?"

9

"All right, all right," Soo-jin said around the mouthful of fir-tip ice cream Osgood had scooped into her hot chocolate. "I'll admit—this is good."

"Told you."

"Yes, you did."

They were in the castle. Most of the town was. Like the other resorts, it used the geothermal hot springs to regulate its heat. Unlike the others, however, its stone walls had provided enough insulation to dull the EMP's effects.

Most electronics still worked, and she'd helped spool its backup reactor in time to take over from the draining emergency battery.

Then, she and Zan had joined Osgood and the rest of the Stirling-Ross clan for their pajama party.

That had been...fun. Cozy. Not romantic, but just...*nice*.

Now, wrapped in the resort's big, plushy guest robes, skin flush and tingling from the hot spring they'd just stepped out of, Osgood was showing her the benefits of having hot chocolate ice cream immediately after a dip in the hot water.

She had to admit—it was pretty great.

She didn't tell him this wasn't her *first* time having ice cream after a hot spring dip. Ice cream freezers were common changeroom staples across hot spring resorts. This was her first time having *fir-tip* ice cream, though, with or without the chocolate they'd dunked it in.

It...literally tasted like a winter festival.

Osgood sat back like a smug cat. "It's the *best* winter drink. Hands down."

"The best, huh?"

"I *dare* you to make a better drink."

"Do you? Dare *me?*"

"I do."

She considered her cup.

Hmm.

"Have you ever had *turmeric* hot chocolate?"

Shadow exploded from the water behind them.

"*Want!*"

"Freezer Burn" is one of many Soo-jin Dokgo misadventures. For more chaos, sarcasm, and questionable decisions in space, including a free prequel to her feature-length series, check out kgorman.ca.

RECIPES: TURMERIC HOT CHOCOLATE & FIR TIP ICE CREAM

From K. Gorman's "Freezer Burn"

TURMERIC HOT COCOA

Ingredients:

- 3 cups milk-ish beverage of choice*
  Whole Milk
- 2 tbsp Cocoa Powder (or however much your heart desires)
- 1/2 tsp Turmeric Powder
- 1/4 tsp Vanilla
- 2 tbsp Maple Syrup

If you're using an extra-sweet milk substitute like almond milk, you might want to tone down on the Vanilla and Maple Syrup. Your taste, your choice!

. . .

Instructions:

1. Pour milk into small pot. Heat on stovetop. Or nuke in microwave in something other than a metal pot.

2. Whisk in cocoa powder, maple syrup, turmeric, and vanilla. Use a vigorous fork if you're desperate.

3. Heat to scalding (or cooler if you prefer). Do *not* bring to full boil.

4. Send self into sugar-coated food coma of happiness.

FIR TIP ICE CREAM

Ingredients:

- 4 ounces (113 g) Fir Sugar (To make, take a 4:1 ratio of fir tips to sugar and grind it all up in a spice grinder*)
- 4 ounces (113 g) ordinary sugar
- 1 cup (125 ml) cold whole milk
- 1½ cups (375 ml) cold cream (heavy cream, if you're feeling fancy)
- 1 ice cream maker

Please make sure the fir tip needles you acquire are from an edible variety and not, say, poisonous yew or else there will be bad times ahead. Remember: Don't contribute to hazardous statistics today!

. . .

Instructions:

1. Put the bowl of your ice cream maker into the freezer twelve hours in advance.

2. Combine sugars and milk in a bowl and stir until sugar has dissolved.

3. Whip the cream until it holds soft peaks, then fold it into the milk and sugar mixture.

4. Pour mixture into bowl of ice cream maker and churn until it is very thick (roughly 25-30min). Transfer to a container and place in freezer.

*If you do not have an ice cream maker, Gods help you. You'll need a shallow container to stick, covered, in the freezer. Take it out after two hours and use a fork to stir the frozen edges into the center. Repeat that ritual <u>every hour</u> until it is frozen and mixed.

JINGLE BELL DOCK

by Peter J. Foote

"DASHING THROUGH THE AIR DUCTS, ON A ONE-DRONE open sleigh..." blared through the *Caissa's* speakers, loud and off-key. Rosario winced, muttering under her breath as she snatched the old headphones from where they hung on the back of the pilot's chair. She shoved them over her ears, adjusting them with a grimace. They weren't plugged in, but it wasn't about the sound—it was about the principle.

Thankfully, a strobing light on the navigation console grabbed her attention.

"Please be an asteroid impact, please be an asteroid impact," Rosario chanted under her breath as she acknowledged the alert. After a quick glance at the inky blackness outside, she shouted into the intercom.

"Liam, dear, can you please be quiet for a second? I think we're here—wherever here is."

The affront to Christmas music paused with all the grace of a bucket of bolts crashing to the floor. A moment later, Liam's voice echoed through the speakers.

"Okay! We'll be right up!" His cheer made Rosario sigh.

"Lord in heaven, save me from husbands who love holidays."

She heard Liam before she saw him—the thump of his heavy work boots on the steel deck, one of the familiar sounds that made the *Caissa* feel like home. His current outfit, on the other hand...

He tied his well-worn coveralls around his waist, the white T-shirt clinging to his slender chest. That wasn't the problem. It was the Santa hat perched on his head and the strands of glittering garland trailing behind him like festive flotsam that made Rosario pinch the bridge of her nose.

And then there was Queen Bee—or rather, her drones—which truly took the cake.

Empirically, Rosario knew their AI companion physically lived in a disguised hazardous waste drum in Liam's mechanical shop. But her ears were the *Caissa*'s intercom, and her eyes were her drones. One such drone—a cross between a metallic lobster and a football—clung to Liam's shoulder, sporting a glowing-red nose. Another, wrapped in holiday paper like a makeshift suit of armor, trailed behind him, dutifully gathering the stray garland.

"We're here?" Liam asked, leaning in to kiss Rosario on the cheek. The pom-pom of his Santa hat brushed the back of her neck, making her shiver.

Rosario couldn't help but smile as she replied.

"Wherever here is. As far as I can tell, we're

someplace roughly where Ceres used to orbit—before Earth's military blew it up."

Grimacing at what his native planet had done during the Earth-Mars war, Liam deflected the barb. "So, where Jeb wanted us then," he said, placing the drones on the back of the copilot's seat.

"This friend of yours is being mysterious. I hope we aren't wasting our time mining air. Fuel pellets aren't getting any cheaper, and we're turning down solid work to be out here."

Liam winced and nodded, rubbing the back of his neck.

"You know how I said Jeb mentored me during those first months I was in the void?"

Rosario nodded, but Liam didn't seem to notice. Instead, he sat cross-legged at her feet, staring at the deck as he spoke.

"I was scared. Terrified. My guts were water every day. What's some orphan kid from Boston doing in space, wearing a vac-suit, learning to weld in zero-G?" He huffed out a laugh. "There were times I wondered if I could keep going. Jeb saw that. He was already counting the days—he'd been smart with his credits, socked them away to buy a rock-hopper. He didn't need to help me, but he did. Showed me the ropes, taught me when to ignore company policy and when to observe it. He taught me a lot—how to take care of the people around you, the difference between right and wrong...and how to cheat at cards. You know, the important stuff."

Rosario smirked. "Real-world education."

"Exactly. The nuns tried their best, but Jeb had life experience. So yeah, I feel like I owe him.

Answering some cryptic message is the least I can do. You can call this my Christmas present if you want."

Rosario grinned, nudging her leg against Liam's. "Don't worry, I already got you a present. It's the—"

"Whoa!" Liam practically bounced on the deck. "You don't tell someone what you're giving them! Is that how they do Christmas on Mars?" Looking up at his wife, his tone softened. "You don't talk about your childhood much. Holidays bring up bad memories?"

Rosario's leg stilled. "Not really. It's just that holidays are different when you're the child of a public figure. It's photo-ops and community engagement, looking like you're in the festive mood when all you really want to do is hang out in your pajamas and play board games with your family."

She wrapped an arm around Liam and turned the question back on him. "I can't imagine the nuns indulging in much merry-making?"

Liam chuckled. "About what you'd expect. But we had no end of classic Christmas vids to watch, and there'd usually be a visit from Santa with new socks or a book. It wasn't much, but we kids made it our own."

A stillness filled the bridge as they each reflected on their two very different childhoods—and how a simple act of charity had brought them together.

To lighten the mood, Rosario plucked the Santa hat off Liam's head, stood, and modeled it herself, the garish red velvet a stark contrast to her gray sweater. Liam grinned, took her hand, and the two twirled around the small bridge—until blue-white strobe lights pulsed across the *Caissa*'s control panels. Their laughter faded as a shadow took form outside.

Another vessel had arrived.

"Am I interrupting anything, Liam?" crackled over the open intercom line.

"Are you sure he's all there?" Rosario whispered to Liam as Jeb Clanton stomped out of the *Caissa*'s airlock.

Jeb stepped out in a faded-red spacesuit, its elbows patched with neon-green emergency seals. His full white beard only added to the Santa-like effect, and Rosario had to resist the urge to straighten the holiday hat on her head.

"Well, he's always been a little pecu—" Liam's sentence cut short as Jeb swept him into a massive bear hug, their belt tools clanging like bells.

"Little Liam! You've filled out since I saw you last. You start eating right?"

"Thanks to my wife. She grows a lot of our food. Jeb, my wife Rosario Vega, Captain of the *Caissa*. Dear, may I introduce Jebediah Clanton."

Jeb, still hugging Liam with one hand, used the other to shake Rosario's, setting the tools ringing again.

"Just Jeb. Only my ma called me Jebediah, and she's long since passed." Jeb released Liam and stepped back. The jovial spark in his eyes dimmed, replaced by something far heavier. His voice dropped to a quieter register. "Just like my son, Foster. And that's why I need your help."

The festive mood fled like atmosphere from an airlock. Liam suggested heading to the galley for something hot to drink, but Jeb shook his head.

"No time, no time. I'll be blunt—I need your help. Two weeks ago, a blowout on H-ring at Endeavor Station killed my son, Foster, and his wife, Katrina. Now their daughter—my granddaughter Mia—is all alone. She's only eight, but sharp as a tack and stubborn as they come. I just need your help to bring her home."

Liam and Rosario exchanged puzzled glances.

"Do you need us to write a character reference or something?" Liam asked.

"You're her next of kin. How hard can it be to adopt your own flesh and blood?" Rosario added.

"Not that hard," Jeb admitted, pulling a bundle of documents from an inner pocket of his spacesuit. "I just need these filed with the Ward of Endeavor Station Institute office on Endeavor before Christmas. Otherwise, Mia will be stuck in the system until she's sixteen—little more than a slave, working for room and board."

All three humans sighed. The red-nosed drone flickered uncertainly, its light dimming.

Life in the void was tough—tougher still for orphans. The stations had taken a page from history books. The Institute system was little more than a mega-corp sponsored workhouse, providing the bare minimum education. When kids aged out at sixteen, they had no real options. Most ended up signing long-term indenture contracts with a mega-corp.

They'd all seen what kind of dead-end life that led to.

Liam and Rosario exchanged another glance.

"We can get you to Endeavor," Rosario said. "Time's short, so we'd better leave soon."

Jeb shook his head, his shoulders slumping.

"I struck it rich, Liam," Jeb said, his voice heavy, as if mourning a loved one.

He handed Rosario the paperwork and pulled a small box from inside his suit. Opening it, Liam and Rosario stared at the hand-carved, blue-white metal star.

"Osmium," Jeb said. "Enough to shield a dozen station-sized reactor cores. I'll never have to work again—and I'll be able to give Mia everything she needs."

Rosario tapped the adoption forms in her hand. "What's the 'but'?"

Jeb hung his head. "You hit the core of the matter. I need to work my claim for ninety consecutive days to register the strike—eighteen more to go. If I leave now, I'll lose it to jumpers. They've been hunting me in this maze of rock." He raised his gaze, but whatever he saw on their faces made him drop it again.

"I know—family comes first. I know it. But without this strike, I'd have to take some station job. And who's hiring an old man? Mia needs more than that. With this osmium, I can provide for her." He nodded at the paperwork. "That has to be delivered and processed before Christmas. They won't take an electronic copy—I already asked. That's why I need you. Take care of Mia for a week or two until I can register the strike."

Jeb lifted his hands. "It's not ideal, I know. But it's too dangerous here for an eight-year-old, and it's only for a couple of weeks. Maximum. It's worth one percent of my claim to you. What do you say?"

Liam and Rosario exchanged glances, but they already knew the answer.

"Excellent!" Jeb exclaimed, snapping the box shut. "Give that to Mia and tell her Gramps is coming for her right away."

Tucking his beard into his suit, he grabbed his helmet. "I have to dash—I've been away too long as it is. Remember, it needs to be filed before Christmas."

"Queen Bee, plot a course for Endeavor Station. I'll be on the bridge in five minutes to review it."

Turning to Liam, Rosario shifted seamlessly from loving wife to ship's captain, as if donning a well-worn uniform. Her posture straightened, radiating authority.

"Christmas is in twelve days, and it's a long haul to Endeavor. Squeeze every bit you can from the engines—we're going to need it."

Her husband and their red-nosed drone sidekick saluted in unison before dashing toward the *Caissa's* waiting engines.

The ship swiftly retraced Jeb's complicated route, weaving through the shattered remains of

Ceres, and emerged into open space—only to be painted by radar.

"Liam!" Rosario shouted as she fed the overloaded sensor data into something comprehensible. "I think Jeb's jumpers found us."

As the heavy pounding of Liam's boots grew louder, Rosario saw they were being hailed.

"I hear, I hear!" Liam huffed, sprinting onto the bridge. A stray piece of garland, caught in his pinchpliers, fluttered behind him. "Stall if you can, I'll see what we're up against. Queenie, I need you on this!"

"I'm on it, Tiger," echoed from the speakers.

Seeing Liam madly typing at his console and holding a cryptic conversation with Queen Bee about sensor algorithms, area of effect, and hull penetrations, Rosario grabbed her headset and plugged in. Exhaling a slow, steady breath, she answered the hail.

"Captain Vega of the bonded courier ship *Caissa* here. Mind telling me why you're trying to overwhelm my sensors?"

A grainy image flickered to life on one of Rosario's screens. The woman on the other end was likely Rosario's age, mid-thirties, but life had taken her down a more violent road. Burns covered the left side of her face, taking an ear and twisting her lip into a permanent sneer. But it was her undamaged eyes that pinned Rosario in her seat. There wasn't a speck of humanity left in them.

"*Caissa*, this is Captain Parkelj of the *Bell 'n' Chain*. I'll make this short and sweet. We know you're out here to meet old Jeb—we watched you enter the asteroid field. Give us the map or whatever you used to find him, and we won't riddle your ship with a thousand holes. You have five minutes. Parkelj out."

"Isn't she a treat?" Rosario muttered, sliding her headphones down to rest on her braid. "We have five minutes. They don't seem like brilliant conversationalists, but I don't doubt their time-keeping skills. Options?"

Liam spared his wife a strained smile before stabbing his screen. Rosario couldn't help but notice his hand shook.

"Their ship's a converted pleasure vessel, probably houses twenty people without straining life support. They welded armor over vital bits and have wire mesh cages connected to large D-rings."

Rosario arched an eyebrow.

"Storage pins for stuff that can survive the void," Liam explained. Tapping the screen again, he continued, "They also have an auto-cannon, homemade from what I can see, firing slugs of solid metal. More than enough to cripple us. I'm sorry, Rosario, I should never have gotten us involved in this."

"You can wash my back later. For now, we need a way out. We can't lead them back to Jeb, so that means bluff or run. And I hate to say it, but I don't think we can bluff Parkelj."

"Never a cop around when you need one," Liam said with a wink.

Rosario blew a raspberry in his face.

"The radiation in the asteroid field gave me an idea. Their ship's tough, but their sensors and comms aren't great. I need at least an hour to put it together. Think you can stay ahead of them that long?"

A light on the communications panel started blinking, drawing their attention.

"I guess we're about to find out. You and Queen Bee get to work. I'll keep them from docking," Rosario said, pulling up her headset.

Liam gave his wife a quick peck on the cheek and dashed from the bridge, shouting into his wrist communicator.

Rosario put on her game face and opened the channel.

"*Caissa*, your time is up," Parkelj said. The distortion on the screen blurred the worst of her scars, but her tone came through loud and clear.

"You don't leave us much choice." Rosario jammed the throttle to max, making the *Caissa* shudder as she darted past the pirates and made for open space.

"Liam," she shouted into the intercom, "I'm taking evasive action around the fringes of the asteroid belt so their gun can't lock on, but they're already in pursuit. Nav says they'll overtake us in fifty-four minutes. I hope you padded that hour?"

The faint melody of Christmas music played, contrasting with the forced levity in Liam's voice.

"Tons of time, tons. Queenie! I said four explosive charges, FOUR! Gotta go, dear, love you."

The bridge suddenly fell silent, but Rosario pushed her emotions aside and concentrated on keeping them alive. Which she did, with seconds to spare.

"Damn, I need to hit the gym after this," Liam huffed as he ran onto the bridge for the second time today.

"We need to survive first, dear," Rosario said, plucking her sweaty shirt away from her skin. "Are you ready?"

Leaning against the copilot seat, Liam nodded.

"Yup. We just need to make sure they don't shoot us before you deliver their presents. Queenie even wrapped it."

Rosario swore under her breath and opened communications as a stream of bullets from the pirates' auto-cannon stitched a line in front of the *Caissa's* nose.

"*Bell 'n' Chain, Caissa* here. We give up, coming to a stop."

"Perfect," Liam said, wiping his brow, leaving a grease stain. "Bring us alongside them so the secondary airlock is in line with their ship. And when I send the signal, shut down all communication and sensors—otherwise, we'll be blinded too."

And with that, Liam gathered his strength and hurried back the way he came.

Captain Parkelj looked even uglier than the last time she appeared on Rosario's screen, and it had nothing to do with her scars. "Why shouldn't I shred your ship and just take what I want?" Parkelj sneered.

Drawing on her training as a former cop, Rosario kept her tone calm.

"Because you run the risk of destroying what you're after. Listen, we both know that you're faster and better armed than us. We just needed time to figure out the best way for both of us to come out of this alive. You can understand that, right?"

Captain Parkelj's sneer softened into something resembling respect. "Go on, *Caissa*."

Monitoring the intercom, hoping that Liam's plan worked, Rosario continued. "We're going to send over what you requested from our secondary airlock. It will be your choice to grab it or us." At Liam's signal, Rosario hastily said, "*Caissa* out," and rushed to shut down comms and navigation.

"Okay Queenie," Liam said as he stared into the open airlock. "It's all up to you."

"I got it, Tiger," Queenie's voice said from the intercom as the red-nosed drone in the airlock waved a metallic claw in farewell.

Laden down with Liam's makeshift device, the red-nosed drone tugged on the cable securing it to the airlock and jumped into the void. Resembling a metallic lobster clutching a used gas cylinder, the drone sped through open space toward the pirates. Queenie snapped some photos, knowing Liam would be interested in the pirates' modifications, then waited until the cable went taut. With the drone's nose shiny and bright to guide the way, Queenie launched Liam's device toward the pirates, waited a minute until it got close to the other ship, and detonated it.

"Merry Christmas, assholes," Liam muttered as

he shielded his eyes from the glare and turned away from the open airlock. Stabbing the intercom, Liam called the bridge.

"Hon, give me five minutes to get that drone back on board and then set course for Endeavor. With a little luck, we should be clear of pursuit."

"What did you do? I barely got my nav board shut down in time, and I'm getting a bunch of warnings on secondary systems. It's like a Christmas tree on steroids up here."

Wincing at the maintenance work ahead, Liam retracted the cable holding the red-nosed drone. Still, he felt a wave of satisfaction as he took in the pirate ship and described the sight to his wife.

"Basically, I made a glitter bomb using spent fuel pellets and some mining charges I had lying around. Lots of radioactive noise to overwhelm their sensors and communications, but no harm to the crew."

The sounds of typing and a shift in gravity told Liam that the *Caissa* was underway. Rosario's next words confirmed it.

"So, a bit like a flash-bang grenade we used in the force. Good thinking. Now for the bad news. That run-in with Parkelj not only delayed us, but the explosion is giving me some weird sensor echoes. I have to slow us down."

Liam's shoulders slumped. "That's my fault. I'm sorry. Can we still make Endeavor in twelve days?"

"We're certainly going to try!"

The *Caissa* and its crew limped into the orbit of Endeavor Station, exhausted but jubilant that they'd reached their destination on time—at least, they hoped so.

"We have time, I'm sure of it," Rosario said as she spared a moment to pat her husband's hand while dealing with port control. When her hand tensed and went still, Liam looked up.

"Our clocks were out of sync, probably something to do with the glitter bomb. Liam, dear, it's 16:13 hours on Christmas Eve."

With fear speeding their steps, Rosario and Liam barely saw the festive mood that encapsulated Endeavor station as they raced through the corridors, the drone clinging to Liam's shoulder. Hand in hand, the pair hurried through holographic visions of snowflakes that disappeared as soon as they touched the metal deck, only to reappear high in the spiraling bridges. Past crowds of excited shoppers who meandered, whiling away the last few magical moments as competing holiday carols floated from permanent shops and temporary stalls. But they didn't see any of it and didn't stop until they skidded to a stop in front of the station's orphanage and saw the sign.

"Ward of Endeavor Station Institute is closed to the public until the New Year to comply with the recent workers' petition. For potential job contracts of the residents of the Institute, contact the management on January 1st for our current manual labor rates."

Liam pounded a fist against the formidable metal door that more resembled an entrance to a jail than a place of care.

Rosario wove her hand around her husband's and leaned against him. "Look at the date on the notice. Look, Liam. The Institute was closed at the same time we were meeting Jeb. None of this was your fault." Once Liam's hand relaxed, Rosario continued. "This isn't over. We're not without friends, we just need a plan. Can your contacts with the Dew Drop Inn help? They're good at smuggling people."

Realizing that they were drawing unwanted attention, Liam gave his wife a weak smile and led them away from the Institute.

"Maybe, given time. But they're used to moving people from temporary housing to the colony ship. Plus, some of those kids likely spent time here, and I wouldn't ask them to return—it would likely bring back painful memories."

Seeing that Liam was thinking again, Rosario allowed her husband to do what he did best: turn a problem into a solution. They had passed a sweet vendor that made Rosario's teeth ache just looking at the selection, but knowing her husband's fondness for artificially processed calories, she considered turning back when Liam beat her to it.

"We're dense! Catherine lives on Endeavor, and what we need is a good hacker right now." And as quick as that, Liam steered Rosario away from the throngs of shoppers and made for a quiet corridor to call their friend.

"So that's it, Catherine," Liam finished, speaking into his communicator. "Can your alter ego, *The Mayor,* gain access to the Institute's systems and wrangle us a pass or something? I know this is last minute, but a little girl's future is on the line." Liam's concern for Mia kept him from asking what Catherine and Hakeema were doing when he called. Hakeema stood like a shops mannequin wearing a half-knit sweater featuring candy canes, and Catherine sat in her wheelchair surrounded by mounds of wool.

Tucking knitting needles into her hair bun, Catherine wheeled out of frame, but the sound of typing reached Rosario and Liam in the quiet corridor.

"It's quick and dirty, and probably wouldn't hold up to an in-depth cyber inspection, but the Endeavor Station Chamber of Trade has invited Liam O'Fallon and Rosario Vega to visit the Institute. Sorry I had to use your real names, but with your time constraints, I don't have time to craft something more solid. Will that do?"

The tension drained from Liam's body.

"Thanks, that gets us in the door. Now we just need to figure out how to get the paperwork in the right folder with no one noticing."

"I have an idea," Rosario whispered. "You'll love it."

"Shout if you need backup," Hakeema called, unmoving in the half-finished sweater. "A good shoot-out sounds lovely right about now."

Catherine wheeled into view and silenced Hakeema with a sharp look before the connection flickered out.

Hugging his wife, Liam breathed a sigh of relief.

"So what's your plan?"

⁓⁓⁓✷⁓⁓⁓

Liam huffed as he struggled to pull the vibrant green tights over his hips. "I thought you said I'd like this idea?" Neither of them had slept well in the few hours afforded to them, and it showed.

"Now you know how we feel," Rosario countered, tugging down the front of her corset for the third time since putting it on. It kept riding up every time she breathed.

"We?"

"Women who dress for the male gaze."

With a wad of green fabric in his hands, Liam tilted his head. "I'm usually more interested in getting you out of your clothes than what they look like, but I must say, that is giving me some ideas."

That being one of the two costumes Rosario had managed to find in Endeavor's market before it closed for the holiday. With limited selection, she had secured a slightly risqué Mrs. Claus costume: thigh-high black leather boots, a red velvet skirt, and a corset trimmed with white fur, topped off with her floppy Santa hat. A quick stop for a red shawl covered her bare shoulders and plunging neckline, bringing the outfit into the realm of decency.

Liam was at least modest, though an affront to good taste. With no Santa costumes available,

Rosario had found something equally festive: a bright green elf outfit complete with tights, a gold-threaded vest, and curved shoes sporting bells.

"I'm not wearing the ears!"

"Think of the children, dear," Rosario said, passing over the large plastic ears.

"Tiger and Queenie are pretty," Queenie's voice chimed through their communicators, and the red-nosed drone snapped its metallic claws in agreement.

Liam had made one purchase for the next stage of their plan—a small set of antlers, now perched atop the drone's head. The rest of their meager funds had gone into practical gifts for the Institute children, packed into a duffel bag beside them.

At 0719 hours, unable to sit still any longer, dressed in their costumes, loaded up with presents and adoption paperwork, they left the *Caissa*.

"Queenie, keep your drone still. Those antlers are poking me in the back," Liam whispered as he adjusted the bag slung over his shoulder.

"Queenie wants to see," came the reply from his wrist communicator.

"You'll get an eyeful soon, Queen Bee," Rosario countered. "But we need you quiet for now, okay?"

Silence was her only answer.

A determined group hurried through the early morning common areas of Endeavor Station, trudging past the castoffs of holiday shoppers. Cleaning robots and human scavengers were already searching for anything of value. Night shift workers, exhausted but hopeful for a holiday, cheered when they saw Liam and Rosario in their costumes.

"I hope you've been good, because Santa's been watching," Liam said, waving a fistful of candy canes. The workers chuckled and stepped aside, allowing them to pass. Rosario's pointed stare ensured the path stayed clear as they plowed forward without stopping until they reached the Institute.

"Ready?" Liam asked, shifting the sack of presents to his other shoulder, his voice heavy with emotion.

Rosario brushed her fingers against his cheek before pressing the door button. Her finger was still on the call button eight minutes later when the heavy steel door finally slid open, revealing a disheveled man in his forties.

"Dip into the eggnog last night?" Rosario asked, straightening her shawl and casting a judgmental eye over him. "Poor example for the children, isn't it?"

Liam, knowing the effect of Rosario's authoritative voice, watched the performance with amusement.

Like a malfunctioning robot coming to life, the man twitched and shuddered, tugging at his shirt cuffs, straightening his collar, and combing back his hair with shaking fingers. Bloodshot eyes flicked between Liam and Rosario, his features puzzled.

"Ah? Hello? I think you might have the wrong address."

"This is the Wards of Endeavor Station Institute, is it not?" Rosario pressed. "We're here to give the children their presents. Didn't you read your mail? We're on a schedule. You've assembled the children, I take it?"

"Presents? Mail? Schedule?"

"Listen..."

"Fuga. Saulo Fuga. Assistant Chief Administrator of the Institute."

Sighing, Rosario shook her head, the pom-pom on her hat bouncing in shared indignation. "Check your records, Fuga. I am Captain Rosario Vega of the courier ship *Caissa*, and we're under contract from the Chamber of Trade of Endeavor Station to hand out presents as part of a mega-corp goodwill initiative. There's talk that vid crews might get involved. Good P.R. for everyone."

Like snow melting, realization slowly crossed Fuga's face. "Come in. I'll need to check into this."

In short order, Fuga led Rosario and Liam into a small anteroom just inside the main door that resembled a holding cell more than a receiving chamber. As Fuga accessed a computer terminal, Rosario positioned herself between him and Liam, smoothly steering the conversation.

With only half an ear on his wife keeping Fuga occupied, Liam spoke softly into his wrist communicator. "Okay, Queenie. It's all up to you. You remember what you need to do, right?"

By answer, the bulging sack at Liam's feet shifted. Moments later, a pair of antlers and a glowing-red nose emerged. A thick elastic held the adoption paperwork securely to the drone's back. Liam smiled and gently pushed the drone back into the sack.

"Ah, excuse me?"

Rosario and Fuga paused their conversation, one face showing understanding, the other confusion.

"Is there a little elf's room around here?" Liam

asked, the bells on his shoes tinkling as he pressed his knees together. "These tights make things a little difficult, if you know what I mean. Been holding it for ages, and we don't want any accidents handing out presents, do we?"

"You'll need time to gather the children, won't you?" Rosario added, turning back to Fuga. "Since it looks like you forgot about us."

Fuga looked between them, then ran a finger along a line of text on his console, shaking his head. "I don't understand how I missed it, but your appointment is right here, logged and confirmed."

"The restroom?" Liam repeated.

Fuga waved a hand at the door. "Third on the left, before the security checkpoint. Ms. Sprude is going to be furious when she hears I messed this up."

Subtly motioning for Liam to slip out, Rosario joined Fuga at the console. "Let's make sure she doesn't hear, then. We can still salvage this. You just need to gather the children, right? How can I help?"

As Liam slipped from the room, sack over his shoulder, he grinned at his wife. Behind him, Rosario was already wrapping the administrator around her finger, keeping him distracted. The latching door cut off all sound.

With a solid metal door between Rosario and him, Liam took a deep breath. The familiar echoes of the Institute and memories of his own orphanage upbringing settled over him like an icy mantle since their arrival. The stark interior, stabbing lights, and ever-present smell of cleaning chemicals reinforced the feeling.

"You will not get this child," Liam muttered, cursing the empty hallway as he hurried to the restroom.

Quickly getting to work, Liam lowered the sack and took the multi-tool the drone held in a claw as it scrambled free.

"Queenie going down the chimney now, Tiger?"

Banishing his dark thoughts, Liam wiggled his elf ears and set to work, removing the grill from the room's life support system.

"Yes, Queenie. You remember the plan?"

"Queenie takes the drone through the ducts, finds the tipsy man's office, and puts the papers in the files."

"In the proper place, Queenie. It's Mia Clanton with a C, not a K. Remember, you get them confused sometimes."

"Mia with a C. Queenie remembers, Tiger."

The sound of voices in the hallway—Rosario and Fuga—told Liam his time was up. He'd have to trust that Queenie was sticking to the plan, playful as ever. Liam hastily replaced the duct grill and watched as the drone scurried down the duct, its red light wobbling.

Liam adjusted his elf ears in the restroom mirror before gathering up the sack.

"Time to go spread some holiday cheer."

*

"Are these all the children in the Institute's care, Mr. Fuga?" Rosario asked as the trio entered a large auditorium that featured bolted-down metal benches, a small play area with well-worn toys, and little else. The blue-white lights that blazed overhead made the assembled children look pale and withdrawn.

"That's right," Fuga replied, straightening his clothes after taking a moment outside to make himself presentable. "We currently have forty-six children aged six to fifteen within our care. That is a little lower than average. We had a class of eight age out last quarter, and I'm pleased to say all eight signed on with well-known corporations."

Whatever reaction Fuga expected from Rosario and Liam, it certainly wasn't the thinly veiled hostility from the couple.

Taking her husband's shaking hand and squeezing it tight, Rosario whispered, "Remember, this is about the children." Feeling Liam return her squeeze lifted some of the concern from her voice.

Husband and wife stepped forward.

"Hey, kids!" Rosario shouted into the metal auditorium, her echoing voice drawing every eye toward her. Suddenly, with forty-six pairs of eyes on her, Rosario found her tongue struggling to make sense, but Liam saved her.

"That's right, kids," Liam said, waving them toward him, "Santa sent his lovely wife, Mrs. Claus, to visit you and hand out some gifts. Let's gather in the play area, and I'll tell a story first. Sound good?"

It took more than a little gentle cajoling and Rosario's firm suggestion that Mr. Fuga remain by the doors, but eventually, Liam had all the children spread out on the foam mats in the recreation area, half the eyes on him and half on the bulging sack laying by his feet.

He'd always been better with children than she was, so Rosario hung back and just listened as Liam and the children had a multi-pronged conversation that made her dizzy, just trying to keep it straight. The rapid-fire conversation must have worn Liam down, too, as he eventually asked the children if they wanted a story.

With half an ear on Liam's efforts, trying to figure out which of the children was Mia, and half an ear on fobbing off Fuga's pleas for them to hurry and leave, Rosario didn't hear the noise above—but the children did, as all eyes looked up at the life support grill. The smile and quick wink from Liam said that he had matters well in hand. Waving off Fuga, Rosario listened.

"When out on the hull there arose such a clatter,

I sprang from my bunk to see what was the matter.

Away to the airlock, I flew like a flash,

Tore open the controls and threw up the sash.

When what to my wondering eyes did appear,

But a miniature sleigh and a tiny reindeer!"

And with this pronouncement, the metal grill popped off, and the drone sporting a slightly cock-eyed set of antlers appeared, its red nose shining brightly. The children cheered as the drone scampered down the wall and made a beeline for Liam's shoulder.

Seeing wheels turning in Fuga's mind, Rosario stepped in.

"Ok, children, who wants a present?"

With nearly four dozen kids yelling, running, and acting like children on Christmas morning, Fuga momentarily forgot about the drone in the life support system. Instead, he shouted into his communicator, demanding help from more staff. From the pained expression on his face, it looked like he wasn't having much luck.

"Ok, settle down, everyone. Mrs. Claus has a gift for all of you, but the first one goes to a special girl named Mia Clanton. Is Mia here?" Liam said as he rooted around in his sack while the drone wobbled on his shoulder.

All eyes went to a sad-faced girl. Standing slightly away from the rest, with hands clenched before her so tight that her knuckles were white, stood Mia Clanton. Instead of wilting under the gaze of her peers, Mia stood tall and stepped forward, but without the cheer the others displayed, instead bracing herself as if for punishment. Rosario and Liam exchanged a look, and each saw the anguish mirrored in the other's face.

"I'm Mia Clanton, but I don't want a present."

The chuckles and jeers of the other kids brought color to Mia's cheeks.

"You're going to want this one," Liam said, holding the box Jeb Clanton gave them. "I'll tell you what," Liam said. "How about we open it together? I happen to know that it's from your grandfather." A spark of something like hope flickered across Mia's face.

"Grampie Jeb?"

Gathering Mia to him, Liam held the box, and

Mia's small fingers opened it, revealing the hand-carved osmium star.

"What is it?" Mr. Fuga said, moving closer as if pulled by gravity.

"Freedom, Mr. Fuga."

Something in Rosario's voice caused Fuga to stand up straight and look at Rosario with narrowed eyes.

With one arm around Mia and his elf ears slightly askew, Liam passed out presents to the milling children while Rosario explained the situation to Fuga.

"We are here to take Mia to her grandfather, Mr. Fuga. Honestly, we expected her to be packed and ready for us when we arrived."

"Pardon?"

"Her grandfather, Jeb Clanton, has adopted Mia. Surely you have the paperwork on file. I'm sure if you check your records..."

Institute staff burst into the auditorium, grabbing Fuga's attention.

"I'll do that right now!" And as quick as that, Fuga rushed to his staff, gave them hurried instructions to watch the children, and raced from the room.

Dismissing the administrator from her thoughts, Rosario felt some of the joy of the season warm her and joined her husband with the children.

"You mean I can go live with Grampie Jeb now?" she asked, her voice barely louder than a whisper.

Liam crouched beside her, his smile gentle. "In about a week. Until then, you'll be staying with us on our ship. How does that sound?"

Mia looked between them, clutching the carved osmium star like it was the only solid thing in her world. She nodded—just once—but it was enough.

Rosario knelt on her other side and brushed a lock of hair behind Mia's ear. "You're safe now, sweetheart. And you're not alone."

Just then, Queenie's drone popped out of a pile of crumpled gift wrap, ribbons tangled in its antlers. It tilted its camera up at the trio, the red recording light blinking softly.

"Say Merry Christmas!" the drone chirped.

Mia glanced at Liam, then Rosario—and for the first time all day, she smiled.

"Merry Christmas," she whispered.

"*Jingle Bell Dock*" *is a story in the* Jupiter's Eye *series.* Encrypted Starpath, *book one, in this series, is available at* books2read.com/u/4NOZW8.

RECIPE: MARTIAN ATOLE

From Peter J. Foote's "Jingle Bell Dock"

*THIS VERSION HAS EVOLVED SINCE COMING FROM Earth.

Ingredients:

- 4 cups milk
- ½ brown sugar cane (normal brown sugar works as well)
- 1 cinnamon stick
- 1 ½ cups warm water
- ½ cup masa harina (fine corn flour)
- 2 teaspoons vanilla extract
- 1 pinch salt
- Ground cinnamon, for garnish

Instructions:
1. Add the milk, sugar cane, and cinnamon stick

to a medium saucepan or pot. Warm over low-medium heat until the sugar cane has completely dissolved. Stir frequently to make sure the milk and sugar cane don't stick to the bottom of the saucepan.

2. Remove and discard the cinnamon stick.

3. In a small bowl, add the warm water and corn flour. Whisk together until smooth.

4. Add the corn flour mixture, vanilla extract, and salt to the saucepan. Whisk to combine.

5. Bring to a simmer, reduce heat to low, and continue to cook, stirring frequently, for 25-30 minutes until thick, creamy, velvety, and smooth. The atole should be thick enough to coat the back of a spoon.

6. Serve and garnish with a touch of ground cinnamon.

ORLANDER'S FOLLY

by Andrew Sweet

THROUGH A THIN PLATE OF GLASS AND THE ROAR of a winter storm, Larken Marche gazed down over the militarized compound she'd helped create. She rubbed her tired eyes and tried her best to focus on a single flake, making up the contour of its edges against a nearly indistinguishable backdrop. She took a deep breath and let it out, fogging the glass. The tent city, little more than a slum, lay sprawled out below, tucked behind walls higher than the birch tree which flipped its weak branches like a dancer at a bolga concert.

"The price of a big heart and a small pocket-book," her childhood friend Joscelyn had said the last time she'd visited. She needed, as Joscelyn stated, to turn people away. But there was nowhere else for these refugees to go. Even in their own country, genetically-altered clones, or models, were considered the dregs of society—and were held in near universal loathing. Here, at least they were mostly safe.

A speck of brown drew her attention amidst the falling white. She focused in on the spot, straining to make out its contours. Larken blinked once, gasped quietly, and covered her mouth with her hand. A giant bulbous-eyed creature—the many-armed little monster-god, Olander—stared up at her. Her cane-hand shook so much that her entire body wobbled like she held a proton rifle set on automatic.

Claws extended upward from the creature as if beckoning her to come down. Sharpened teeth clamped to interlocking points in a wide, malevolent grin. She shivered as much from the god's growing smile as the chill of standing only a breath away from the double-paned office windows that separated them.

I'm seeing things, she thought. *The Martian god isn't real. It's because of the day, that's all.*

Larken closed her eyes and shook her head. By the time she opened them, the god had disappeared.

"All those children down there," said Dandelion. "Is it safe?"

Dandelion's voice startled Larken, who had all but forgotten the android in her surprise at seeing a mythical deity. She twisted to see Dandelion staring out toward what had by now become a snowbank. Tiny dots of children moved around atop it, now that the storm had lessened some. Dandelion grinned and pointed a thin synthetic finger toward the children below. Then she lifted a hand to her mouth, half-covering her smile with her fingers. At that reaction, Larken's rattling cane slowly stilled as she managed to bring it back under her control.

"How can they stand the cold?" she asked, wrapping her free arm tightly against her chest.

"A child runs hotter than an adult on median," Dandelion said. "When they're running around like that, their internal temperatures can exceed one hundred and five. Those rags they wear retain nearly sixty percent of their body heat. That means to them it feels between forty to fifty degrees. They won't *feel* cold for another fifteen minutes. If—"

"I didn't need—"

Dandelion's widening smile interrupted Larken's interruption. Larken could tell the woman wasn't going to stop.

"—if only they had warmer clothes. Then they could stay out for hours more even." A whisper of a sigh followed at the end.

"We do the best we can," Larken assured, feeling heat rising to her face. "Too many children, and not enough donations."

"I know," said Dandelion, her eyes still following the running, screaming children. Her gold-flecked green irises pivoted in Larken's direction, drilling directly into her brown ones. Then Dandelion squinted *past* Larken at the wall behind.

"Orlander?" Dandelion asked, causing Larken to contort her body once more. An Underworlder calendar clung to the wall, named after a table-top role-playing-game. Larken's fear tugged at the back of her neck at another Orlander sighting. This one was only their image as the god-of-the-month for December. The celebration on December 12 this year—the date was based on a Martian calendar and skipped around Earth time—was for a holiday called Orlander's Folly.

"He's hideous," Dandelion said.

"*They're* not a *he*. They're a god," Larken corrected, the same way Larken had been corrected the last time she'd assumed the monstrosity was a male. Her Underworlder friend had pointed out that gods could be whatever they wanted, and so it made little sense to categorize them by sex.

"What are *they* the god of?"

"Small children," Larken said with a grin, knowing how well that would go over with the still-sometimes-literal Dandelion.

"Do they *eat* them?"

Larken laughed at the *very* valid observation. The image of the god belied their being the god of small children. Four arms, each adorned with thick, clawed hands, were covered in sparse hairs interpolated with scales across the skin's surface. The face, with overlarge eyes so big they seemed fake, rested atop a head that itself resembled something from kabuki theatre, with giant sharpened fang-teeth that forced its mouth open most of the time.

"No," Larken said, laughing until a pain in her side reminded her that she was very much injured still. "Well, they used to. It's kind of a long story."

"Look at us," Dandelion said. "We're in the office, in the middle of a snowstorm. We have time."

"Okay," Larken said. "Okay...let's see what I can remember."

"Wait, I have an idea," Dandelion said, darting toward the food replicator that sat on a shelf by the door, usually relegated to coffee production. She punched in fifteen digits and, thirty seconds later, pulled out two plates, steeped in the acrid aroma of acetic acid. Larken scrunched up her nose.

"Vinegar cobbler," Dandelion explained, shoving a plate toward her while reciting words that Larken already knew from the quote on the calendar: "Orlander's Folly is traditionally celebrated by eating vinegar cobbler, vinegar being a replacement for rhubarb which doesn't grow in Martian soil."

"Nobody on *Earth* eats that," Larken added, accepting the dish with a scrunched nose.

"Somebody programmed it into the replicator," Dandelion said.

"Probably as a joke," Larken retorted.

Dandelion disappeared from the room and reappeared moments later with two forks from the break room.

"Okay, now we're ready," Dandelion said, settling onto a chair and shoving a bite of the bitter-sweet cobbler into her mouth. Larken accepted the fork as well, and placed this and her plated "dessert" down on the counter beside her. Then she began.

"Orlander is the god of prosperity. That's the purpose of all those teeth and the arms: arms for grabbing as much as they can, and teeth allowing them to consume anything they grabbed."

She rubbed her jaw for a second before continuing.

"On Mars, you have to remember the generations of terraforming families. Mostly subsistence farmers, nobody had enough to eat or drink. They sometimes lacked air to breathe. If you had *enough*, that meant you were probably stealing from others."

"It was bad," Dandelion replied. "I remember. One could get stabbed just stepping out of a volantrae."

"I forget how old you are sometimes," Larken said with a sigh. "You're sure you haven't heard the story."

"Guarding interplanetary freight means a lot of alone time and very few stories," Dandelion said.

"I guess. Well, Mars, as you know, is where Orlander originated as a deity," Larken said, stabilizing herself on her good leg and cane. "At least, according to Joscelyn. She said it doesn't really make sense here on Earth, having a god of plenty be also the god of destruction. It resonated on Mars, though."

Larken balanced her cane across her arms. "On Mars there was just *less*. Especially during the age of the warlords, before the planet was brought together under Liu Jian."

"I knew Liu," Dandelion said between mouthfuls. "I met her at a reception dinner after a delivery once."

"Before or after Reunification?" Larken asked, referring to the renegotiation of interplanetary treaties after the emperor's ascension, and her very quick demise after negotiations went sour. After Reunification would have been a matter of less than an Earth year.

"Before," Dandelion said. She wiped a bit of crust from her lips. "I thought she was nice."

Larken had never heard the murderous warlord referred to as *nice* before. But the extremists against whom Larken struggled were often called *nice*, too. Their hate-filled hearts were anything but. She clenched her fist at the unwelcome memories the thought pulled up, breathed, and continued her story with a forced smile.

"As I said, Orlander was the god of prosperity. But they didn't *bring* prosperity. They *ate* it, usually appearing on the eve of bouts of scarcity or droughts, and vanished leaving devastation behind... according to legend. One day, Orlander appeared to a young boy. This boy saw that Orlander was about to eat his family home, and stood defiant. Orlander would have usually eaten such a boy, as happened in some of the older stories. Yet, something about the boy's confidence as he blocked the way caused Orlander to be curious."

"What'd the boy look like?" Dandelion asked. She rested her chin on her hands, eyes wide as a child's while she listened.

"It's not important to the story," Larken said.

"He had to have looked like *something*," Dandelion replied, craning her neck and then scraping her plate while eyeing Larken's. "Are you going to eat that?"

"You can't even digest it," Larken said.

"The flavors are so complex," Dandelion replied. "And I *can* too process it. I just can't derive *energy* from it."

"Have at it then," Larken said. Dandelion wasted no time in shoving half the entire piece of cobbler into her mouth.

"Okay," Larken said. She didn't know what the boy had looked like, so she described her nephew instead. "Thick, curly black hair rested on his head. He had a face full of bright white teeth and eyes as big as cash-coins."

"I can see it," Dandelion said.

"Good. So...Orlander asked the boy why he stood there. The boy said that it was his home that he protected," Larken continued. "Orlander felt their first twinge of empathy. The boy's house was only a shack hammered together with rough nails and wires and tarps. The roof was torn open in places from an earlier storm. There wasn't that much to protect. The boy himself wore tattered clothes, falling off a frame that was too skinny to be upright, yet impossibly was. Even as destitute as he was, the boy stood firm, ready to die to protect his family and their belongings.

"Because of this, Orlander decided to give the boy a chance to not be eaten. He—they—said that they would spare the child, if he could prove that his love for his family was real. If he could do this, then Orlander would spare the boy."

"How would you prove—"

Larken shrugged as she tried to rub out the pain in her lower back just above the tailbone.

"The boy didn't know how. So he did what children always do. When Orlander asked the boy for proof of his love, the boy went into the shack and emerged with his mother, who, being an adult, was far more terrified than the child. But when Orlander repeated their demand, she laughed, ducked inside, and came out of the shack with an armful of photos."

"Nobody has photos anymore," Dandelion said.

"The refugees do," Larken said, motioning out of the window toward the huts. "And paintings and sculptures. They can't afford the screens and technology that most of us have. Anything they have they make."

Larken paused for a moment, staring out into the easing snow. The children still played, though they indubitably felt the cold by now. They seemed happy, despite that they lacked so many of the things that she surrounded herself with. Watching them in their rags, playing, Larken's heart grew heavy enough to force out a sigh. She turned away from the window.

"Anyway, the photos. There were so many, and she showed them to Orlander one at a time. Orlander had seen such photos before, but had never had the context to *understand* them. The woman explained each smile, and each hug. She explained every image where they touched and where their eyes were locked together, and what that meant."

Dandelion shifted to lay with her legs over one arm of a chair and her head over the other arm. The woman's eyes were locked onto Larken as she began again.

"You understand that she was only stalling, as she had no idea how to get out of the situation she and her son were in. Therefore, she talked for hours and hours, not just about the photos, but about every memory she came across for the last year, from the joys to the tragedies, and how they supported each other through them. Orlander had never heard or thought of any of it before, because nobody had ever taken the time to explain these things to them. She had almost run out of stories when night fell, and Orlander's stomach grumbled. When she heard that, she related about the times they'd had to go without food in the hopes of endearing their plight to the god.

"Orlander listened. For the first time, they understood some little bit of what it meant to be human. And if you know anything about Martian gods, you know that the only thing that exceeds their self-interest is their curiosity. Every story generated within Orlander millions of questions, so that when she finished, the god blurted out a hundred in one breath."

"The boy's mother and the boy answered each, to which they offered still more questions, and more questions, until the boy yawned, and held up his hand. To the mother's surprise, Orlander stopped mid-question at this.

'We have to sleep,' said the boy, as his mother tried desperately to hush him. 'Do you believe me yet?'

Orlander did, but said they wanted more information. This was really just curiosity, and the boy knew it. So he seized the moment to make an offer.

'We need sleep, but if you come back tomorrow, we will tell you more stories,' the boy said.

At first, Orlander did, but after a hundred nights of this, the boy and his mother ran short on stories. The mother, afraid that Orlander would eat them when they exhausted their stories, despite the deal, devised a plan with her son. They told Orlander that there were millions more stories, all of the children in the world had stories. And they said that if Orlander gave them a year, the boy could get all of the children in the city to come up with new stories to give the god."

"And that's how we have Orlander's Folly celebrated every year?"

"Well, not every year exactly. And it moves around, but yes."

"But why is it called Orlander's *Folly*?"

"In his village, the boy told the other children what happened. By the next year, the children had all written stories for Orlander. And the following year too. The practice spread so that even today on Earth, children write stories for Orlander in exchange for gifts. The folly was that Orlander could never be satisfied after that. He craved more stories forever. And because there are always new children born, and new stories written, Orlander changed. They ceased being the god of plenty and devastation, and became the god of small children. By protecting them, Orlander also protected their stories. The plentitude that Orlander once consumed was freed to be shared among the people as Orlander's insatiable hunger morphed from craving physical things, to lusting after the ideas and stories that children tell. The other gods, especially Vrenofed—remember her?"

"The goddess who ate her own children and vomited and created the satellite belt from their remains?" Dandelion asked. "Yes. And...ew."

"That's the one. She considered this to be a poor trade, from consuming everything, to consuming only words. That's why it's called Orlander's Folly."

"I like that story," Dandelion said. The gold flecks in her eyes glowed. Larken's heart lifted, and she turned her attention out the window to where the children played. All of the ones still out wore coats and sweaters. The rags must have gotten too cold. Larken bit her lip as she watched the wind picking up and flinging newly fallen snow over the huts and shacks.

"I wish we had enough for them all," Larken muttered quietly. "It never seems like it's enough."

The storm resumed in force, then began to escalate, re-affirming its grip on the Bremerton compound. Flakes swelled in size, changing from pinky-tipped-sized drifters to cojoined clusters of flakes half the size of Larken's thumb. The children stayed out as much as they could until, eventually, even those with decent looking coats had to succumb to the forces of nature and retire into the tiny shacks. Within each, Larken knew, were two or three families forced together.

"Do you think we're doing the right thing?" she asked Dandelion. The android raised an artificial eyebrow at her. Larken nearly giggled at the look. It was a clunky maneuver, arching her brow nearly to her hairline and making her attempt at inquiry into more of a clownish sad face.

"What is the right thing?' Dandelion asked. "I've

been wondering a lot about that lately. How do humans decide? You know, between right and wrong?"

"You want to help those kids, right?" Larken asked. "Why?"

"Because they need help," Dandelion said, without hesitation.

"Why do you care?"

Dandelion seemed to ponder this for a moment, before swinging her legs up onto her desk and directing her stare out into the snow that looked now like a solid blanket of white falling from the sky. "I've never wondered about that."

"That's because you're a good person," Larken said with a sigh. "And I guess maybe I am too. For me, it's pretty easy, I suppose. I help those who need help when I can. That's all it takes."

This was true. When someone asked for help, her default response had always been to say yes. Often even when others failed to ask for help, like after her friend Sam had been kidnapped the year before, Larken forced help upon her. A fault, perhaps, but as far as she was concerned, it wasn't the worse fault to have. She could be flawed like Christine Hamilton. That woman acted as though every other person on the planet was created to serve her. In many ways, as the owner of Beckett-Madeline Enterprises, she wasn't wrong about that.

As though she'd summoned the woman just by thinking her name, Larken's pink, lipstick-sized communicator flared up on her desk, printing out Christine's name on the side of it. Dandelion pulled her feet up and swiveled toward where Larken sat.

"Are you going to answer?"

Larken tented an eyebrow. "Why?"

"That woman doesn't call without a reason," Dandelion said. "She doesn't work that way."

"I know," Larken said. The communicator stopped buzzing. As she was about to say more about how annoying Christine Hamilton was, it began to buzz again. Larken closed her eyes and took a breath, steadying herself.

"I guess," she muttered as she crossed the room with her cane and retrieved the communicator. When she pushed the button on the side, it projected a ballroom, wherein stood Christine Hamilton, wearing the traditional red-orange of Orlander's Folly. The scene beyond Christine caught Larken's attention and made her whistle slightly between her front teeth. Four chandeliers the size of cars hung from the ceiling, bathing the room in a warm red-orange glow. Red-orange table runners covered the tables flawlessly over the blue-green background of Earth on one side of the divide, and the rust-brown color of Mars on the other. The shock of the decor was only supplanted by the wide-toothed grin on Christine's face and her pinkish eyes, perhaps colored by the lighting, or maybe by the half-empty Martian Snakebite glass in her hand.

"What?" Larken asked.

"No greeting, Ms. Marche?"

"What are you calling me for?"

"Can't a girl call her friend on the other side of the country for no reason? Or just to say have a Happy Orlander's Folly?"

"Yes, a girl can," Larken said. "But not you. And we're not friends."

She looked genuinely hurt. Larken had to wonder whether Dandelion or Christine took longer to *learn* how to express that level of hurt. The difference, as Larken figured it, was that even though she was an android, *Dandelion's* emotions had always run deep. Her expression of them was hard to learn, whereas Christine, she was pretty sure, faked having emotions at all.

"Okay, maybe you're right *this* time. I do have an ulterior motive. The model laws are being challenged in New York, and I want you to testify."

"I'm not testifying," Larken said. "Not against the model community. Find someone else."

Again the hurt look.

"I'm not asking you to," Christine said. "I'm talking about discussing the complexities of housing models who haven't learned to take care of themselves or how to properly exercise their agency. We need to know how much time and money it takes to care for them. I understand that you have your Bremerton compound—"

"Why do you need to know?"

Dandelion shook her head, but Christine didn't seem to see. Dandelion pointed a long finger out of the window toward the snow, which now covered everything in a thin white sheet, but showed no signs of letting up. Larken followed her finger down to where the children had been playing.

"For the children," Dandelion seemed to mouth.

"Fine. The truth?" Christine said.

"Yes," Larken said, shaking her head and

furrowing her brows, and mentally preparing to filter Christine's "truth" to discern the meaning beneath.

"Because the laws are going to change," Christine said. "One way or the other. We need to know the impact to our bottom line if things don't go our way."

Just as Larken was about to respond, and just as Dandelion made some strange face the Larken was thinking *might* be an attempt to communicate something she was supposed to translate and pass on to Christine, a swirl of snow hurled past the window slamming briefly into the glass. Larken jerked backward, seeing in the miniature flurry two giant eyes that seemed to drill into her soul. Then the lights in the building flickered and the ansible connection cut out, saving Larken from any further condescension or a need to reply.

Something heavy thudded unseen against the glass.

"What was that?" Larken asked, as she stared into the white. The swirling stopped and the snow dropped to the ground. Everything beyond the window looked exactly as it had a few moments before. The huts were covered in white, thick up to at least a few centimeters, maybe nearer to ten or twenty—it was hard to tell from so high up. Nothing moved in the world beyond a gust or two in the far distance shaking loose clumps from one of the many trees on the compound.

"We should check," said Dandelion, already on her feet. As Larken began to reach for her cane, Dandelion continued. "I meant I should check. Stay here. I'll be back in a moment."

Dandelion ran out the door. Larken grabbed her cane and tried to follow, stepping out into the hallway beyond the office, but she couldn't even compete with walking speed, so catching up to an android at a dead sprint was impossible. She stopped and stood, wobbling slightly, heart pounding in her chest. The most likely situation this high up was that a bird had gotten caught up in the gust and slammed into their building. Larken didn't think she could handle seeing a tiny broken body, especially coming down off of the jarring unexpected conversation with Christine. She turned to go back into the office when she saw a flash from the corner of her eye.

Step by slow step, she started her own investigation. The light appeared to come from a nearby closet, which, considering everyone else in the building should have gone home hours ago, she couldn't explain. Her rational mind told her that she'd probably left it on, or maybe Dandelion had—though doubts niggled at her brain stem.

Larken approached with hesitation, poking out her cane first, and pulling herself to it. When she arrived at the doorway, she leaned forward to peer inside and see what she could without disturbing the door further, just in case someone had broken in. That was unlikely, given the level of fortification: anyone making it this far would have had to get into the compound in the first place. Most of her money, she reminded herself, was spent on an enviable security posture. Sucking in a bit of air, she used her cane to shove the door open...and gasped.

---❋---

"You see him?" a voice from behind asked. Larken turned and saw a black-haired woman, the same woman who'd frequented her when she was recovering from a violent HPM attack that nearly killed her. The remnant of her fever dreams sported a strong jawline and hazel, woeful eyes, as though in the nearly four decades since her death, she'd never had a moment of happiness.

"*Same*," she thought, thinking of her own near-death experiences, and commiserating with her hallucination. "I must be in trouble to see you again, Aayushi. *That's* a he?"

"Inasmuch as they could be anything, I suppose. He's always called himself a male. But he's also a god and a trickster, so there's no telling whether or not that's true."

The creature hadn't noticed them. At least, he hadn't seemed to. Larken turned her attention from her more docile hallucination to the other, and squinted slightly as her eyes adjusted to the light. She recognized the creature as Orlander, though the god had six arms now, all too thin to be human and finished with thick claws. His head was a morphology of a human face with that of a lion, in the creepiest combination possible. Orlander seemed to have been spared the lion's mane, yet had the folded lips of cats and she was close enough to be able to count all of those razor-sharp looking teeth.

He turned and stared directly at her.

"Aayushi," Larken said in a whisper that barely

materialized, unable to look away as the creature shoved the messy end of a mop through his teeth. "Aayushi!"

"Back here," Aayushi said, matching her whisper. "What?"

"I think he sees me," Larken said, her cane starting to wobble frantically as her heartbeat made its way into her arms.

"Maybe you should run?"

"From the god of small children?" she asked, gulping and holding fast to her determination not to flee in terror as the beast took a step toward her.

"And the god of plenty," Aayushi reminded her, "of which he likes to eat. And I don't see any small children here."

The god took three huge bites to finish the mop before moving on to a bottle of cleaning agent, which his mouth stretched to accommodate without opening the bottle. The entire thing fit somehow into his jaws, and he clamped shut and chewed, giving her what might have been a thoughtful gaze.

"What have you to offer me?" he demanded. More closely, the voice sprang out of nowhere and everywhere at once, shaking her bones.

"I—I have nothing," she said. "Nothing but what you see here."

"Perhaps you?" he said, no effort at intimidation in his intonation. He rubbed his stomach with two left hands.

"I'd prefer if you didn't," she said, in a bit of a whisper again, unsure how to properly address a god who was also likely to kill her, and who was probably a hallucination all the same. This seemed to annoy the god, who drew himself up to his full height, still somewhat shorter than her. Yet she knew better than to take his size for granted, even if the creature was entirely in her head. Larken rubbed her eyes.

"What would you give me?" he asked, rephrasing. "To ease this hunger. I see all you have here. Will you give it all?"

She considered this.

"I can't," she said, as the god progressed closely enough to her that she could smell the bleach on his breath.

"Give," he said.

"This isn't for me," she said. "It's not mine. None of it. This is for them." She pointed out into the snow toward the huts below. "I would give anything if I had it. This is not mine."

"You own it," he said.

"I keep it," she said. "I protect it, so that I can protect them."

"Good. Keep *that* hallucination at bay," Aayushi said behind her.

"You're not helping," Larken muttered between her teeth. In her mind, she recognized that both were hallucinations, but then her eyes told her other stories, and her ears worked against her too, so she flitted between belief and disbelief. "And you're a hallucination too, remember?"

"You're doing a poor job of keeping *me* at bay," Aayushi said, and Larken thought she detected a note of sarcasm in the woman's voice.

"You own—" Orlander started.

"I don't," Larken said. The god grabbed at another bottle of cleaner and opened his mouth to down that one too. Larken surprised herself by yanking it out of his clawed hands; he seemed admonished for a handful of seconds before one of his claws found its way around her throat. For such a little creature, the god was amazingly strong. He lifted her into the air. His mouth extended wider than she'd thought possible as he lowered her toward his teeth.

"I thought you were the god of small children," she said, desperately grasping for something with which to distract him.

"Small children," he muttered in his gravelly tones. "And of the plenty, and the hoarders, and the capricious. I am the god of reckoning."

He continued to lower her, ever so slowly as though the delight of her panic was the appetizer to her demise. She slammed her staff into his face, but it seemed to have no impact. Nor did the batteries from the shelf, or the loose cabling that she found, or the mops and brooms that she'd managed to grab. Nothing slowed him or even made those monstrous black voids he had for eyes blink. She squirmed in his grip, twisting her body in pain trying to get herself free, while telling herself that he wasn't real.

"You can't eat me," she said. "You can't eat this. This is all for the children."

He stopped and lowered her, gazing her up and down with one giant eye.

"Those are for the children?" he asked, twisting her in the air so that she faced the pile of cleaning supplies that she'd bounced off him, which now lay on the floor.

"Yes," she said. "We are a village, and we support

each other. Those are so that the children don't get sick and can stay clean."

Not directly, but she was grasping at whatever she could at this point. There wasn't a world in which the mop directly helped any child, except perhaps to produce what somehow was deemed "character," by asking them to use these tools. Still, the tools kept the place clean, and that kept disease down, which was one small, but important, thing to her—and apparently to Orlander, who placed her back on her feet.

"Why did I see children without warm clothes, without toys, in the snow?"

"We're limited," Larken said. Somewhere in the background, she heard Dandelion approaching. When Dandelion arrived, she would finally have proof of her delusion, and could then use that proof to break free. But right now, Orlander's teeth and the dripping orange drool that pooled in the bottom of his mouth seemed too real to ignore.

"Limited?"

"People only give so much, Orlander. We have to start with safety, and then food, and then *any* clothes. By the time it comes to warm clothes, we've spent everything we can afford to. The children can stay inside."

Orlander's face, hairy and brown at first, now turned a bright shade of red.

"My stories," he said, "must be protected. Children can't *think* indoors. The stories they come up with when they do are all about walls. Children must be free, must be out and in the world in order to create. *Leaving* is as vital as eating."

She pondered this while also pondering how it was that the gravelly voice he formed into words ever made it past the garden of pointed teeth that was his mouth. He growled low as Dandelion's footsteps approached around a far corner.

"Nobody gives," she said. "It's barely what we can do to keep them warm and fed, Orlander."

"Then I will change this," he said, glowering now, if she read his god's face correctly. "I will *change this*."

A hand on her shoulder caused her to turn quickly, and nearly collide with Dandelion. Behind the head of blond hair and green-gold-speckled eyes, she saw Aayushi's face, fading into nothing. She spun back and Orlander was gone as well.

"Are you okay?" Dandelion asked, steadying Larken with a hand on each shoulder.

"I—I'm fine," she said. "Let's go back to the office."

"Or we could go home," Dandelion offered. Larken ignored her, as tempting as the offer was. She was too rattled to chance the snow yet.

"What was the thud?"

"A snowball," Dandelion said with a smile. "Another group of children played alongside the building over there." She pointed to the general direction from which she'd come. "I sent them home. It's too dangerous out there."

"Did they have warm clothes?" Larken asked, unable to shake the image of the many-toothed god from her head.

"Half did," Dandelion said. "That's why I sent them home. One was nearly blue with cold."

"Children have to play," Larken parroted, then

scooped up her fallen cane and took Dandelion's offered arm as she thought through what just happened. She pondered what her hallucination meant by the "change this." Was it something she had to do herself? She didn't know, and tried her best to expunge the god of small children from her mind.

They took the elevator down to the main level, then walked past the reclamation vats that Larken had insisted on keeping as a sobering reminder of what the Bremerton compound used to be. She ran a finger along the brim of one of the large vats, approximately a meter in diameter. The lives that were lost within seemed to scream out at once when she touched it. Larken yanked her finger away.

"Come, Larken," Dandelion said, giving her a tug. Larken began to move again.

"What do you think Christine was really calling about?" Larken asked.

"I think she was calling for exactly what she said."

"On the day of Orlander's Folly? She think's it's appropriate to invade people's family time on a day of celebration."

Dandelion raised an eyebrow. She did better than she'd done earlier, raising it only half a centimeter and looking decidedly less like a circus clown. Larken scrunched her lips.

"What?"

"You and Christine are the same," she said. When Larken glared at her, Dandelion smiled and continued. "I mean you are both working during

Orlander's Folly. She is your kind, and like her, she knows you're not celebrating anything."

"She was definitely celebrating something," Larken said. "Did you see that dress?"

"She's at a business celebration in downtown Seattle, at the H Hotel. It's a networking event."

They approached the front door of the building and pushed through. Beyond, the snow stopped as they stepped out into it. The path to Larken's home cut over the sidewalks that were now invisible beneath the white coating.

"Dandelion," Larken said, contemplating her recent run-in with Orlander. "Do you want to spend the night tonight?"

"I'd planned on it," Dandelion said. Then a second later, "Call."

"Call who?"

"No. A call for you," she said. She canted her head to the side and seemed to disengage for a second before she shook slightly and blinked. "You probably want your communicator for this."

When Larken fished her communicator from her pocket, she saw that she'd already missed several call attempts, likely while she was entertaining her hallucinations. She flicked a button on the device to connect and got a projection of Christine Hamilton in the snow.

"What will it take?" the woman asked, her face deadly serious. A strand of her sandy-brown hair fell down across her face, stealing some of the sobriety of the situation as she blew it back up.

"What will what take?"

"To get you to help," Christine said. "Share your secrets. What?"

------*------

Larken's mind shuffled through the last ten minutes. Orlander had accused her of having too much, of being a source of plenty, and she hadn't understood what it meant. Every dollar that came in through the door went to the village she attempted to protect and maintain. Yet as she saw Christine standing there, in her lacy ball gown with an impatient glare and people glistening around her like stars, it finally began to dawn on her what he, or since he was a hallucination, she had been trying to tell herself. She had more leverage than she'd thought. Her eyes lifted toward the snow-covered buildings, many with smoke tendrils rising from makeshift chimneys, and smiled.

"Clothes," she said. "Children's winter clothes. Coats, jackets, scarves...and lots of them."

Christine's eyebrows curled up, changing her glare into an inquisitive stare.

"You want to know what it takes, right? I'll tell you everything you want to know. All you have to do is send children's clothes *tonight*." She glanced up at the still-overcast sky. "Preferably before it starts snowing again."

Christine licked her lips slowly. Then she seemed to catch the eye of someone off camera, mouthed words that Larken couldn't quite make out, before she nodded briskly and turned her attention back to Larken.

"Done," she said. "Expect them within the hour. And—"

"And nothing," Larken said, feeling her stomach churn as she interrupted the most prominent person in the modeling communities. She swallowed. "I mean, thank you. We can discuss the rest tomorrow, yes? It's Orlander's Folly, after all."

"I didn't realize you are the sentimental type," Christine said, as she lifted a bite of something that Larken could only assume was the traditional dessert of Vinegar Cobbler to her mouth, by the way her face screwed up as she chewed.

"I am tonight," Larken said, just before hanging up. She let out a massive sigh as she finished. Larken turned to Dandelion, who looked like she might split in two with laughter.

"What?"

"I can't believe you did that," Dandelion said, gold flecks dancing in her eyes.

Larken puffed herself up now that the intimidation was gone. Then she giggled.

"I can't either," she said. "But we're in the big leagues now. Got to use what we can."

An hour later, lights broke through the overcast gloom of the storm clouds. Out plodding through the snow toward them, Dandelion in tow, Larken saw a massive flattened equilateral triangle hanging in the sky. The vehicle touched down in the middle of a snowy clearing not far from where the children had been playing earlier. An opening formed in the side. A walkway extended down, crunching into the snow in the distance.

Her guards joined her in the snow, eyeing her

warily for instructions. She motioned to them to do nothing. Christine's lackey, a man with a beard and a suit too expensive to wear during a snowstorm, exited the vehicle carrying an armful of children's clothes. The eyes of the handful of children from the village out to witness the intrusion widened. Some parents had emerged as well, and clung tightly to their offspring. Only when Larken nodded did the children squirm free to sprint to where the man stood. He dropped the pile of clothing into the snow, and went back inside, to reappear a moment later with another pile and a poorly-concealed grimace on his face. He stood, watching as the children divided up the clothes, giving the warmest to the ones who'd been in rags earlier. Then, to Larken's great joy, the children formed teams to play her favorite game of Lofting.

The lackey re-boarded the vehicle and lifted into the air without so much as a word. Partially blinded from the lights, Larken noticed movement behind where the ship had been. She bit her lip as she concentrated on the space, and thought she made out the snaggle toothed mouth of a hairy beast, now with eight arms. For a half-second, fear peaked in her heart, until she realized the god was smiling. And just beyond Orlander, with a faint glowing aura the color of hazelnut with a dim blue outline, stood Aayushi, waving. Larken smiled at her hallucinations, and waved.

"Thank goodness," Dandelion said, rubbing her hands together unnecessarily, mimicking Larken's actions. "I thought I was the only one who saw him."

Larken blinked once, then turned toward Dandelion. Dandelion said nothing, and didn't seem to register her glance. The android stared toward the same spot that Larken had. Larken interwove the fingers of her free hand between Dandelion's frigid fingertips. A second later, warmth channeled through Dandelion's hand into her own. Dandelion lay her head on Larken's shoulder as the sounds of playing children filled out the soundscape of their lives.

In the distance, Larken thought she saw a hint of brown and the flash of pointed teeth atop a distant snowbank.

"Orlander's Folly" is part of the Virtual Wars saga. Learn more at andrewsweet.net.

RECIPE: ORLANDER'S FOLLY VINEGAR COBBLER

From Andrew Sweet's "Orlander's Folly"

WHEN SETTLERS FIRST ARRIVED ON MARS, THEY brought with them specific staples from Earth. These staples included food items like flour, sugar, and the certain fruits that could survive the months-long journey. Protein packs and regular electricity for replicators couldn't be expected for another ten to twenty years, so raw ingredients was the surest way to feed the first wave of settlers, who held the thankless obligation to terraform the planet into something livable for others. The initial wave of people struggled to survive the harsh, Martian terrain, and things like fruit became luxury items as the struggle to standardize shipments often provided crates of rotting goods, having failed to appropriately account for the shift in relative distance between the planets of Earth and Mars.

The ten to twenty years turned into half a century, and the daily struggles of life on a planet where half of newborns died from malnutrition gave rise to a new mythology: the gods of the solar system, popular myths on Earth that led rise to the Underworlder Tabletop Role-Playing game. One of these gods, the god of plenty, Orlander, originated during this time of hardship. Orlander was something to be hoped and feared, as seeing the god was translated to mean either that one would lose everything, or one would become wealthy, depending on the circumstances. It was only after stability was achieved some century after terraforming that the god's story morphed to make them the God of Small Children, eventually the rough equivalent to the Earth-born caricature of Saint Nicholas.

Vinegar being simple to make from spoiled wine, which could be made from the late, nearly rotting deliveries, the colonies had it in abundance. Sugar as well proved to be a crop that habituated well to the Martian soil, when a bit of water was supplied. The dish of Vinegar Cobbler was revived due to the simplicity of the ingredient list and the lack of any better result for sweet treats. This recipe is the closest the author has been able to identify to the traditional dish for celebrating Orlander's Folly, the nearest thing to Christmas that Martian settler children experience, and a roaming holiday that Earth adopted in the late twenty-second century.

Ingredients:

- 3 cups All-Purpose Flour
- 0.5 teaspoons Kosher Salt
- 1 cup Shortening (butter-flavor is best, but

white, solid shortening is traditional -
both work)
- 0.5 cups White Vinegar (cider-based
vinegar for a more traditional appeal)
- 2 cups Sugar (cane or beet sugar will
suffice, to flavor)
- 2 teaspoons Vanilla (optional, this was not
available to Martian settlers, but
improves the taste)
- 4 cups Water

Steps (no replicator):
1. Pre-heat oven to 425 degrees.
2. Whisk the flour and salt together and cut in the shortening using a pastry blender until crumbly. Divide into thirds.
3. Roll out each portion into a thin, 1/8- to 1/4-inch-thick oval and cut into strips the width of a dinner fork's head.
4. In a pan suitable to be oven-fired, and about 10-inches wide, holding 4-8 quarts, combine the:

- Sugar
- Vinegar
- Vanilla (optional)
- Water

5. Bring to boil over high heat. Note that on Mars, the boiling point is significantly lower, reaching as low as 0 degrees. If on Mars, start with more water to account for boil-off, and ensure with a

digital thermometer that the temperature of 100 degrees has been reached.

6. Set aside 8 of the pastry strips from above. Tear or cut the remaining into grape-sized pieces and drop into the boiling liquid. Boil for approximately 5 minutes Earth-time.

7. Remove the pan from heat. Criss-cross the last 8 strips to make a pie lattice atop the thickened filling made of the now-pastry dumplings from the torn/cut pieces absorbing the liquid. Any extra can be pushed under the surface of the dumpling-syrup mixture in the pan.

8. Place the pot and contents in the oven until the latticework is golden brown. Earth-time, 25-30 minutes.

9. Serve warm or with ice cream if available.

Steps (replicator, standard):

1. Verify that the protein packs are at least half-full:
- P-23345
- P-8093
- P-73205

2. Punch in the following code: 9974857

3. Dish code for plating (if desired): 3545

4. Wait approximately 5 minutes if using a standard replicator. Using an older model may increase processing time.

5. Serve warm or with replicated Vanilla Ice Cream (code 2546548 in most standard models).

ON ICING

by Heather Texle

Reliance Sinclaire 1.5

CHAPTER 1

DeAjamae hopped her butt onto my desk. She wore a red headband with jingle bells that rang whenever she tilted her head. The color matched the new highlights in her curly brown hair.

"What are you bringing to the Exploration Day potluck tonight?" she asked.

I saved my mug of artificial coffee from sloshing over and moved it to the other side of the desk where it would be safe. "Is that mandatory? I planned on staying in tonight."

"Eww! Exploration Day is all about hanging out with your family and friends. You can't spend it by yourself. Hey, Wright!" DeAjamae called over to our boss. "Tell Reliance she has to come to the party."

Wright spun around in his chair. He'd been filling out a report at his desk console but seemed pleased for the distraction. "Absolutely. Consider it a mandatory team-building exercise."

I groaned. In previous years, I'd spent the holiday playing *Fox Hunter* holovid games with my best friend, Jarrett. He'd been murdered last year, and I didn't know if I felt like celebrating without him.

"Ha!" DeAjamae gloated. She'd been inviting me to outside-of-work activities since I'd joined the team a few months ago, but for some reason, I'd been resisting. This was a big win for her.

Ravi, the fourth member of our team, wandered over at the sound of our conversation. He folded his arms and rested them on top of the cubicle wall.

"Can't argue with the boss's orders," Ravi said.

"What would I even make?" I asked. "I know my way around a mycoprotein proofer, but after that, it's pretty much downhill to hellaberry bars and whatever I can scrounge in the precinct vending machine."

The look of abject horror on DeAjamae's face made me laugh. "Please don't tell me you eat anything out of that," she said. "I haven't seen the food replaced since I arrived here from the academy. Come over to my apartment after work and help me make Big Mamma's sugar cookies. We can ice and decorate them, too."

"Fine, but don't expect me to be a big culinary help."

"You can bring the wine."

"Now, that I can do."

"How about you, Johnson?" Ravi asked the forty-year-old officer as he walked by the end of our row. "What are you bringing tonight?"

Johnson waved a beefy hand dismissively. "Nothing. I'm stuck on patrol. The lieutenant has us looking for that toy-store thief. The media is calling him the Red Bandit."

"You still haven't caught him?" DeAjamae asked. "I read the bulletin. How hard can it be to find a guy who wears a bright-red jumpsuit and drives a convertible LAV?"

"*How hard can it be?*" Johnson parroted back in a snarky voice. "The guy's like magic. He hit three Toybox Trinkets stores this week. We can't figure out how he gets in without tripping the alarms."

Wright folded his arms behind his head and rocked back in his chair. The move showed off his toned arms, something I shouldn't be noticing about my boss.

"Are you posting officers to each of the stores?" he asked.

"On Exploration Day? I'm short two people and happy that it's only that many. We're running extra patrols by the stores, but there are too many to cover them all."

"Security cameras?"

Johnson shook his head. "Disabled. And his entire LAV is covered with ov-ex material. It's just one big, overexposed blob of white streaking through the air on the traffic drones. The automated system doesn't even register it as a vehicle. And get this, he only steals the new Star Tourist model spaceship. He's made off with fifty so far."

"My niece wants one of those," Ravi said.

"Yeah, her and every other kid on Andaress-4," Johnson grumbled. "It's this year's new 'it' toy. Do you have any idea how much flack I'll get if we don't catch this guy? Speaking of, Cruz is over there, and I need him to refile a witness statement for me. Hey, Cruz!"

Johnson walked off, hiking up his duty belt on his way to intercept Cruz.

"Those poor kiddos," Ravi said. "It's rough not getting the present you wanted on Exploration Day."

DeAjamae uncrossed her legs and kicked her feet back and forth. "I remember wanting this electronics kit when I was five. It had all these cool projects that taught you about circuits and things. Big Mamma said I was too young and would break it. I was so disappointed, but then on Exploration Day, it was on the kitchen table when I came down for breakfast. It was wrapped in the prettiest sparkly red paper and white ribbons. She told me she figured future explorers probably needed someone who knew about electronics. Playing with the set got me interested in computers. How about you, Ravi? What was your favorite Exploration Day present?"

"Hmm, probably concert tickets. I took my best friend, and we waited around the back entrance after the show. The guitar player threw us a couple of picks." He smiled at the memory.

"What about you?" DeAjamae asked Wright.

"A lint roller with a hoverbike figurine for a handle."

She cocked her head to the side. "A ... lint roller?"

"It was from my little brother."

"Ah," she said and gave him a sympathetic smile.

I knew Wright's younger brother had died when they were teenagers, but not much else. He didn't talk much about his days growing up on Ritru-6.

DeAjamae turned to me. "Your turn."

"Well, I guess I'd have to go with the Captain Stardust ray gun my dad gave me. A neighbor kid and I pretended to be Captain Stardust and her first mate out exploring the galaxy and fighting space pirates. We had a lot of fun, but I don't know how much his cat enjoyed always playing the pirate. It led us on many a merry chase."

"Do you still have it?" DeAjamae asked. "The ray gun? Not the cat, obviously."

"No, I lost it during a move."

That was a bit of a lie. After my dad left us, my mom and I had to move to a smaller place in a cheaper area of town. I'd been so mad at him I'd thrown the toy away rather than pack it with the rest of my stuff. It had been stupid. I had great memories of playing with that ray gun, and I hated that I'd let him take those from me, too.

CHAPTER 2

Five hours later, I double-checked the address DeAjamae had given me and knocked on the door. She greeted me with a big grin and pulled me inside.

"Nice place," I said, handing her a bottle of white wine imported from my home planet, Brione-5.

Her apartment was small but bursting with color and energy. It had dark-green walls, a pink velvet couch, and a gold lamp that looked like a rabbit using the ruffled shade as a dress.

"I can't believe this is the first time you've been here. You can throw your stuff on that chair."

The kitchen and living room flowed into each other, and I set my cross-body bag onto the faux-leather chair as I passed by it. Holiday music played through a nice set of built-in ceiling speakers. It was a rock version of a classic song, but I couldn't name the band.

DeAjamae tossed me an apron. "Is that what you're wearing tonight?"

I looked at the long-sleeved shirt that I'd worn all day. "What? It's red."

She'd changed into a sequined top that shifted from red to white, depending on the angle you looked at it. Black leather pants and boots completed the ensemble. I could never pull off something that chic without feeling self-conscious about it. She made it look effortless.

"It's fine," she said, tying on her apron. "I just thought you'd put on something more festive since it's a *party*."

"A party held in the same smelly bullpen and conference rooms we hang out in every day."

"Yes, but there will be streamers. And alcohol."

I slipped my apron over my head, tied the strings behind my back, and pushed up my sleeves. "And cookies, apparently. How can I help?"

"You can pour the wine."

She retrieved two glasses from a kitchen cabinet and set them in front of me. I made mine a small pour even though it was a low-alcohol variety, because I'd be piloting my hoverbike later.

DeAjamae pulled out a pile of ingredients and set them on her small island. I stared at the sugar, butter, and flour dubiously. The last time I'd tried to bake something, fire suppression measures had been deployed.

I picked up an amber jar filled with a dark liquid, unscrewed it, and sniffed. Creamy, warm notes of vanilla filled the air.

"Try this one." DeAjamae handed me a second bottle. "Saper lemons. They're only in season a few weeks a year, but there's a specialty shop that makes an extract from the juice."

"Mmm." That one smelled bright and citrusy. It tickled my nose. I thought the two scents would have clashed, but they didn't. The blend was homey and reminded me of sitting by a sunny window on a warm summer day. Since Exploration Day fell during winter here in Salin, I appreciated the reminder of warmer times.

"Shoot, I'm out of powdered sugar for the icing. Hang on while I order some." DeAjamae launched the holoscreen projection from her cuff, aerial scribed to her grocery delivery program, and placed an order. Then she opened a file with a list of ingredients and *chill 2 min, zap 3 min* written on it.

"Okay, we're making Big Mamma's sugar cookies. Don't tell her I let you see the recipe."

I squinted at it. "That looks like a shopping list."

She dug out a few teaspoons and a coffee cup. "Measure with your heart."

"Pretty sure that's not how baking works."

"Pfft. No one will be sober enough to care how the cookies taste. The important part is that they're cute."

"Fair point."

We mixed up the ingredients into a passable-looking dough and shoved the ball in the hyper-chill freezer for two minutes.

DeAjamae's parcel delivery port dinged, signaling the drone had dropped off her order of powdered sugar. She used her cuff to unlock the small door beside her living room window and withdrew the reusable delivery box. By then, the dough was ready to be rolled out. She handed me a tall, cylindrical glass to use.

"This might be my kind of baking," I said and flipped the glass around to use the open end to cut out round shapes.

We placed the cookies on a tray and slid them into the zapper while DeAjamae mixed up the icing. By the time the last cookies finished baking, the first batch was ready to ice and decorate with glittery red sprinkles. They were wonky around the edges, but the sweet frosting covered a multitude of sins.

"What do you think the guys are bringing?" DeAjamae asked, licking the spoon. "I bet Ravi ordered something from a bakery."

"Sure, but it'll be from a *good* bakery."

"The guy does have exquisite taste."

I transferred the cookies to two containers and sealed them tight. "Wright's probably making some fancy-schmancy Corsica dessert—macarons or croquembouche or something else I'm afraid will break if I touch it."

DeAjamae gave me an assessing look. "Hmm, yes, that sounds like something our fearless leader would make. You're getting to know him pretty well."

"Not really," I said, but I was sure my cheeks matched my shirt. Maybe I should have poured myself a bigger glass of wine. "I noticed that he likes to cook, is all."

"Mm-hmm. That's very observant of you."

I tossed a towel at her. She caught it and laughed.

DeAjamae put the bigger container of cookies in her backpack, and I snuggled the smaller one into my cross-body bag for the ride back to the precinct. We double-checked that the zapper was off, locked up, and carried the cookies out to the parking lot. It was a little chilly since the sun had set, and I wished I hadn't left my jacket at my desk.

I removed two helmets from the storage compart-ments over the thrusters and handed her one. She put it on and activated the interface. My Intell neural impulse chip immediately detected it and popped a notification up in my mind's eye. Usually, I tried my best to ignore all the beeps and boops the Intell threw at me, but in this case, I opened the notification to connect our comms.

I threw my leg over my hoverbike. She climbed on behind me. Once she settled, I took us up to the skylane. My Intell searched out information, feeding data from my bike, the city net, traffic drones, and nearby LAVs to be processed. I hadn't asked for the illegal technology to be implanted in my brain stem, but flying my hoverbike was one of the few times I truly enjoyed using it. The seamless integration of information, tech, and physical responses almost made it feel as if I were flying, like a bird.

Most of the time, though, the implant was a giant pain in my rear end.

The precinct wasn't too far from DeAjamae's apartment building, so I kept to the lower lanes that wove between buildings. Truth be told, I wasn't in a hurry to get to the party. I'd only joined the Salin Department of Enforcement of Criminal Affairs a few months prior, and I hadn't done much with my team outside of work. We were in that awkward getting-to-know-each-other stage, and I didn't want to mess it up by doing something dumb.

About halfway to the precinct, DeAjamae tapped my shoulder and pointed at a building.

"Do you see that?" she asked over our comms.

I followed her finger to a convertible low altitude vehicle parked near the rear exit of a Toybox Trinkets. A portly man with white hair came out the back door lugging a bulging brown sáck over his shoulder. He heaved the sack over the wing and into the backseat of the LAV before climbing into the pilot's seat.

"Is he wearing a red jumpsuit?" I asked, already braking hard and bringing the hoverbike around for a closer look.

"Hard to tell from this high, but it sure looks like it."

His thrusters fired, blasting a cloud of sinnafuel exhaust around the LAV. Then he shot up to the highest skylane and sped off toward the edge of the city.

"Call it in," I said over the comms.

I craned the handlebars to the side, nearly dumping us as I spun my bike around to pursue the Red Bandit. Once we got heading in the right direction, I heard DeAjamae contact Dispatch. She gave them our location and a description of the suspect.

Ahead, the convertible LAV zipped through traffic. I increased my speed to keep from losing him.

"The only officer on this side of town is tied up at an accident," DeAjamae said. "Johnson's the next closest, but he's at least ten minutes out."

"Tell Dispatch we're taking lead and in pursuit."

"Already did. Johnson's going to be pissed when we catch this guy without him." I practically heard her grin through the comms.

We neared the edge of the city limits, and the Red Bandit showed no signs of slowing down. Ahead, the salt pan surrounding Salin glowed blueish-white, like snow under the light of the two moons.

Traffic thinned as the last building dropped behind us until it was only us and the convertible LAV. I rolled back the throttle to push my hoverbike faster. It responded with a low growl and a kick that had DeAjamae grabbing onto my waist for balance.

Using my Intell, I pulled up a map of the area. The semi-transparent image projected in my mind's eye still felt weird. I was getting better at using the advanced tech, even if doing so often left me with a wicked headache.

I calculated our current trajectory. "He's heading toward Saper."

"We'll never find him if he gets into the mountains."

DeAjamae was right. The salt pan extended approximately fifty kilometers out from Salin until it ran into a mid-sized mountain range. Saper was the largest city, but small farming towns dotted the border. They grew food and spices up into the foothills and lower levels of the mountains. There would be hundreds of places for him to hide.

"We need to take him down before he leaves the salt pan," I said.

"How? We don't have our blasters."

"I'm going to jump into his LAV."

"You're going to *what*?!"

We'd closed about half the distance between us and the Red Bandit already. My plan could work, but we'd have to move fast.

"When we pull up beside him, I'm going to jump off our port side. You need to lean toward starboard to counter my weight and grab the throttle with your right hand."

"Uhhh…" DeAjamae squirmed behind me. "That doesn't sound like a smart idea."

"You've flown a hoverbike before, right?"

"Once, in the academy."

It was a good thing the helmet hid my expression. "It's fine. Acceleration is on the right handle. Brake is on the left. Use the auto-landing function after I get control of the Red Bandit's LAV. Super simple."

"Hmm, simple." DeAjamae's sarcasm was thick,

but I saw her request permission to connect to the bike's control system through her cuff and granted her access.

We pulled up closer to the convertible LAV. I didn't recognize the model. It was red and trimmed in shiny, reflective gold along the body panels. That must be the ov-ex striping Johnson had mentioned. Twin thrusters were mounted to the bottom of the wings, leaving ample room for the open top. In the pilot's seat sat an old man with a potbelly, white hair, and a thick beard that flapped wildly in the wind. He wore a red jumpsuit and gold-rimmed flying goggles.

The Red Bandit finally noticed us when we drew even to his starboard wing. He veered left and down until he skimmed the surface of the ground. Giant plumes of salt dust swirled up, obscuring our vision like a snowstorm in the dark.

I increased my speed, hoping to get a clearer view. Up ahead, through the blowing salt, I spotted the red anti-collision light on the front of his LAV shining like a beacon. We came in for a second approach. This time, I positioned us to his side, right over his wing.

"Ready?" I asked DeAjamae.

"Yeah?" she responded, but she reached her right hand under my arm to take the handle.

I stood on the footrests and brought my right leg under me, so that I sat sidesaddle on the bike. DeAjamae leaned to the right, counterbalancing my shift in weight. She contorted her torso around mine to get both hands on the handlebar. We eased the bike closer.

"Steady," I said, easing my weight onto my back foot so I could push off. "Another meter and I'll be close enough."

"Copy that."

Salt dust pelted my helmet, but through the enhanced optics of my visor, I could see well enough to line up my jump. The Red Bandit couldn't go lower, so he tried to swerve left again.

I leaped into the LAV before he could get any distance between us.

"Ho!" the Red Bandit grunted as I landed on top of him.

The LAV rocked to the side. DeAjamae stuck close, but she fell back when the wing almost clipped the hoverbike.

"I'm with DECA," I said, raising my voice to be heard over the rushing wind. "You're under arrest for stealing these toys!"

I tried to grab onto the Red Bandit's wrist, but the slippery material of his jumpsuit prevented me from getting a good grip.

"You're not being very nice, young lady," he said, yanking his arm away.

"Land the LAV now."

"Not now. I can't tonight. I'll go in tomorrow."

"That's not how this works." I made another unsuccessful grab for his hand and really wished I had my blaster.

Fine. We would do this the hard way. My Intell was equipped with non-standard, illegal hacking capabilities thanks to a company that coveted the limitless profits of the black market and an inventor who had used me as a disposable guinea pig.

I connected to the LAV's main computer system and initiated the emergency landing procedure. Our speed and altitude decreased.

"What's happening?" The Red Bandit tried aerial scribing commands into the computer console to no effect. He banged his fist on the dashboard.

"I've taken control of your vehicle's computer. After we land, DECA officers will arrive to transport you to the detention center, where you may contact your attorney or request that one be appointed to you."

The LAV skimmed the ground. Salt crystals kicked up, coating the interior in a fine, white dust. My Intell notified me that the landing gear was about to lower.

"Listen," the Red Bandit said. "I'm very sorry to do this, but the children are depending on me."

He jerked the steering wheel hard to port and sent the LAV into a barrel roll. In an instant, my world flipped upside down. I tumbled through the air, flailing my arms for something to grab on to. My connection with the LAV broke as I dropped out of range. Everything was a blur of red, white, and black.

I hit the ground rolling and cocooned my head into my arms until I slowed to a dizzying stop. My breath came in ragged gasps. I unfastened my helmet, pulled it off, and spit out a mouthful of salt. Crisp night air flooded my lungs.

The Red Bandit righted his LAV and circled around me. His harness had held him fast to his seat, so he hadn't fallen out. He lifted his goggles from his face, revealing twinkling eyes and cheeks that were rosy from the wind.

"A good Exploration Day to all!" he yelled before speeding off toward the mountains.

CHAPTER 3

I sat up, feeling bruised but not broken. Salt coated my pants. My sleeve was torn, and the heel of my boot had busted off. Several meters away, I spotted my cross-body bag lying on the ground.

Another blast of air stirred up the salt when DeAjamae touched down with the hoverbike. She ripped off her own helmet as she ran over to me.

"Are you okay?"

I stood, brushed off my pants, and hobbled over to retrieve my bag. A peek inside the container revealed a fluffy pile of yellow crumbs and red sprinkles. "I'm good, but I can't say the same for the cookies."

DeAjamae handed me my helmet. It had a large dent on one side.

I stared off in the direction the Red Bandit had flown. He was so far gone that I couldn't even see the anti-collision light on his LAV against the night sky.

"Do you want to keep after him?" she asked.

"I don't see how. Unless you saw him land or something from the air."

"Nope, but I threw a tracking bug in his back seat while you were distracting him."

My jaw dropped. "Where'd you get a tracking bug?"

"I keep a couple in my backpack. Doesn't everyone?"

I laughed, shaking my head as we walked back to the hoverbike. "No, I don't think they do."

She woke up her cuff and projected a map between us. A blinking light indicated the location of the tracking bug.

"Huh, that's weird," she said, zooming in. "It looks like he's at the hospital in Saper."

"He might have hurt himself doing that barrel roll."

"We should probably turn this over to Johnson when he gets here and let him figure it out."

"Sure, we could do that," I said, climbing onto the bike. "Or, we could tell Johnson we lost him and go check out the hospital ourselves."

DeAjamae grinned. "We're almost there already. There's no reason to make Johnson fly all the way out here."

"Exactly. Hop on."

We landed near the Red Bandit's convertible LAV in the parking lot of the Saper Pediatric Hospital. DeAjamae arched her perfectly sculpted brows in surprise. The general hospital wasn't far. In fact, he had to have flown past it to get here.

Both the Red Bandit and the sack of toys were missing.

"He must have gone inside," I said, seeing no sign of him elsewhere. "Let's go check."

DeAjamae reached inside the pilot-side door, popped the hood, and went to the front end to disconnect several wires. She slammed the hood closed. "This way, if he comes back and we're not here, he won't be able to fly away again."

We entered the building and stopped at the patient sign-in desk.

"Excuse me," I said to the nurse aerial scribing something into a chart on a wall console. "Did you see a man come through here? Red jumpsuit, white beard, and carrying a big bag?"

"Sure, he's in the children's play area." When the nurse finally looked up, she eyed my ripped and tattered shirt. "Do you need to see a doctor?"

"No, thank you. Which way to the play area?"

She pointed down the hallway to her left.

We thanked her and followed the signs to a large room painted in bold primary colors with kid-sized furniture, toy baskets, and art supplies lining the walls. Through a plastiglass window, we watched a group of about thirty kids sitting in a ring around the Red Bandit and his sack of toys.

Most of the kids wore hospital clothes with snaps along the seams and warm socks with grippy material on the soles of the feet. A few had immobilizers around their limbs. Three sat in hoverchairs with blankets tucked around their legs. All of them sat with wide-eyed, rapt attention as the Red Bandit told them an animated story.

"On the night before the first deep-space explorers were set to leave Earth, they gathered with their families to say goodbye. They shared a meal and exchanged gifts, not knowing if this would be the last time they ever saw each other."

"But they did, didn't they?" asked a little boy with light-brown hair. "They got to see their moms and dads again."

"That's right, Timmy! Because after that, many more explorers took to the stars. Some of them were your great-great-many-greats grandparents. That's why on Exploration Day, we spend time with our families and friends, and why we share gifts with one another—to honor our ancestors and those early explorers."

We stepped through the door, and I cleared my throat.

The Red Bandit looked over at us, and his shoulders slumped. He reached into his sack and pulled out a small bag of saltwater taffies wrapped in wax papers and handed them to a boy with a GraftPatch on his temple. "Timmy, can you help me pass these sweets around?"

Timmy bobbed his head as he took the bag. The kids swarmed him as the Red Bandit waded through the mob to walk over to us.

"I'm glad you're all right after that tumble. Sorry about that—and the clothes," he said. "You see why I had to get here. The children expected me."

"We're going to have to arrest you...?" My voice trailed off when I realized I didn't know his name.

"Nicholas," the Red Bandit supplied. "But most people call me Nick."

"Nick, please come quietly so we don't upset the children."

"I understand, but can I give them their toys first?" he asked.

"The toys aren't yours to give. They belong to Toybox Trinkets. We will have to take them into custody and return them to the store."

Nick's face turned red, and not just his rosy cheeks from the flight to the hospital. "Toybox Trinkets is the real thief. I ordered these toys three months ago when they first came out. Then five days ago, I received a notice saying they canceled my order. I only took what was mine."

"Why would they do that?" I asked. "I heard these model spaceships were the season's hot new toy."

Nick glanced over at the kids, who were having as much fun pulling the taffy into long strings as they were munching on the treat. "I wondered, too. So, I went to the store I'd ordered them from, and there was a huge display of the spaceships marked up three times what I'd paid for them. When I talked to the manager, he pretended he didn't remember me or placing the order."

"Did you show him your invoice?" I asked.

"He said to come back after the holiday rush, and we'd sort it out. But that would be too late! I needed the toys by today. I've already given the rest away at other hospitals. This was my last stop."

DeAjamae frowned. "Can I see your receipt?"

The Red Bandit pushed his sleeve up past his cuff, launched the holoscreen projection, and pulled up an invoice from Toybox Trinkets. It was marked PAID across the top.

"And the cancelation notice?" DeAjamae asked.

She studied the holoscreen, flipping between the two documents. "Have they refunded your credits yet?"

Nick tugged at his snowy-white beard. "No, that's why I had to take these toys. They were paid for with donation funds. I'd promised the hospital I would deliver them to the patients this week, but I didn't have enough credits to buy new ones without the refund."

"Wait here," DeAjamae said and motioned for me to step back a few paces. She lowered her voice to a whisper. "The paperwork seems in order. He bought the toys."

"We also caught him at the store."

"Hmm, that is kind of a problem."

We watched as one of the braver kids scooted closer to Nick's bag and tried to peek inside without being noticed. Her friend played lookout but was doing a terrible job, because he wanted to know what was in there, too.

"Do you want to arrest him for breaking and entering?" I asked.

DeAjamae screwed her mouth to the side. "No, but Johnson will go straight to the lieutenant if he finds out we had the Red Bandit and let him go."

"How did you get into the store without setting off the alarms?" I asked Nick, who was turning out to be less of a bandit by the minute.

"Oh, that was easy," he said. "I work for their security company. We set up their cameras and sensors. The default access code is ACCESSCODE, and they never bothered to change it."

I turned back to DeAjamae. "It sounds to me

like he had a lawful right to be in the building, and he only left with his own property. If Toybox Trinkets wants to take it up with their security company, that's their problem."

The little girl who'd been sneaking around Nick's bag ran over and tugged at the bottom of my shirt. Her big brown eyes sparkled with excitement. She squirmed from one foot to the other as she pointed to the bag. "Can we thee what'th in the bag, now? *Pleeeeeathe?*"

My teammate and I shared a look. DeAjamae slid her backpack from her shoulders, bent down, and took the container of Big Mamma's sugar cookies from it. She handed it to the girl.

"Why don't you pass these cookies around to the other kids? Then we'll see about opening that bag."

The girl grinned from ear to ear, revealing two missing front teeth, and ran back to the group with the cookies. She tossed a half-forgotten "thank you" over her shoulder.

"Does that mean you aren't arresting me?" Nick asked.

"It's your lucky Exploration Day," I said. "Come down to the precinct tomorrow, and we'll get it sorted out."

"In that case, would you like to help me hand out these Star Tourist model spaceships?"

"Oh, we definitely would!" DeAjamae said.

Nick gave a jolly laugh, and we couldn't help but join in.

CHAPTER 4

After we'd handed out all the toys, candy, and cookies, a massive sugar rush hit the kids. They'd tackled
DeAjamae and me to the ground, declaring us void
monsters. Then they zoomed around the room with
their little model ships, making flying noises and
screaming if they got too close because we
pretended to attack them. The nurses let this
continue for a few minutes, then declared it was
bedtime and shooed the kids off to their rooms.
They weren't too strict about it, though.

Nick left after that, promising that his days as
the Red Bandit were over. He expected repercus-
sions from his job, but thought it was worth it to see
the smiles on the kids' faces.

DeAjamae and I climbed back on my hoverbike
and sped across the salt pan to Saper. With any luck,
we'd make it back before the office party ended.

We landed in the precinct LAV lot, stowed the
helmets on the bike, and made our way to the
bullpen. Someone had taped red sparkly streamers
from the ceiling, and a holographic spaceship floated
around the perimeter. A speaker drone hovered over
the lieutenant's desk, playing music loud enough to
discourage anyone from standing by it for too long.

Ravi spotted us walking in and waved us over.
His normally charismatic smile faltered as we drew
closer. Between the long bike ride and borrowed
helmet, DeAjamae's curly hair had frizzed out. Her
red highlights looked like the rocket flares periodi-
cally shooting from the back of the holographic
spaceship.

Wright looked me up and down, taking in my disheveled hair, salt-coated clothes, and broken boot heel. He set his drink down on the nearest desk. "What happened?"

"Let's just say this has been one of the most interesting Exploration Days that I've had in a long time."

"Yeah," DeAjamae agreed, throwing her arm around my shoulder. "It was a wild ride."

The guys—understandably—looked confused.

Ravi rubbed at the back of his neck. "Did that, uh, happen while you were baking? I know you said baking wasn't your thing, but..."

I handed the container of cookie crumbles to Wright. "Take them. They're all yours."

Wright cracked open the top and peeked inside. "Were they ... cookies?"

"I'm sure they still taste perfectly fine."

Ravi reached inside to snag one of the larger chunks. He popped it in his mouth. "Mmm."

He grabbed a second piece. When he went for a third, Wright passed the container over to him.

"Well, cookies delivered. It's been a long night, and I'm going home."

"You're not staying?" DeAjamae asked me.

"I'm going to grab my jacket from my desk and then I'm out. Happy Exploration Day."

My desk was on the far end of the bullpen. The lights on this side had been turned down to encourage everyone over to the designated party area.

I reached my darkened cubicle and grabbed my jacket off the back of my chair. When the chair spun around, I noticed a white box with a red ribbon tied around it on the seat. There was no tag or card.

Curious, I opened the box. Inside was a vintage Captain Stardust ray gun, complete with all the accessories. It was exactly like the one I'd had when I was a kid.

I carefully lifted it out, turning the toy over in my hands. The handle felt small when I gripped it, but my fingers remembered all the little bumps and groves in the molded plastic. When I flipped a switch on the side, a neon-blue light shone out from the barrel—Captain Stardust's iconic ray beam. It also doubled as a handy-dandy light for kids if they weren't old enough to have their own cuffs yet.

So many nights had been spent playing space pirates in the backyard, blasting at toys and pretend flying through obstacle courses made of sticks and scraps of junk we'd hauled back from around the neighborhood.

Our parents had *loved* that.

Who put the toy on my chair? I looked around to see if anyone was watching me. No one was. My team had moved over to the food table, and Ravi was filling a plate. DeAjamae ate a brownie, laughing and catching the crumbs with her free hand. One of the other lead agents had pulled Wright into a conversation.

They were good officers and good people. Even though I'd only been on the team for a few months, they'd welcomed me in without hesitation.

I placed the ray gun back into its box and slipped it into my bag. Maybe Exploration Day wouldn't be so bad now that I had people to celebrate it with, and maybe I didn't need to get home right away, after all.

I laid my jacket and bag back on my chair and rejoined my friends.

"On Icing" is a story in the award-winning Reliance Sinclair series. To see how this sci-fi thrill ride began, download the free prequel at heathertexle.com/Newsletter or jump straight into the action with On Impulse (Reliance Sinclair, #1) at book s2read.com/On-Impulse.

Either way, fasten your harness, because this ride is about to take off!

RECITE: BIG MAMMA'S SUGAR COOKIES

From Heather Texle's "On Icing"

COOKIE INGREDIENTS:

- 1 cup sugar
- ½ cup butter, softened
- ½ cup shortening (regular or butter flavor)
- 2 eggs
- 3 tablespoons sour milk* or cream
- 1 teaspoon vanilla extract
- 1 teaspoon lemon extract
- 3 cups flour
- 1 teaspoon baking soda
- ¼ teaspoon salt

Frosting Ingredients:

- 2 cups powdered sugar
- 1 tablespoon butter, softened

- ½ teaspoon vanilla extract
- Milk (a few tablespoons)
- Optional: food coloring and sprinkles

COOKIES:

1. Preheat oven to 425°F.

2. Cream sugar, butter, and shortening together. Beat in eggs, sour milk, vanilla extract, and lemon extract.

3. Mix flour, baking soda, and salt.

4. Add the dry ingredients to the wet ingredients.

5. Form into a ball and cover with plastic wrap. Chill for at least 1 hour.

6. Roll the dough out to a quarter-inch thick circle and cut with cookie cutters. Bake for 6-10 minutes.

FROSTING:

1. When the cookies are cool, mix the powdered sugar, butter, and vanilla extract together. Slowly add a little bit of milk at a time and whisk until smooth.

2. The frosting will be more of a thin glaze than a fluffy frosting. The more milk you add, the thinner it will be. You may add food coloring to tint the frosting.

3. Top the cookies with frosting and decorate with sprinkles.

. . .

*To make sour milk, mix 1 teaspoon of vinegar with ½ cup of milk and let sit for a few minutes. This can be used as a substitute for buttermilk.

ALL THEY SEE ARE STARS

by Jeannette Bedard

FROM MY USUAL SPOT IN THE PILOT'S SEAT, I frowned as I scanned through the latest list of auction items coming up for sale. At the moment, the field of stars out the windshield was empty of other ships. We'd gone off the main routes to give ourselves time to plan what to do next (and I'd gotten distracted).

"Is there something wrong with your face?" Tud's tone was flat as usual because he was a robot—a fact I kept reminding him of.

"I was hoping there would be something good coming up for auction on New Venus." I sighed. "But there's nothing worth making the trip for."

"What could you possibly need? Everything required to sustain a meatbag like you is already on this shuttle." He gestured to the spaceship around us.

Raising an eyebrow, I stared at him—considering his processing power, he was often surprisingly thick. "What keeps this shuttle running and a 'meatbag' like me sustained is my work. That's also what keeps you in lubricants and credits."

Tud made a sound that could have been a snort, except robots didn't have those kinds of emotions.

I stood and made my way back to the common area. My ship wasn't big, but it suited me fine. It was an old survey vessel with a lab in the rear, a basic kitchen/common room, and a small cabin originally with four bunks, but I had converted it into nice quarters for me; if I ever took on passengers, they'd have to sleep in the old lab. The only other spaces were the engine room, a tiny bathroom, and the bridge (where Tud stayed 90% of the time, he'd even installed his charging port next to the co-pilot's seat).

After filling my mug with coffee, I sat at the table, hoping for a few moments alone. With Tud as my only crew member, I'd thought I'd get more solitude, but it turned out Tud was as chatty as any human.

With a squelch, the intercom activated. "Hey, meatbag, there's an incoming message for you." Tud was literally on the other side of a wall, yet he, once again, insisted on using the intercom. Not for the first time, I was shocked how lazy the decommissioned military robot was—but then his military model was TUD, which people joked stood for Totally Useless Device (I never made that joke in front of Tud).

"I should just get the intercom removed." I slowly sipped my coffee. The whole point of solitude was not rushing at other people's whims.

"I'll pipe the message to the common room," Tud said seconds later, again using the intercom.

I ran a hand over my face and wondered who could possibly want to talk with me—and could I just ignore the call. But Tud didn't wait. A millisecond later, in a cascade of pixels, a holographic head materialized in the air over the table.

"Chen," I said at seeing my old friend's face. I hadn't seen him for years. He was almost the last person I'd expected. At least he was someone I liked.

Chen smiled, dimples formed on both cheeks, but the expression didn't reach his eyes. "Darla, it's been a long time."

I took another sip of coffee. "It has. Was it three years ago I dropped you off on Hamber's Hole to set up your new noodle shop?"

"About that." His face took on a more serious expression.

I frowned. "Are you having business troubles?" Chen's food was always among the best I'd ever eaten.

"I set the restaurant up, and it's doing fine. As I suspected, the miners love spicy noodles." Chen bit his lip. "But I called to ask for help."

"It better not be for a romance problem," I said.

Chen shook his head. "No, I was hoping you'd pick up something for me. A shipment of dried jazzy peppers."

"You need me to do a grocery run?" I cocked my head. "Aren't those grown on Blue Moon Colony?"

"Not these ones." Chen's hand appeared in the hologram as he scratched his cheek. "I know a guy who grows them on Jade Outpost. He uses a special growing process to ensure the peppers are both hot and sweet—I've never found peppers as good from any other grower."

"Are these peppers legal?"

"Well..." Chen's words trailed off.

I almost groaned. "Are they impounded by the Protectorate Trade Authority?"

Chen took a deep breath. "The grower exposes the pepper to special radiation as they grow. The PTA has a blanket ban on radiation growing from uncertified farms. But I've had them tested, and the peppers are totally safe to consume."

My eyebrows pulled together. "Did you say whether they were impounded?"

Chen looked behind himself, and the hologram shimmered, threatening to de-pixelate. He met my gaze once more. "No, they haven't impounded the peppers. I got them before PTA did."

"Wait, are you physically in trouble?"

"Maybe." Chen sighed. "I panicked and darted onto the closest ship leaving Jade Outpost."

"And that ship is..."

"*Stardust 3.*"

This time, I let out a groan. "You stowed away on a Star Cult ship?" I wasn't terribly familiar with the Star Cult, but I did know all of their ships were named Stardust.

Chen nodded.

"Stay hidden, and I'll come and get you and your irradiated peppers."

✳

Luckily, *Stardust 3* was only one gate away, so within twelve hours I was approaching it.

"Why are we helping this human?" Tud asked as he brought up the cult ship's specs.

"We've been over this. He's a friend."

"You don't seem like the sort who makes friends," Tud said.

I sighed and shifted my attention to the *Stardust 3* specs. It was a converted long-distance cargo hauler, probably at least a century old. The Star Cult bought up this kind of ship whenever they could, giving their followers very unsafe homes. It was their central belief that all beings were just stardust waiting to be returned. The first thing they did when they acquired a new ship was to remove all locks on the airlocks and get rid of the escape pods along with every spacesuit. If the ancient ship had any kind of issue, there was no refuge for those who lived there—they would literally become one with the void (another central tenant of the cult).

"There it is." Tud pointed a metal finger towards a glimmering speck in the distance.

The *Stardust 3* was reflecting the blue light from the system's star, giving the ship a shine. I checked our scanner and confirmed it was the ship we were after.

"Is it true the meatbags on that ship all have a death wish?" Tud rotated his head to face me.

"I don't know. I've always avoided them." I zoomed in to the ship. The scanners beeped for a moment, forcing me to fiddle with the settings. Then it showed there were over one hundred people on board—no doubt families. "They creep me out, though."

I rubbed my chin as I continued to stare at the other ship. The Star Cult actively recruited new members whenever they stopped at the space stations, but would they accept a new member randomly out in space?

"How are we going to rescue this 'Chen?'" Tud asked, his synthetic voice laced with disdain he shouldn't have.

"I was thinking of asking about becoming a new member."

"That won't work," Tud said. "Their manual states that out in open space, new members are required to endure trial by the stars."

I raised my eyebrows. "What the hell is that?"

"They want a new recruit to survive the vacuum of space."

"I won't survive that."

"That's why that plan won't work." Tud's voice took on an 'I told you so' tone.

With my lips pressed together, I consulted the cult's manual. For a few minutes, silence fell over the cockpit. The coffee pot in the common room pinged.

"Can you grab me a mug of coffee?" I asked as I kept scrolling through the document.

"No," Tud said.

"Fine, I'll go get it myself." I stood and took the few paces back to the common room. I turned on the tap to rinse out my mug (because, like everyone, except perhaps Tud, I had a favourite mug). A healthy flow of water came out of the tap, and an idea struck me.

"Hey, Tud, check their manual to see if they provide aid to other spaceships."

I filled my mug, took a moment to savour the scent of the steam, then returned to the cockpit.

"Like all ships in Protectorate space, Star Cult ships are required to provide assistance if another ship is in need." Tud turned off the document on his side screen. "Their manual directs all of their members to follow this rule."

"So they have to help us if we ask?"

"Correct. However, they have excellent scanners and already know we do not require assistance."

"Hmmmm." I took a long sip of coffee and stared at the other ship. The brew was bitter as only discount coffee could be. "Dump our water."

With a whirr of servos, Tud turned his whole torso to face me. "May I remind you that all meat-bags like you require significant water to survive?"

"A catastrophic failure of our water tanks, along with losing all our water, would count as an emergency then." Darla eyed the ship ahead.

"Correct."

"Then do it."

Tud hesitated for a moment, but wisely said nothing, before he worked a side control screen. Then, a thunk reverberated through the ship. The whoosh of flowing water passed through the hull, but the plume of ice crystals would be behind us (no doubt, I could see it through the window of the airlock, but I was comfy, sipping coffee and didn't want to move).

······✸······

A few minutes later, long enough that the billowing plume of ice crystals would be obvious, I opened a comms channel to the other ship. "*Stardust 3,* this is the survey ship *Mallard.*"

"This is a foolish plan." Tud didn't even glance my way. "But I can survive forever without water."

"Good to know." I kept my gaze fixed on the other ship.

"*Mallard.*" An unfamiliar voice answered. "Our sensors indicate that you have lost a lot of water."

I smiled, delighted they fell for it. "That's correct. We've had a catastrophic failure in our plumbing. We can make repairs; however, we've lost our entire water supply. I'm requesting an emergency resupply of water."

The line went silent for a few minutes.

"Why would your water tank suddenly fail?" the voice from *Stardust 3* asked.

"We haven't had a chance to investigate yet," I said.

"Perhaps it is the will of the stars that you join them." The voice sounded cold.

I clenched my jaw. "Perhaps it is the will of the stars that you are close enough to provide aid." I muted my microphone and took a deep breath.

"You should tell them that the Protectorate regulations are clear about rendering aid," Tud said.

I shook my head. "I'm not sure that logic would work."

"It's not logic, it's law."

A burst of static came from the comms. "Of

course, that must be the will of the stars," the voice said. "You can become stardust later when your time comes."

A shiver ran up my spine as I unmuted my end—dealing with the Star Cult was as creepy as I'd expected. "Thank you. Can I bring my ship into your cargo bay?"

"We require proof," the voice said.

"Proof of what?" I already hated having to deal with these people.

"Proof that the stars have a plan for you. You must pass the trial."

I closed my eyes and mouthed a swear word that no robot should hear. "What is this trial?"

"Trial by stars."

After muting the comms, I let out a long exhale.

"Told you so," Tud said.

I frowned at the robot, then unmuted the comms. "Please describe your trial by stars."

"One of your crew needs to transfer from your ship to ours without the protection of a spacesuit."

I cocked my head. "Does it matter which member of my crew endures this trial?"

"That is for you to decide," the voice said. "You may approach our cargo bay. At a distance of ten metres, your chosen one must come over."

With the comms muted, I looked over at Tud.

"Let me guess, I am your chosen one." His tone was flat, clearly not a question.

✳

We reached the required distance to *Stardust 3* an hour later, after I'd checked our airlock seals and scarfed down a package of mediocre instant noodles that smelled like cardboard (why write spicy all over the packaging when the only real flavour is salt?).

Back in the cockpit, I stared at the worn hull of the other ship. They weren't going to like my work-around for passing their trial. But would they respect it? I didn't care as long as they filled my water tank and allowed Chen and his precious peppers to board.

"We are now ten metres from the *Stardust 3*," Tud announced. "I have set the autopilot to prevent you from crashing into the other ship while I'm out."

I frowned. "I've been a pilot my whole life. I'm not going to just crash because you aren't here."

"That remains to be seen." Tud stood and left the cockpit.

Leaving the autopilot active, I opened a comms channel. "*Stardust 3*, my chosen one is about to begin the trial."

"We will await their arrival," said the voice on the other end, their tone as flat as before.

A clunk reverberated through my ship, and then I saw Tud fly by the windshield. He easily grabbed onto the other ship's hull, like he'd been designed to leap from ship to ship in the vacuum of space (which, of course, was exactly what he'd been designed to do). Hand over mechanical hand, he pulled himself towards the airlock and opened the door. I bit my lip, hoping the fools over there had closed the inside door—whether that thought crossed Tud's circuits or not, I don't know. Without hesitation, he entered, quickly closing the door behind himself.

They made me wait for a half hour. Unsure what to do with myself, I paced the length of my ship repeatedly. Finally, a ping alerted me to an incoming message. I raced back to the cockpit and activated the comms.

"This is the *Stardust 3*," a very bland voice said, that may or may not have belonged to the same person I spoke to before (at least they didn't sound angry).

"Hello."

"Despite sending an artificial man as your chosen one, we have agreed that you may land in our cargo bay."

In front of me, the massive cargo bay doors slowly opened.

"Thank you," I said. "And I should point out that my artificial man will ultimately end up as stardust, just like you and me."

"That is what he pointed out." With a click, the line went dead.

Taking the open cargo bay doors as an invitation, I flew my ship through their atmo field (which was probably dodgy and prone to failure) and landed on the open deck. I left the ship powered up and ready to take off.

I opened the comms channel Chen had used before. "Hello? Chen?" My voice was barely a whisper, just in case that mattered. After a few minutes without a response, I gave up. As I rubbed a hand over my short hair, I hoped he was okay.

From my seat in the cockpit, I could see no one in the hangar. Which was odd. Even weirder, the cargo bay was empty. I stood and proceeded back to the airlock. I put my hands on my hips and stared at my favourite spacesuit (my new orange one with silver trim).

"Should I go out in a spacesuit?" I asked my empty ship.

No doubt the cargo ship was unsafe, but showing up in a spacesuit might make the cult members angry. I'd have to take the risk. But I did pull on my AR goggles. They'd been helpful more than once. With a knot forming in my gut, I left the safety of my ship.

The first thing I noticed was a water hookup on the bulkhead. "That's what I'm here for, and they already agreed to help," I said to myself (I really should talk out loud to myself less).

I took the nozzle and connected it to my ship, then started the pump—at least we'd have water for the trip out of here (assuming we made it out).

Turning around slowly, I hunted for any hiding place that Chen might be in. He did say he was hiding in the cargo bay. But there was nothing, not even a single crate. The other rumour I'd heard about the cult's ships was that families lived in the cargo bays—which apparently wasn't true, at least not here.

I headed to the doors leading to the rest of the ship—I had been on this model of cargo ship before and knew where the bridge was, which was where I'd hopefully find some people with answers. As for where Chen was, that was a different matter completely, but I wouldn't leave without him.

The ship's main corridor was as vacant as the cargo bay, and I could hear no sounds of humans moving about. The lights in the corridor dimmed to nothing towards the aft section of the ship as if that part of the ship was running minimal power. I headed forward wondering where the hundred or so people my sensors had picked up were.

The bridge was up on the top deck, so I took the first set of stairs heading up I could find. This level was as deserted as down below. The knot in my gut churned as I headed towards the bridge. Just outside the bridge, the lights winked out.

Before I could activate night vision on my goggles, someone tackled me from the right. My attacker was big enough to slam me into the wall and drive the air out of my lungs. I didn't have a chance to fight back, but I got my night vision activated as I slumped down to the deck.

As I struggled to pull in a breath, my attacker cuffed my arms behind my back.

"On your feet," they said, pulling me up.

"What the hell? Your people invited me here," I said in gasps. My goggles only gave me a rough outline of their face.

"The First Star has changed their mind."

Someone hauled me along the dark corridor away from the bridge. I deeply regretted not bringing along my Emerg-Blast; it was charged and ready to go...back on my ship. An EMP pulse would have been handy.

"I should remind you that your manual requires you to provide aid to fellow space travellers," I said, well aware this goon wasn't going to just let me go.

The goon didn't say another word to me. Instead, they pulled me along until the end of the corridor. Then they opened a door, filling the corridor with light, and shoved me inside. As I stumbled forward, they slammed the door shut behind me. The night vision in my goggles automatically turned off.

"Hi, Darla." It was Chen. He sat on a bench on the far side of the small room, his hands cuffed together behind him just like mine were. He had always been a small man, but here, he looked gaunt, as if he hadn't slept or eaten in days. Even his skin had taken on an ashen hue.

"Are you okay?"

He gave a nod, then hung his head. "I'm sorry about this." He sighed. "It's my fault you're here."

I snorted and sat down next to him. "Is this a jail?" It was a small room painted grey with no windows and only one door. The space smelled like lemon cleaner. Seemed like a jail to me.

Chen shrugged. "They caught me right after I called you." At his feet was a large case—no doubt his precious dried peppers.

"They were tracking outgoing comms?" I looked around as if answers were written on the wall. "Why would the cultists do that? I mean, they aren't known for worrying about security."

"I don't think this is a Star Cult ship." Chen's expression was bleak.

"They seemed culty to me." But as I thought about it, bits and pieces just didn't add up. There were supposed to be a hundred people here, and I'd seen only one—and assuming that the goon wasn't who I spoke to on the comms. That made two. "My scanners picked up lots of people on board. Where are they?"

Chen shrugged. "I never saw many. Just a few workers. They might have equipment to fool your sensors."

"But why bother?"

"I don't know."

"If this isn't a Star Cult ship, why pretend to be?" Whoever felt the need to pretend to be Star Cult people had to be much worse than the actual cult.

"I don't know."

I bit my lip. "And where is Tud?"

Chen cocked his head. "Who?"

"He's a robot on my crew."

"I haven't seen him." He pulled his eyebrows together. "Wait. You hired a robot? That doesn't sound like you."

I frowned. I needed at least one crew member, and humans had proven to be too hard to deal with —of course, now I knew robots also presented challenges. Instead of answering Chen's question, I looked around again as if Tud was just hiding in a corner (he wasn't).

"We need to escape—and soon." I wiggled my arms, but the cuffs held them tight.

"Agreed, but how?"

I sighed. I didn't want to admit I had no idea. The one thing I had was my goggles. Good thing I'd activated them. I scrolled through the menus simply by moving my eyes...but most of what I had access to proved unhelpful. I could activate my Hank the Hippo projection—but, sadly, my favourite holographic hippo couldn't open a door.

Instead, I brought up the ship schematic and projected it into the air in front of us. Turns out, whoever these not-cult members were, they hadn't bothered to lock down their internal network. It was easy to overlay blue dots corresponding to where everyone was.

"So there are only seven of them," Chen said.

My nose itched, but I couldn't scratch it. "Not exactly the hordes of people I'd expected to be here —but still, seven people might be hard to escape from."

"Especially cuffed as we are." Chen smiled. At least he'd perked up a bit.

"Step one has to be get out of the cuffs." I froze as one dot raced right for our room. I deactivated the hologram just as the door opened and held my breath.

"Good, you two meatbags are together." Tud sounded irritated, which was the way he always sounded.

I exhaled. "Thank the stars it's you."

Tud came into the room. "Who else would come save you?"

"Never mind. Can you undo the cuffs?" I stood and turned to give the robot access to my bound wrists. It only took a few moments for Tud to release both Chen and me.

After rubbing his wrists, Chen picked up his crate of jazzy peppers. "Let's get out of here."

"Affirmative." Tud headed back out into the hallway, where the lights remained off.

"I got you," I said to Chen as I activated my night vision and grabbed onto his elbow.

The three of us made our way down the corridor. Unfortunately, I couldn't run the map showing everyone's positions alongside my night vision.

Just outside of the bridge, we slowed. Voices came from inside. At least two people with low-ish voices discussed something I couldn't quite make out. Gently placing down each foot, we turned into the stairs leading down to the lower level. I let Chen go ahead of me, and Tud followed behind. I gritted my teeth and told myself I'd be back in my ship and on our way soon, leaving the not-cult people behind.

The lights flicked on, and the three of us froze half-way down the stairs.

"Stop!" someone shouted from below. The person pointed an energy weapon at us (definitely not a cult member—they banned weapons of all kinds).

"Activate the TUD unit's override," someone said from above. (Did I mention that Tud was a surplus military robot? In service, they were called Tactical Unit Droid, or something like that, TUD for short.)

I turned and stared at Tud.

"This might be unfortunate," he said. His body jolted as though hit by a surge of power.

I backed up, forgetting that I stood on stairs. Tumbling backwards, I slammed into Chen. He did his best to stop my fall (I dwarfed him, after all), and in doing so, he lost his grip on the case of hot peppers.

"Noooooooooo." Chen sprinted down the stairs after his prized ingredient.

The case hit the ground next to the person at the bottom of the stairs and burst open. A cloud of powdered pepper rose into the air. The person started sneezing, then ran away—we had an opening.

"Apprehend them," the person at the top of the stairs ordered.

"Affirmative," Tud said.

I grabbed Chen's arm and pulled him into a sprint, right through the billowing pepper cloud, holding my breath all the way.

"My peppers," he said as we ran (I was amazed he didn't start sneezing).

I was able to see solely due to my goggles. Enough got on me that my exposed skin started burning. "We'll go to Jade Station and get you more." Why he wanted to use the stuff was beyond me.

Heavy footfalls behind us announced Tud was right on our heels.

I continued to pull Chen along as I tried to think of how I might 'deactivate' the military bypass in Tud. He was here because of me, and I wasn't going to leave him behind. Also, why hadn't I looked into this kind of programming when he first joined me?

At the cargo bay, I pushed the door release button, panting now. As the door opened, I glanced back to where Tud chased after us, half-expecting his eyes to be glowing red (they weren't). He had slowed to a walk, but he was close. We wouldn't escape his grasp—but I'm stubborn as hell and foolish enough to never give up.

Chen raced ahead towards my survey ship, and I followed.

"Get inside!" I yelled as I went to disconnect the water hose.

"Meatbag!" Tud called as he came around the shuttle. To my ear, his tone held more disdain than usual.

I bit my lip and backed up, holding the disconnected hose. As he took another step towards me, I blasted him with water. Dropping the still-discharging hose, I bolted for the door. Tud beat me to it.

"You did not properly seal our water supply. I would hate for you and your passenger to dehydrate."

"Tud?"

"We need to get going," he said. "I will start up the ship. You need to seal the connector."

In somewhat of a daze, I returned to where the water hose had connected to the ship. Tud was right. I didn't seal it properly—the water would have vented right into space. I fixed it and entered the ship. I took extra care sealing the door, then headed forward.

Chen sat at the table in the far corner with wide eyes. "The robot's through there." He pointed to the cockpit.

I nodded, then pursed my lips together as I approached. Tud sat in his usual seat, going through the pre-flight checklist like he always did. I took my place in the pilot's seat.

"Let's go." Tud lifted us off and flew out of the hangar. He set a course for the nearest gate at maximum speed.

"Tud?"

He swivelled his head to stare at me.

"Are you *you?*"

"Affirmative." He swivelled back to face forward.

"What about the military override?" I asked. "Do you have one?"

"All TUD units do," he said as if the answer was obvious. "I, however, refuse to be controlled. I had it removed shortly after you took me into your employ."

I let go of a breath I hadn't realized I'd been holding and slumped back into my seat. "You were pretending."

"Affirmative. That remained our optimal escape option."

I closed my eyes and leaned my head back into the headrest. "Thank you."

Later, after I'd explained Tud's ruse to Chen, calming him down, he headed to the kitchenette. Cooking up a storm had always been his way of dealing with anything.

"It'll take us a couple of days to get to Jade Outpost," I said as I leaned against the wall next to the stove.

Chen paused and looked at me. "Thank you for coming for me."

I smiled (a genuine one, for once). "I'm happy to help."

"Do you know who those people were?" he asked, returning his gaze to the carrots he was chopping.

"I don't, and Tud doesn't either."

Chen nodded. "I guess that's a mystery for another day."

"I guess so," I said, hoping it wasn't me who'd have to figure it out.

"Anyway, the celebratory noodles are almost done." He shifted his attention to the boiling water and lowered the dried noodles in. "But I have to warn you, your food supplier didn't give me much to work with." He pulled out peanut butter and a tub of miso.

I had randomly selected food at our previous stop—but I didn't tell him that. "I'm sure the noodles will be fantastic. Yours always are."

"All They See Are Stars" is a Lost Orbits story. To see how Darla and Tud ended up together on a ratty old survey ship check out The Lost Star Chart *at books2read.com/ TheLostStarChart*

RECECIPE: CHEN'S CELEBRATORY NOODLES

from Jeannette Bedard's "All They See Are Stars"

(FOR WHEN THERE'S NOT MUCH IN THE CUPBOARD, time is short and everyone is hungry)

4 servings

Ingredients:

- 14 oz udon noodles (or whatever noodles are on hand)
- 1 tsp oil
- 1 broccoli crown cut into small florets
- 1 medium red pepper sliced
- 1 cup frozen edamame

Sauce:

- 1/2 cup peanut butter
- 1 tbsp white miso paste

- Juice of one lime
- 1 tbsp soy sauce
- 1 tbsp maple syrup
- 1 tsp sesame oil
- 1 tsp jazzy pepper sauce (or sambal oelek, or whatever hot sauce is at hand)
- 2 cloves minced garlic
- 1 tbsp minced ginger
- 1/3 cup hot water

Optional toppings:

Cilantro, diced green onion, sesame seeds, chopped roasted peanuts.

Instructions:

1. Put all sauce ingredients in the blender and blend until smooth.

2. Cook noodles according to the package instructions.

3. In a medium saucepan, stir-fry the broccoli and red pepper. When almost done, add edamame and cook until warm.

4. Toss everything together in a large bowl.

5. Serve up and add toppings.

NEVER STOP ROLLING

by A. Webster

LOADED DOWN WITH CAMERA EQUIPMENT, Lamont pushed through the door of his studio apartment, squatting just slightly so his shoulder would fall below a newly hung wreath adorned in crimson ribbon. Startled by the intrusion, a cockroach scuttled out from behind the bow and over Lamont's arm.

"Jesus Christ," he said, juggling—almost dropping—the thousands of dollars worth of borrowed-from-his-buddy-and-promised-to-give-them-back-he-just-needed-them-for-a-job lenses.

"What? You don't like the wreath?" his girlfriend called from the couch. Chuckie was curled up in a blanket, barely visible under the flickering light so dim they could never really tell whether it was on or off. He didn't expect to see her there, right where she'd been when he left that morning.

He set the lenses down in the small opening between the toilet, kitchen sink, and nightstand. "How much was it?"

"Two grand. I pawned one of your friend's lenses that you left behind." Chuckie smirked when Lamont bristled at the thought, then she continued, "You really need to give up on trying to break into showbiz. You can't even take a joke anymore. It was $15.99."

"$15.99?!"

"Not just for that. I also got us a Christmas tree." She motioned to a sad, one-foot tall, Charlie-Brown-looking excuse for a tree sitting on the microwave.

"Chuck, don't waste your money. You don't even live here."

"I don't really live anywhere." She patted the space next to her. Lamont joined her on the couch, and she tousled his hair and kissed him. He was perfectly happy to stay locked in that embrace all evening—until he caught a glimpse of his phone.

"I have to edit."

"Whatever." Chuckie pulled the blanket over her head. "At least close the shower curtain so I can get some sleep."

Lamont enclosed himself in the jerry-rigged cubicle setup inches from the couch. He sat on an old crate and propped his laptop up on an empty box, pulled the curtain to block the glow of the screen, and got to work editing his passion project when he should've been focusing on his paid gig.

The next morning, Chuckie was still curled up on the couch fast asleep when Lamont got up to leave. Little circles of light dotted her body, reflected from the tiny Christmas tree. Lamont smiled and shook his head, then pushed the tree further back on the counter so the light wouldn't shine in her eyes and wake her before the sun moved off the horizon. Then, gear in hand, he quietly slipped out and made his way down to the bus stop.

Today was day three of a cringey commercial shoot for a local business with a marketing budget pulled out of a tip jar. It was the last thing he wanted to do and the last thing the business needed to waste their money on. With the level of acting they had access to, they'd be better off having a waiter film something on their phone. Oh well. It was their money to waste and a week's worth of work for Lamont. And anyway, it's not like he had anything else important going on.

Greyish slush sprayed onto the bus shelter as richer people than Lamont drove by in their beater cars. Forget T-travel or automated chauffeurs or even a ten-year-old electric car. Lamont just wanted to be able to go wherever you wanted, whenever you wanted, without paying any attention to bus schedules or how deep the snow was and how many Ziploc bags that meant you had to wrap your feet in to keep your socks dry inside your holey boots. No one else making you late except for yourself—and *where is this damn bus, anyway?*

Lamont braced against the biting wind and reluctantly slid his hand out of his pocket to check his phone. Of course he was late. He hadn't needed to check his phone to know that. The client hadn't called him, either. Not really a good sign.

The long slow screech finally signaled the bus's arrival, followed by a horde of people trudging out into the snow like they had nowhere to go. Lamont squidged through the slush, leaving deep footprints next to the bus, then balanced his bag of lenses as he shuffled to the only open seat in the back. He closed his eyes and sighed in relief. Too much relief. After a long night of wasting time editing true crime that no-one-is-watching-anyway-*Lamont,* highway hypnosis set in, and the bus jostled him to sleep.

"End of the line. Everybody get off." Lamont woke with a jolt to the driverless bus's automated announcement, which had been eerily, needlessly tuned to the brusque tone of a human driver.

Shit. Shit!

Thank god his stop was only two blocks back.

Squish, squash. Clink, clank. Lamont lumbered-stepped-jogged down the street through the slush, trying not to slip with all of his friend's gear, only to find the client already set up with another videographer. He snuck up to the set without anyone noticing and waited for the take to finish.

"The stakes are high, so order High Stakes Steaks today for a chance to win a free steak." The owner recited his horrible line and smiled a cheesy grin, complete with a thumbs up.

"And cut!" the videographer yelled and stopped recording.

Clap.

Clap.

Clap.

No one else joined Lamont's slow clap. They *did* all turn to face him.

"Were you going to tell me you fired me? I wasted my whole morning coming here." Lamont said. "Do you know how hard it is to get over here without a car?"

"You couldn't respect me enough to *ever* be on time. Why should I respect you? Get out of my parking lot. We've got a commercial to shoot."

Middle finger up, Lamont walked towards the bus stop and called over his shoulder, "I'm giving you a one star review."

"I pay to have those removed!"

"Piece of shit," Lamont muttered to himself.

The jostling bus was less soothing this time. Lamont fussed with the lenses, trying to keep them from smacking into one another. A fleeting thought crossed his mind: *I could sell these.* The brief feeling of hope dissipated when he remembered they weren't even his. He could ask that same friend for money. *He already let me borrow his lenses. That's worth more than money...*

He should at least text Chuckie and see if she could cover half the rent for once. She was always there. But then he would have to tell her he got fired from his *only job* this week and she'd probably leave his sorry ass. He pulled out his phone. Maybe this would be the week he went viral... nope. 342 views.

Just before he slid his phone back in his pocket, he noticed a DM.

This is sick dude. You've got a future in true crime. If you ever need work lmk.

He looked up to see he'd already missed his stop. Not that it mattered. He wasn't supposed to be home this early. Might as well ride around.

Thanks man. What shoots you got?

Big studio gig. Just lost our B cam to a Marvel movie. Can you start tonight?

"Jesus. Who responds that fast?" Lamont muttered to himself.

Yeah. Tell me where to show up and I'm there.

Can you meet me in an hour to talk more about the job?

The mysterious producer—Lamont didn't even know their name—dropped a pin with the location of a coffee shop. He didn't have anything to lose...

Lamont shook his head at the irony. A future in true crime—as a victim, probably. *Better a stranger killing me because I'm naive than Chuckie killing me because I'm a deadbeat,* he thought.

Sure.

Lamont meandered around the city on the bus to pass time until the meeting, reflecting on what he had just gotten himself into.

When he had waited long enough that he wouldn't be awkwardly early while looking for a person he didn't know, he exited the bus and proceeded to Starbucks—the most stereotypical of all "let me buy you a coffee" business meeting locations.

Lamont ordered a tall hot water with lemon and moved off to the side to wait for his order. He ran his hand up and down the strap of his bag to calm his nerves. "Lament!" the barista called out.

"It's Lamont, actually," he smiled politely, took his drink, and looked around. Still unsure who he was meeting, he noticed a man in business casual perk up at the sound of his name, then take out his earbuds and close his laptop.

"Lamont!"

The man's eagerness startled Lamont, causing him to spill a bit of his drink on his hand. He lapped up the drip and greeted the man—who had a much friendlier and less sinister face than Lamont had been expecting.

"Hi, I'm Matt," he introduced himself, extending a hand. "I just realized I should've told you my name earlier. Please, have a seat."

Lamont scanned for the exits before taking a seat. *Surely, no one would be so bold as to commit a crime in broad daylight* and *in public.*

"Thanks for meeting me so quickly. The studio is on a really tight schedule, and even with our B cam dropping out, that wasn't a good enough excuse to push the shoot. I asked if we could do it with just the one camera, but the director said it wouldn't be the same without multiple angles. He told me to find someone or he's dropping out, and there's way too much money on the line for that. So, here we are."

Lamont gulped his water and swirled the lemon at the bottom of the cup. "If there's so much money on the line, why go with a nobody?"

Matt leaned across the table and played Lamont his own reel from last night. "Because of this. With social media, you don't *need* to be anyone. Talent speaks for itself. Besides, everyone is booked up. Who's going to have the same night open other than people trying to break into the biz?"

Lamont nodded and smirked, sucking on the dregs of his drink. "So, tell me about this job."

"Double homicide on a Christmas tree farm.

Unknown motive. Framed as a murder suicide to make it look like a crime of passion. Owners were a married couple with a meet-cute out of a Hallmark movie. They were known for their over-the-top spectacle. Beloved by the entire community. Perfect story to air right before the holidays."

"Yeah, I'm interested," Lamont said. "But why haven't I heard about this? My girlfriend Chuckie loves places like that, so we've been to almost all of them in town."

Matt ignored the question, instead shoving an iPad with a contract and non-disclosure agreement in Lamont's face. "I have a feeling their farm is out of your price range, but if we like you and keep you around, it won't be for long." He tapped his stylus on the day rate.

Lamont took the final swig from his empty cup, choked on his no-longer-existent beverage, then signed without reading.

Matt shook his hand and welcomed him to the team. "I'll airdrop you a location and a time."

Lamont watched Matt leave, as all of reality seemed to slow down around him. The smaller, self-actualizing facets of life came into focus—the ones that blur away when you don't know where the money for your next meal is coming from.

I guess Chuckie was right about the wreath. And even the world's saddest Christmas tree is better than nothing.

Should I decorate even more?

Would I think my apartment was less of a shithole if I got plants?

Fuck my apartment. I could move somewhere with parking...and actually have a car to park there.

I could even pay for Chuckie's driving test.

I could buy her a minivan. She can drive our future kids around in it like the suburban soccer mom she deserves to be.

Somehow, he was home. He paused in the hallway, appreciating the sounds floating around him. An ode to a paper-thin-walled apartment: Babies crying. Dogs barking. Couples fighting. And overtones of holiday music that Chuckie must have been blasting because it only got louder the closer he got to his door. The low-income cacophony sounded like a symphony to Lamont. Nothing could dampen his mood.

He pushed open the door and stood in the threshold, watching Chuckie before she noticed he was there. An empty family sized container of vanilla yogurt on one side of the impossibly-narrow counter, an empty container of Cool Whip on the other. She had just poured a box of red-and-green store-brand holiday Funfetti cake mix into the bowl and was singing along to the Christmas music at the top of her lungs while she whisked the mixture together. She opened a container of red-and-green sprinkles to add to the bowl, all without looking up once.

"Hey, Chuck."

Sprinkles rained down around her as she gasped and jumped, her concentration broken. Time still felt slow for Lamont, and the scene almost created a prismatic effect in his mind.

"I swear it was less than 10 bucks for everything. I bought all of this at the dollar st—"

Lamont ran his fingers through Chuckie's hair

and kissed her passionately. She braced herself against the gritty sprinkled surface with one hand and embraced him with the other. He pushed her up onto the counter, empty boxes toppling to the ground, then nibbled her ear and said, "You'll never have to worry about money again."

She kissed him back, "Oh, yes sugar daddy. Make love to me on your yacht."

He pulled away, held her hands, looked directly into her eyes, and said, "No, Chuckie. I'm serious."

She rubbed his hands against her face. "What?"

"Well, first, I got fired."

"You *what*?!"

He hugged her and kissed the top of her head while he tried to find the rest of the words. "I got fired...But then some producer DM'd me. We met for coffee and he offered me a big studio job. It's more money than I've ever made—and it starts tonight."

She scooped a fingerful of dip and fed some to Lamont. "Well, then. I guess this will be the last night we have funfetti dip. At least for both dinner *and* dessert."

Lamont looked at the pin on his phone. Then looked at the time. Then looked around at the empty industrial park full of abandoned buildings, most of which appeared condemned.

"I got fucking scammed."

He turned to walk back towards the bus stop,

then stopped when he heard, "Lamont? I'm the director, Griz."

An older man with a camera bag slung over his shoulder and a cigarette hanging out of his lips stuck out his hand. "I wish Matt wouldn't tell new people to get here so early. Makes me look bad."

Lamont visibly relaxed as they shook hands, then followed as Griz walked off towards one of the abandoned-looking buildings. Griz talked the whole way, though he never looked back at Lamont.

"Small crew. Just you and me. We have to T-travel to get to our location."

Lamont's face lit up—not that Griz could see it. "Oh shit, are we filming in the past?"

"Something like that," Griz laughed. "You've never T-traveled, have you?"

"T-traveled?! I've never even been on a plane."

"You're in for a real treat then." Griz unlocked a rickety door and the inside of what appeared to be an old warehouse that had seen better days. Lamont looked around and watched a spider spin its web.

"I always imagined T-ports to be... nicer? Less... empty?"

"The commercial ones are. You at least know what a private plane is right?" Lamont grunted an affirmative response, following Griz down a dark stairway into a basement. "This is like our own private hangar. It allows the studio to be more flexible with our time travel."

Griz motioned for Lamont to have a seat in an ordinary looking office chair. He punched their intended coordinates into his phone, then sat in an identical chair facing Lamont.

He might have been imagining it, but the air around Lamont seemed to get... thicker?

"Ever had surgery?"

Lamont gripped the armrests, which were now vibrating. So, he hadn't imagined it.

"Um... no."

"Well, then my analogy won't make sense, so I'll spare you. Anyway, you might want to count backwards from 10."

"10, 9..."

Lamont woke with a start, standing in the middle of a desolate Christmas tree farm, the perimeter roped off by caution tape. While getting his bearings, he held his head and almost stumbled in a pile of fresh snow. He caught himself on a tree to steady his balance. Griz had clearly done this before, already holding his camera and tugging Lamont's arm to move him down the well-worn, muddy path.

"This way. You don't want to leave new tracks. And get your camera out. Never stop rolling."

As they walked up the path, Lamont filmed the trees. Zoomed in on the caution tape. Followed the thick tracks to the house where the viscous brown earth had started to mix with the blood that was splattered across the snow.

The trail led them to the victims. Griz was already inside, shoeless, filming handprints on a blood smeared wall. Lamont sat on a stool outside of the house to remove his shoes and set them next to Griz's.

Without looking up from his camera, Griz said, "Be careful to keep your feet dry when you come in. Don't touch anything except the blood-free parts of the floor. Don't leave any evidence that we were here. Treat it like a crime scene. Because it is."

Lamont had never seen murder victims in person before, but through the lens of his camera, it was eerily similar to looking at archival footage.

Looking at real bodies shouldn't feel like looking at photos should it?

Am I dissociating right now? Is any of this real?

Am I? Real?

He sucked in a big breath of air to ground into reality.

Similar. Except for the smell.

The stench of death seeped into his clothes like campfire smoke. He wondered if it would travel home with him across time.

He held the camera close up on the woman's face. Eyes wide open. Hair matted with blood. Then panned to the man. His head was turned to face the woman, staring towards his beloved during the last harrowing moments of their lives.

Pst. Psst. Psssst!

Still filming, Lamont looked up to see Griz running toward him with soft footsteps, holding onto their shoes and clearly trying not to make much noise. He crouched down next to Lamont and said in his ear, "Time to get out of here. I heard a noise out back. It's probably the cops but we don't want to find out. Follow me and start counting backwards."

"10, 9..."

Lamont woke in the same office chair with Griz

sitting across from him. Griz stood and bro slapped Lamont.

"Nice work kid."

Lamont patted his clothes, once again trying to feel into what was real and what wasn't. He sniffed.

"Don't worry, that's just your own BO you smell. You don't have stinky death clothes or anything. Not everything travels with us," Griz said with a smile. "I sweat through my shirt my first time, then hurled by the steps. Right over there."

Lamont tried to look up where Griz was pointing but the room was spinning. He saw two sets of stairs. Griz continued, "You'll be fine in a few minutes. I'll be setting up my computer. Let me know when you're ready to offload."

Once Lamont's dizziness passed, they offloaded the footage from their cameras and made their way back upstairs and out of the T-port. Lamont started to trudge through the snow towards the bus stop when he heard Griz say, "Check your account. Order yourself a Lyft. See you tomorrow night."

Lamont nearly dropped his phone in the snow.

Lamont couldn't believe how quickly he was able to get home.

He curled up next to Chuckie, who was sleeping on their couch. As soon as he closed his eyes, he was also asleep.

The next morning, Chuckie woke Lamont up by jingling the bells on her ugly reindeer sweater. He sat up slowly, still a little bit disoriented from the night before, as she happily futzed with the Charlie Brown Christmas tree—moving it from the microwave to the countertop back to the microwave. Lamont squinted as her holiday light leggings flashed in his eyes.

The tree now situated to her liking, Chuckie grabbed some graham crackers with dip and sat back down on the couch next to Lamont. "I found a Groupon for half off admission, food, and drink for this Christmas tree farm we've never been to. We should go today to celebrate your new job."

She paused, hoping he would fill in the obvious gap in conversation with details about the previous night, but he just sleepily agreed to her plans. She rolled her eyes and went a more direct route: "How was last night?"

Feeling more awake now, Lamont put his arms around Chuckie's neck and said, "Chuck, I got to T-travel."

"Damnnnnn! What was it like?"

"Really weird. You can't even feel the jump through time. You just wake up and you're in the past. Then the victims—"

Chuckie cut him off. "I'm *eating.* And you know I can't even handle you describing pictures. I'm just glad you had a good night." She kissed him on the nose. "Now hurry up and get dressed—we've only got seven minutes or we'll have to wait another three hours."

"Send me the address?"

Chuckie did. Lamont tapped his phone.

"No need to rush. Our Lyft gets here in an hour," Lamont winked and kissed her hand.

At the Christmas tree farm, they stepped out of the gray slush of the city and into a winter wonderland. Family fun, cozy sweaters, and snow-kissed evergreens surrounded them as they walked arm in arm towards a sleigh meant to take them deeper into the property.

They cuddled into the high-backed seats, tucked under a blanket, enjoying the ride without a care in the world. Chuckie whispered in his ear, "In the wise words of Ariana Grande, 'Whoever said money can't solve your problems must not have had enough money to solve them.'" They chuckled and took turns singing Ariana Grande lines back and forth to each other for the rest of the ride.

The sleigh dropped them off between the concession stand and gift shop. Lamont stepped inside to get them each a hot chocolate, and Chuckie couldn't resist the temptation to look at the ornaments on display racks outside. A few minutes later, Lamont came out, cocoa in hand, looking for Chuckie. Instead, he spotted a building in the distance that looked eerily familiar. He started to walk up the path a bit to get a closer look–

"Hey!" Chuckie called to him, startling him out of his curiosity. "I'm over here."

Lamont walked back to Chuckie and handed her the drink as she pulled him over toward the gift shop window. She pointed out a porcelain ornament the size of a grapefruit and said, "I didn't buy anything, but maybe we can stop on the way out." Then she winked and added, "You have all the money."

They took their time touring around the farm.

Looked at trees. Thought about buying one. Decided against it. *Where would one fit in Lamont's apartment?* Talked about moving in together. Dreamt about where they could move. Then finally circled back to the gift shop.

A jingle bell tinkled above the door as they walked in, and the person behind the counter greeted them with a warm smile. "Welcome back and welcome in."

Lamont looked up, expecting to nod politely then move on to shopping with Chuckie. Instead, he stopped in his tracks, locking eyes with this perfect stranger.

His memory flashed to the murder victim's face —the same one staring back at him now.

Alive.

Chuckie called for him to come look at something sparkly, once again bringing him back to the present. She had collected an armful of ornaments that she planned on making Lamont buy. Lamont dreaded walking back to the checkout counter, not ready to see the cashier again.

Once Chuckie was satisfied, they made their way back, and the woman with the victim's face scanned the ornaments. "Did you find everything ok?"

Lamont cringed when Chuckie asked, "Actually, there was one that I found that said 'display only, not for sale' but I was wondering if you had any more in the back."

The woman nodded and then yelled to someone in the back. "Hey, honey can you come out here?"

Sweat dripped from the bridge of Lamont's nose

onto the counter, which seemed to annoy the woman ever so slightly.

Lamont tried to say something, but started wheezing instead. Chuckie responded for him, "He gets wheezy whenever the temperature changes too drastically. I'm pretty sure he has asthma."

She smiled and kept her air of customer service as she wiped the drips up with a tissue. "We like to keep the heat up in here because it's so cold outside."

A man appeared around the corner, squeezing the woman's shoulder and pecking her on the lips.

The other victim.

Lamont's vision started to blur, and he had to catch his breath, leaning against the counter.

"Sir, are you ok?" the woman asked. He nodded and dripped more sweat, which she wiped up once again, then turned to her husband and asked, "Do we have more of this display?"

"I'll go check."

"Sir, would you like a seat?" the woman said, offering him her stool from behind the counter.

"NO!" Lamont said just a little too loudly, causing the other customers to turn around. He lowered his voice, "Thank you. No, thank you."

Chuckie mouthed, "Lamont, what the fuck?"

He shook his head and mouthed back, "Just hurry up."

The man returned and they finished their transaction. Lamont nearly pulled Chuckie's arm out of its socket as they were leaving, blissfully unaware of his suddenness as she admired her new set of ornaments.

Later, in the back of the Lyft that Lamont couldn't order fast enough, Chuckie said, "You really should see a doctor and get an inhaler now that you can afford it."

Between labored breaths, Lamont said, "I have something to tell you when we get home."

"If you don't die on the way there," Chuckie responded. "You're really freaking me out."

Inside the apartment, Lamont locked the door behind them and sat Chuckie down on the couch. He took a moment to slow his breathing, then said, "Those were the murder victims."

Chuckie stopped unboxing her ornaments and stared at Lamont.

"I swear to God. Chuckie. The people behind the counter? They haven't been murdered yet. But it was them. We didn't go to the past. We're filming crimes that *haven't been committed yet*. What am I supposed to do with that?"

Chuckie shrugged then continued unboxing.

"You show up tonight when you're supposed to, and you film them."

Lamont shook his head.

"Do you not see how messed up that is? They're *still alive*. And you want me to just *film them?* After they've been *murdered*."

Chuckie crossed her arms and said, "You think you can stop the world's biggest studio as some broke nobody?"

Lamont looked at the ornaments lining Chuckie's lap. "I didn't expect this from you—who can't even stand me *talking* about cold case footage."

"You think I don't think this is wrong?" Chuckie

said through exasperated laughter. "You can't save them, Lamont, but *you can save yourself*. This is the most money you've had in your account and it's only been one night. I'm serious about going to the doctor. Remember that time you almost died of an asthma attack because you wouldn't let me call you an ambulance? You made us walk to the ER. In the middle of the night."

"I just think that if I tell someone, somewhere, then... somebody will do something about it," Lamont said as he paced in the kitchen.

"*Who*? Do you hear yourself?" Chuckie responded. "They're going to sue the shit out of you if you say anything. Did you even read your contract? Do you know what happens if you violate the NDA?"

Lamont fell silent for the first time since they got back.

"Of course you didn't. You were so greedy you didn't read the contract before you signed it. And you're accusing *me* of being unethical."

"10, 9..." Adrenaline caused him to hold on for a beat longer. "8..."

Lamont almost dropped his camera after the jump. He struggled to hold it steady as the bodies came into view nearby, the faces now familiar. He kept filming, though—*never stop rolling*—even as he confronted Griz.

"Why didn't you tell me this was the future?"

Unfazed, Griz kept filming too. "Oh, you figured

it out. Groupon deal? My wife and I went to their farm today too. We must've just missed each other."

"They're still *alive*. They have families. We have to stop this!"

Griz turned his camera to film Lamont.

"We all start out like you kid," Griz said. "It's the Harvard undergrad problem. Everyone writes their entrance essay about changing the world, but by graduation they're signing with investment banks and oil companies. Consider this your internship with ExxonMobil. Now shut up before you ruin the shot."

Griz got his shot, then moved onto the next angle as Lamont tried again.

"But I don't want to work for the film equivalent of an oil company. I don't even want to change the world. I just don't want anybody to get murdered."

"Of course you don't. Neither do I. Doesn't mean I can do anything about it."

They alternated in this way for a while, each filming an angle of the crime scene then the other person, until Griz finally said, "Look, *this* is the present. When we go home, *that's* the past. And right now—the real right now—they're dead. And there's nothing we can do about it."

There was no convincing him.

And maybe he was right.

In their current reality, what else was there to do except film?

Plus—past, present, or future—Lamont was a captive of that time. He couldn't leave without Griz.

As the night wore on, Lamont's hand steadied.

Eventually, Griz was satisfied with the footage, and the countdown began.

10...9...

Then, slowly, silently, they walked up the basement stairs, their footsteps echoing through the hallways.

Griz broke the silence first, "You can talk to Matt if you want. See if he can get you a meeting with an exec. I don't really care. There will always be another desperate up-and-comer to fill your shoes. But he was right about you. You've got a future."

Griz waved without turning as he walked away. He called back, "Have a nice life, if I don't see you again."

Lamont's phone shook in his hands, as much from the nerves as the cold. He dialed Matt.

Straight to voicemail. Lamont paced in the snow as he dialed again, muttering to himself, "I'm losing my mind. None of this makes sense. This feels like it can't be real, but it is real. I saw them... dead... alive... then dead again."

DEAD.

The thought of the victims steeled his nerves.

Ring. Ring. Ring.

A sleepy voice answered, "Hey, it's Matt."

"I need a meeting with whoever is in charge," Lamont started, then the rest tumbled out. "I know what you're doing. I don't even care if you sue me. What do I have to lose? I've been poor my entire life. But this can't keep happening. I will tell the entire world what you're doing if I have to."

"Lamont," a much more alert Matt cut him off. "Hey man, we've all seen stuff we haven't done anything about. You've seen couples fighting in public. Have you ever intervened? The stats for the domestic violence to murder pipeline are pretty grim. Or what about—"

"It's not the same!" Lamont shouted before lowering his voice. "You know for a fact that these people are going to be murdered."

"We don't pull the trigger."

"Ok, then if I leak this tonight it shouldn't matter either."

"Woah, woah, woah, you don't need to do all *that*," Matt said. "I'll get you a meeting to talk to Veronica Raven in the morning. I bet she'll ease your worries."

The next morning, Matt sent for a car to pick up Lamont, who'd been instructed to dress in his best— whatever he had. No need to buy anything new. Before they got to the studio, the driver took Lamont for brunch at a place that probably cost more than his entire day rate. He was woefully underdressed. The whole red carpet service dynamic felt less like kindness and more like "we're trying to bribe you" and "don't do anything you'll regret."

Matt greeted Lamont at the studio door and prepped him for the meeting with Veronica as they walked. Other than being lined with Christmas movie posters for the holidays, the long echoey halls felt eerily similar to those in the T-port.

At the end of the hallway, Matt opened the door and motioned for Lamont to sit down before he closed the door and left. Veronica sat across a long table. She smirked as she waited for him to speak.

"Ms. Raven," he began. "I'm Lamont—the B

camera operator who's been working with Griz. I have some...ethical concerns about how we're filming," Lamont cleared his throat. "It's...just...if you time travel to the future, that means that the victims are still alive, which means that you could use this technology to stop crimes from happening. People wouldn't have to worry for their safety. People could live—"

"What kind of filmmaker *are* you?"

"Excuse me?" Lamont wasn't quite sure what she meant.

"Haven't you seen Minority Report? Don't you know what kind of trouble stopping future crime causes?" Veronica asked.

"I...I have, but that was science fiction. This is re—"

"You wanna stop crimes?" The studio executive swiveled in her chair and stood, looming. "Go be a cop. Justice might help you sleep at night, but my ratings keep people like you from sleeping on the streets."

"Once people find out the victims are still alive, you won't have those ratings."

Veronica laughed like she truly thought Lamont was funny, then buzzed in Matt. "Can you show Lamont what happens if he violates the terms of our NDA? Feel free to use my office."

She left the room, walking past Lamont without any acknowledgement to his existence. She picked up a call on her way out the door, and Lamont could hear her laughing as she walked down the hall, talking about how their next show was sure to be a blockbuster hit.

Matt dimmed the lights when he entered the room.

A giant screen came to life on the wall, flickering briefly before an image appeared that made Lamont's stomach turn. It was Chuckie, curled up in the corner of the couch in Lamont's studio apartment, dead—in full 4K resolution. Lamont's vision went dark as soon as he took in the gruesome remains. Skin carved off the bones. Blood mixed with shards of glass, her brand-new ornaments broken all over the floor.

Matt shook Lamont awake and offered him a bottle of water. He refused to drink it.

"Don't worry, man. She's still alive," Matt said. "We don't alter the trajectory of our reality unless it aligns with our strategic goals or mitigates any undue risk. Changing different conditions upstream leads to desired—albeit undesirable—outcomes. Small changes, the butterfly effect and all that. And before we make any of those changes, we simulate alternate realities using AI." Matt gestured to the blank screen where the image had been, raising his eyebrows to make sure Lamont understood his meaning.

"Do you have any further questions about your contract?"

Lamont shook his head, and Matt escorted him off the property.

Having five months of rent banked after just two days of work made the shock of the whole situation a bit more bearable. Lamont was darkly grateful that he could afford to mope around, processing whatever it was that had just happened. He could eat cookies with Chuckie. Clear his head. Reset his moral compass. Cuddle on their new bed, which took up all the space that was left between the toilet, kitchen sink and nightstand. And watch *A Christmas Tree Farm Tragedy* on their brand new iPad.

Chuckie swiped a bit of funfetti dip with her finger and fed it to Lamont as his name rolled by in the final credits.

Stay tuned after the show for an interview with the future victims.

RECIPE: HOLIDAY FUNFETTI DIP

from A. Webster's "Never Stop Rolling"

(IT'S VERY EASY!)

Ingredients:

- A box of holiday Funfetti cake mix
- A 16 oz container of Cool whip
- A 32 oz container of Vanilla yogurt
- Sprinkles if desired
- Whatever you'd like to dip in it—graham crackers, ginger snap cookies, pretzels, etc.

Instructions:

1. In a large mixing bowl add the box of cake mix, cool whip and vanilla yogurt. Stir well with a wooden spoon until fully combined.

2. Cover bowl with plastic wrap and chill for at least 1 hour.

3. Enjoy!

JAY AND CHAR MAYBE SAVE THE GALAXY: THE LATKES EPISODE

by MJ Blehart

JAY WASN'T A FAN OF RUNNING LATE. CHAR WAS utterly against it. Not that it was their fault.

It had been almost a year of nonstop press inquiries, accepting and rejecting interviews, and coping with notoriety that neither of them had ever wanted. That was the downside to having helped save the galaxy.

Jay still found it utterly crazy. How many times were they going to be asked to answer questions about how they—Jay and Char—had saved the galaxy? Two middle-aged humans, one a specialized project manager, the other a pilot and starship captain, in the right (wrong) place at the right (wrong) time. Even when they tried to share their status with the new Rangeen King and his husband, Imaro and Kukeb, most of the attention stayed on Jay and Char.

A little more than a year had gone by since all the events that had transpired, and Jay and Char had just done their first real transport job since before their fame. Yet, despite the legitimate work and normal pay that came with it, they'd been invited to a special celebration in honor of what they had done.

(Want to know more about what happened that made them celebrities? Read Jay And Char Save The Galaxy, *available from multiple retail sources in eBook, paperback, and audiobook formats. Thanks. – Your Sponsor)*

The celebration had actually been a lot more fun than either Jay or Char had expected, but that had made them depart late. Their next stop was a space station between multiple sectors that Jay's family could get to via a short hyperspace hop.

The holidays had arrived. Jay's mom had a near-obsession with the need for the family to gather for the holidays. This was something of a challenge, as his mom and stepdad were on one planet, his sister and her family on another, and Jay and Char out and about aboard *Audacia*.

This year, Jay and Char had agreed to host. *Audacia* might have been a transport, but the starship was their home, too. They could easily and comfortably entertain Jay's family.

Char's parents had passed away years ago, and her sister's family did their own thing for the holidays. While Jay loved his family, they could often be a tad too much.

Still, plans were made, and now found Jay and Char en route to the space station to meet everyone. They would be arriving about ten minutes late. That irked Jay. Char's version of "on time" tended to be half an hour early, so she was particularly stressed.

Jay was a little stressed, but knew better than to expect his family to be on time. Hence, it came as no surprise when Essie, his sister, let him know that she, her husband Exeter, and daughter Emberly, were running at least an hour late.

Despite this, Char was about halfway through prepping the main part of their holiday meal. She'd also prepared a lot of cookies. Char always said she'd only make three to five types of cookies for the holiday. Jay properly translated this to six to twelve types, which tended to be more accurate.

Fortunately, baking was a form of stress relief for Char. The *Audacia*'s main galley featured a professional kitchen setup. Thus, baking a large number of cookies, even on a starship, wasn't crazy.

Jay was playing sous chef, cutting up vegetables and pulling oils and spices out of the pantry for Char. He liked to cook but acknowledged that she was far more skilled at it than he was. For this reason, Jay let Char organize the galley, both the main one and the smaller one, on their private deck of the ship.

Jay, however, would be making the traditional potato latkes that had been a family recipe for a surprisingly long time. The biggest issue with making latkes came from the rarity of potatoes in the galaxy.

While virtually every fruit or vegetable could grow in the soil of nearly any world, potatoes didn't. The only planets on which you could successfully plant and grow potatoes were Earth and Mars.

No other human world, or nonhuman world, for that matter, could grow them. For a crop that had been fairly abundant pre-interstellar travel, now it was a delicacy.

Potatoes were not cheap anywhere that was not Earth or Mars. Still, no matter what potato substitute was available, his mom insisted on real potato latkes for the sake of tradition and authenticity.

Jay knew that potatoes could always be purchased at the station they were going to. He would contact the vendor as soon as they arrived to purchase a bag and then deliver it to the ship once they were docked.

Preparation was easy enough, and Jay had already pulled out the blender, flour, oil, eggs, salt, baking powder, and an onion. He just needed the potatoes.

Jay's tablet, lying on a nearby table, began to chime. As if summoned, his mom was calling on the 'cator.

"I'm busy and not talking to her," Char said as Jay reached to answer it.

"I know," Jay said. He accepted the connection, saying, "Hi, Mom."

"Hello, dear," his mother said. "We're on our way to the station now. We should be there in an hour or so."

Jay glanced at the nearest chronograph. Unsurprisingly, he and Char, despite running late, would beat his mom and stepdad there by ten to fifteen minutes.

"Sounds good," Jay said.

"Now, where will we find the *Audacia*?" his mom asked.

Jay forced himself not to sigh and replied, "Personal craft docks, level thirteen."

His mom hissed dramatically and said, "You know that thirteen is an unlucky number, right?"

"Not for me," Jay remarked.

"Be that as it may," his mom pressed on, "what specific dock will you be in?"

"I don't know yet, Mom," Jay told her. "We haven't arrived, so it hasn't been assigned to us."

"They don't pre-assign docks?" his mom questioned. "That seems inefficient."

"It's standard operating procedure, Mom," Jay remarked.

She sighed dramatically. "But, Jay, honey, you and Char are famous. Shouldn't that mean you get preferential options?"

Jay could feel Char's eyeroll from across the galley. He said, "Frankly, Mom, even with that being a possibility, Char and I don't like to use it."

"What?" his mom questioned. "You and Char are famous for what you did. Shouldn't you reap the benefits of that?"

Jay translated that to mean shouldn't *she* reap the benefits of that. Before he could say more, Char said, "Actually, Ma, that's been more trouble than it's worth. It's frequently bothersome."

"Fame is a bother?" Jay's mom asked incredulously.

"Often," said Char.

"Mom," Jay started, "it was a novelty, at first, but you know Char and I like our freedom. Being constantly tailed by the press everywhere we go became a real nuisance to work and living our lives on our own terms. Fortunately, things are finally beginning to return to normal."

"Normal?" Jay's mom questioned. "But isn't normal boring?"

"No," Jay replied. "At this point, it's rather welcome. Really, what we did might have given us this fame, but it was more about the actions that Imaro and Kukeb took."

"If you say so," Jay's mom said. He could tell she wasn't buying it. This was no surprise. Jay's mom loved the attention, and the idea of being in the spotlight held an appeal to her. Yes, that had appealed to him in his youth. But he'd let go of that desire long ago.

"Oh," his mom took up a new thought. "Will your rangeen friends be joining us?"

Jay couldn't help himself and laughed. "No, Mom. Imaro and Kukeb are not going to leave Rangeenavelt to come to Yonna Em station for a holiday they don't even recognize."

"The rangeen don't recognize the holiday?" Jay's mom asked in a tone of utter dismay.

"No," Jay said. "The rangeen, and for that matter many other races, don't get the whole idea of holidays, celebrating them with special meals and gifts and gatherings, and why or how they're more special than any other day. So no, they don't understand nor recognize holidays because they celebrate none at all."

"But that coronation," Jay's mom started.

"Not a holiday," Jay interjected. "A special event that represented a change."

"I guess," his mom said. "Still, I don't see why they wouldn't care to make the time to spend with the people who helped them get where they are."

Jay had no good response for that, but was saved by Char saying, "As it is, Ma, they're relatively on the other side of the galaxy from Yonna Em station. But the next time we talk to them, we'll let them know you asked about how they were doing."

"Oh, thank you, dear," Jay's mom said.

"We'll let you know, Mom, what dock we're in as soon as we are assigned it," Jay said to conclude the conversation. "We'll see you and Bob soon."

"So long as we don't get lost traversing this meshuga station," Jay's mom replied. "Love you both. Bye."

"Bye, Mom," Jay said. The transmission ended.

Jay and Char basked in the silence for a moment. Then, Char said, "How many times have we met her at Yonna Em?"

"At least four or five," Jay commented. "Even Essie agrees it's the easiest, most accessible point for us all."

"And you can always get potatoes there," Char said, glancing toward the empty blender.

Jay sighed, feeling his frustration. He checked on the source at the station for the potatoes and groaned. "Damn. Prices are up again."

"They low on supply?" Char asked.

"No," Jay said. "They have plenty. I suspect this is a way to gouge us for more EVILC. It's a pity that Mom and Bob can always tell when I use a potato alternative."

Char laughed. "Not like there aren't a lot of those out there. Starcherons, otatops, aptotos, and muunnas are plentiful and way cheaper options."

"Sure," Jay agreed. "They just come in colors less

appealing to the human eye and a subtly different texture. I think it's mostly the color that makes them unappetizing to my mom and Bob."

"Aptotos are obscenely blue-grey," Char commented.

Jay sighed. "Yeah, yeah. I dunno. Even with Essie, Exeter, and Emberly running as late as they are, maybe I should just say to hell with it and skip the latkes this year."

Before Char could say anything in response, the *Audacia* lurched. Jay got the distinct impression that they were being yanked out of hyperspace. But that was impossible. Still, Jay felt as if something wasn't right. Then had that confirmed when, across the internal 'cator, his robot copilot, Quinn, called out, "Captain? Something is wrong."

Jay looked at Char, and the look on her face told him she also sensed the problem. Jay left the galley and walked across the deck to the bridge.

Looking out the viewport immediately confirmed to Jay that something was amiss. Rather than the usual blurred "lines" of stars as they traversed hyperspace, or the stars you saw in normal space, the sky beyond the viewport was a strange, cloudy, lavender color.

"Quinn," Jay queried as he joined the robot on the bridge. "Are we still in hyperspace?"

"No," Quinn replied.

Jay continued, "Are we in normal space, then?"

"No," Quinn replied.

"Okay, then where the hell are we?" Jay asked.

"We are somewhere that is nowhere or elsewhere but not hyperspace or normal space," Quinn replied.

"That doesn't tell us anything," remarked Jay under his breath. He sat in the pilot's seat. "Well, how did we get here?"

"I have no idea," Quinn responded. Then, he added, "Before you ask, I also do not know where, how, why, or what happened, but I do know who, which would be the three of us. Apart from that, I have no answers."

Jay just sighed. He started to turn on sensors and run scans. Looking out of the viewport, he felt awed and disturbed at the same time. There were no stars nor starlines out there. Just a cloudy, lavender-colored, unmoving sky. It was beautiful and eerie and unexpected.

The scans were not reading anything. They didn't show where on the starcharts *Audacia* was, nor register anything about the space outside the ship. No readings about gravity, motion, radiation, tachyons, or anything else. It was as though they were in a total void of absence.

"Quinn, run diagnostics on all scanners, sensors, radar, lidar, and everything else," Jay requested.

"I am already doing so," Quinn stated. "So far, no results. All systems are registering as functioning normally. Diagnostics show no anomalies."

Jay stared out the viewport into the impossible sky. This was more impossible than the time the phased-reality drive had somehow failed. At least that had dumped them from hyperspace to normal space. This was surreal.

Char entered the cockpit. Jay could tell she was pausing to look out the viewport before she asked, "Where are we?"

"Nowhere," Jay replied.

"Where is nowhere?" Char asked.

"Well, that's the problem," Jay said. "We are not anywhere. *Audacia* isn't in hyperspace or normal space or anywhere that our sensors can make heads or tails of."

"How can that possibly be?" Char asked. Jay could hear a note of concern in her tone.

"No clue," Jay said. "But we're working on it. Anything, Quinn?"

"No," Quinn replied. "All systems are operating within normal parameters, and there are no malfunctions of anything ship-wide. Before you ask, I am running deep diagnostics on all systems. I..."

Quinn stopped abruptly. If he'd had a head, Jay would have expected it to have been tilted to one side as if he were considering something. Then, Quinn said, "Intruder alert. One life form detected on the central deck in the galley."

Jay and Char exchanged a look. That was more or less the middle of the starship. There were no hatches to the exterior anywhere near the galley. The only way to access it would have been to materialize from nowhere into it.

They had no guns aboard the ship, as neither Jay nor Char were fans of guns. He had his 'lectro-bo staff, which was a collapsible, mostly non-lethal weapon that expanded to a 1.6-meter staff that could deliver a charge to disable. Quinn could act as a taser, but that was the extent of their armaments.

Jay and Char, without any verbal communication, left the bridge and crossed the deck to the galley. Jay had his 'lectro-bo staff clipped to his belt but didn't reach for it. Instinct told him this wasn't a threat; it was an explanation.

They arrived at the galley and entered it cautiously. The person within had their back to them but turned as they crossed the threshold from the corridor.

At a guess, Jay figured she was a little more than two meters tall. Her skin was a light purple; she had a long, thin, orange tail, ruby-colored hair, and ears that were somewhat more forward on her head than human ears. But her eyes were brown and very human.

Jay knew only one other half-human, half-rumel individual. This one looked incredibly familiar, but Jay couldn't place where he might have seen her before.

"Hi, Uncle Jay. Hi, Aunt Char," she addressed them.

Jay was too stunned to speak.

"Emberly?" Char breathed.

The half-rumel, half-human female nodded in response.

"How," Jay began, a half a dozen questions clamoring all at once to be asked before he settled on, "How can that be? You're only, um, 13 or 14 right now."

Emberly grinned and said, "It's complicated, but it really is me. And to prove it, I know that when you told grandma about my baby-tail growing in, she said, quote 'I thought the first child of an inter-species couple was always the most human.'"

Jay couldn't help himself and laughed. While he'd told the story before to many people, the impersonation of his mother's tone that she did was perfect.

"Emberly," Char said. "How is this even possible?"

"Like I said, it's complicated," Emberly answered. She did not elaborate further.

Jay and Char had seen many strange things in their travels across the galaxy. This was near the top of the strangest. Sorting through the mad jumble of questions in his head, Jay asked, "Why are you here?"

"That's the right question to ask," Emberly replied. "Simple. To make sure that you and Aunt Char know how important it is that you follow through on the holiday plans, lest disaster befall the galaxy."

"What are you talking about?" questioned Char, sounding as confused and distressed as Jay was feeling.

Emberly withdrew a device from a pocket on the jacket she was wearing, and it expanded in her hand until it was the size of a tablet. Jay realized that's what it had to be, albeit a futuristic-looking expandable one.

Emberly gave it a slight shake, and an image projected above the tablet. It showed people Jay didn't recognize. After a moment, however, he could tell that there was something not right about them. They were all moving with what could be best described as a shambling gait.

More images appeared. Again, the people they

showed were discolored, as if they were washed out, and they moved in that strange shuffle, like they were being dragged by an unseen force. Jay found it deeply disturbing but oddly familiar.

"This looks a hell of a lot like a zombie flick," Char commented. Char was a fan of horror and had watched many programs that featured monsters of that ilk. While Jay was not a fan, the trope was well-known and appeared in many entertainment programs that he was into.

"That's because they are zombies," Emberly confirmed.

Jay gasped. "Please tell me that Char and I bankroll a horror flick you're directing, and it offends multiple races so badly that war is threatened, and you're going to tell us this idea at the holiday gathering that we're on our way to now, and we should discourage you?"

Jay could feel Char's eyes on him as Emberly shook her head and said, "No, Uncle Jay. This is all too real."

"How is that even possible?" demanded Char. "Zombies are an ancient terror that are as improbable as vampires, werewolves, or other undead attacking."

Emberly sighed. "Not so impossible as that, Aunt Char. As far as my associates and I can tell, it all begins with a microscopic organism. That organism is from some far-out world that was being explored by the crew of a transport when they experienced an impossible phased-reality drive failure that shot them into nowhere."

"I suspect I know where this is going," commented Jay.

Emberly nodded, then continued, "While lost, the crew found and explored said alien planet. That's where the microscopic organism came from."

"No good is going to come of that," Char remarked.

"Too true," Emberly said. "That transport managed to work out how to return to hyperspace, get back on course, and resume their normal work. One job involved transporting potatoes from Mars to other worlds and stations, including Yonna Em. The shipment to Yonna Em began to turn. When the potatoes developed eyes, the microscopic organism came to life, and then the potatoes developed spores. Those spores were also microscopic, and when they went into the air unseen, they quickly spread to the nearest people."

"No way," Jay breathed.

Emberly continued, "Before long, it was spreading across Yonna Em, then the cities the people first exposed visited, then the planet, and on and on. By the time it zombified people, it was already too late, and half the galaxy had been turned into zombies."

Jay and Char were both silent. Jay was stunned and was too preoccupied with his thoughts to consider how Emberly's story impacted Char.

It was Char who came out of it first. "That's truly horrific. But what does that have to do with your uncle and me hosting the family holiday party?"

Emberly's face became serious. "Because we

know that those are the same potatoes that Uncle Jay was going to use to make the latkes."

"What?" Jay asked, initially too stunned to ask for more details. Before Emberly replied, he added, "How does me buying or not buying potatoes to make the latkes impact everything?"

Emberly took a deep breath, then said, "So, you see, by you buying those potatoes and turning them into latkes, between the blending of the raw potatoes, mixing them with flour and salt, then frying them in oil, the microscopic organism is destroyed before the potatoes rot and it mutates to harm everyone."

Jay didn't know what to say to that. It was too fantastic and too impossible to believe. Char recovered first again and asked, "But won't that harm us? The family? Won't we be eating the microscopic organism?"

Emberly shook her head. "No, it won't harm any of us. You see, we've traced the mutation of the microscopic organism specifically to its interaction with the rotting potatoes. It's inert and harmless in a healthy potato that hasn't started to rot or develop eyes."

Jay was incredulous. While he was convinced he was talking to his niece as an adult, he was finding it hard to believe what she was telling him. Hence, he asked her, "How can you be so sure of this? Seems pretty damned random to me."

"There has been extensive research," Emberly said. "We took a lot of effort to trace the origin from at least 3 different angles. The research has been deep and thorough. I work for some very smart people."

"Who would that be?" asked Char.

"King Imaro and Consort Kukeb," Emberly replied.

"How did they get involved with this, and how are you part of it?" asked Char.

Emberly sighed. "I don't have the luxury of filling you in on my whole life history without causing some potential problems. But what matters is I work for Imaro and Kukeb, and we've turned over every stone and looked in every possible place for the answers. This is where it began, with the potatoes you are supposed to buy and use for the latkes."

"No offense, Emberly, but you must be able to tell us more than that about how you've been researching this," pressed Char.

Char had always loved research. On more than one occasion over the years, she'd put considerable time and energy into learning something that interested her on the deepest levels she could.

"Without getting too technical," Emberly began, "King Imaro and Consort Kukeb have been working closely with the roptera, since much of this has required making use of their unique connection to all things temporal and the shared rangeen, sutac, and soetub resources."

"The same resource Imaro's father nearly started an interstellar war to keep exclusive," remarked Jay.

"The same," agreed Emberly. "As you know, part of why it's used in all the 'cators and other communications devices across the galaxy is its unique temporal qualities. The roptera inherently understand this in ways no other race can. And that's how I'm here to talk to you now, too."

"Time travel?" questioned Jay.

"In a manner of speaking," replied Emberly, her tone somewhat evasive.

"How is time travel even remotely possible?" Jay pressed. "I'm no expert by any stretch of the imagination, but the physics of time travel has never worked out without major potential problems. Like, what about the danger of creating a paradox? If the multiverse theory is correct, won't we just be shunted to a wholly different timeline where you'll still deal with the aftermath of this zombie apocalypse?"

"It feels a lot like lazy writing and hacking time travel tropes," commented Char almost under her breath.

Emberly sighed. "Look, Aunt Char, Uncle Jay, Imaro, Kukeb, and various roptera science types have assured me that this all works itself out. Even though none of them can give me the specifics of that, save lots of technobabble mumbo-jumbo involving temporal adjustments and pan-galactic hyper-continuance theory and quantum engines and the like, it works. So, here I am, warning you about a potential future that you can change. All I know is that if you don't buy those potatoes and then turn them into latkes for the family holiday party, their rotting will lead to the zombie apocalypse we're fighting in your future."

Jay and Char were both silent for a moment. Jay was working on digesting what Emberly was saying. His currently 13- or 14-year-old niece had somehow materialized as an adult he guessed to be in her 20s or 30s, on his starship, in the middle of nowhere. Literally, nowhere, as the *Audacia* was currently neither in hyperspace nor normal space.

Jay was being presented with one implausible, if not impossible, concept after another. Unknown microscopic organisms from previously unexplored, alien planets. Transport crews inexplicably thrown out of hyperspace to parts unknown. Potatoes leading to a zombie apocalypse. Natural resources with bizarre temporal properties. Time travel. It was a lot all at once.

Jay was typically an optimist, but sometimes a skeptic. Or was it a cynic? He could never remember which was which and which applied to him. Whichever it was, he was incredulous despite the evidence before him.

There was also another statistical aspect of reality he couldn't wrap his head around. "Emberly, while you've given us a lot of evidence that has vague plausibility to it, this is really hard to believe. Char and I, against all odds, are credited with saving the galaxy from a massive, devastating war. Now you're telling me that, for a second time, Char and I, against even more impossible odds, need to save the galaxy again. But doing so involves making potato latkes?"

"And if your Uncle Jay doesn't make the latkes," Char added, "we're responsible for destroying the galaxy we previously saved because of a zombie apocalypse?"

"That's the crux of it, yes," agreed Emberly.

"That's incredibly distressing, and really hard to swallow," said Char.

"Yeah, it is," agreed Jay.

"Imaro and Kukeb thought you might react this way," Emberly said. "Would you like me to explain further?"

"Please," encouraged Char.

Emberly took a deep breath. "Okay, so, the odds of any one person saving the galaxy are so preposterous that no sane mathematician has ever tried to work them out. Even adding a second person to that doesn't change the numbers to anything more reasonable. Both probability theory and improbability theory work in a combination of real and imagined numbers and hypotheticals that, again, factoring in the potential for any individual or two individuals saving the galaxy, is nonsense. However, if a person or two beat the utterly insane, impossible odds against—and manage to save the galaxy—the probability of saving the galaxy yet a second time are dramatically more probable."

She took a breath, then Emberly continued, "On the other side, by the way, the odds of the person or people who saved the galaxy being involved in its collapse and ruin also increase to a dramatically more probable percentage. However, in both instances, the numbers involved only barely make sense to the most seasoned and not-entirely-sane statisticians and theoreticians across the galaxy. But they are such that, while deeply impractical and implausible, they are not non-zero. Along that same line, the potential for time travel that we are working with, which has allowed me to come visit you in my now and your now—which is my past and your future, respectively—works out in much the same way as a phased-reality drive allows for faster-than-light travel via hyperspace. Which is also, according to various branches of science, impossible. Still with me, Aunt Char, Uncle Jay?"

Jay just nodded his head, not trusting himself to speak or to show that his eyes were glazing over. He didn't look to see Char's reaction but guessed it was probably similar.

"Okay," Emberly started again. "Now, given all the math and diverse scientific fields that all of this encompasses, and the convoluted nature of it all, when investigations by the rangeen and roptera, who happen to be two of the only races not impacted by the zombie virus—which I didn't previously mention—began, Imaro and Kukeb had an intuitive hit that it somehow tied to *you* once they knew where the microscopic organism originated and how it most likely found its way to human space. When they knew you were anywhere near that point of origin, in the same timeframe as the spreading infection, they sought me and my team to get involved in the investigation. When you factor in the added familial connection, plus your connection to Imaro and Kukeb, it all works out in a mathematically and scientifically compelling sum. That's how we know that you both are and aren't responsible for saving the galaxy and ending the galaxy."

Emerly paused a moment. After taking a breath, she said, "That's how we traced this whole thing back to you two. Do you want me to give you a more thorough explanation of how I am visiting here to your present from my past and my present, which is your future?"

"No," Jay replied, probably a little too quickly. "No, Emberly, I get it. Okay, I'm willing to buy this wacky thing."

"As am I," added Char.

"So," Jay prompted. "All that I have to do is, what, agree to make the damned latkes, and then make them?"

"Yes," replied Emberly.

"Fine, then," Jay said. "Yes, I promise you and the unseen maths and sciences and deities of the galaxy that I will buy the potatoes and make the latkes."

"Wait a second," Emberly said. Jay noted she cocked her head to one side, as if listening to someone on an earpiece. He didn't see one in her ear, but then again, being from the future, she might have had technology or an implant of some sort that neither Jay nor Char could see.

"Yes!" Emberly said, her voice excited. "It worked!"

"It worked?" Char asked.

"I could explain it," Emberly began, "but it's some pretty mind-bending science."

"I'll pass," said Char.

Jay was shaking his head. "Well, this is going to make for a hell of a story at dinner."

Emberly sighed. "Actually, Uncle Jay, Aunt Char, no, it won't. See, now that you've agreed to make the latkes, you will. When you do that, all of this will have never have happened. You see, that's because it never does happen, which is because the future I come from never was, or, rather, will be. Crazy, I know, but it all works out for the best. That's the most important part of all of this. I love you both. Thanks for saving the galaxy, again, by not being responsible for destroying the galaxy by making the holiday potato latkes."

Jay blinked. He felt terribly disoriented. He had a momentary feeling as if he had been somewhere else doing something else.

Jay vaguely thought that he'd been in the galley. But no. He was on the bridge.

Wasn't Char in the galley with him and... someone else? He glanced to the side and saw Quinn in the co-pilot's seat.

For a moment, he felt as if something had happened to the *Audacia* and hyperspace. Looking out the viewport, however, he saw the starlines typical of the ship in hyperspace.

Jay found that he had a sense of confusion and disorientation. Why did it feel like he was missing something?

Jay looked at Quinn again and asked the robot, "Quinn? Did anything happen to us or the ship recently?"

"Define recently?" requested Quinn.

"As in just now. Or within the past, I don't know, half an hour?"

Quinn paused for maybe half a second, but Jay knew that was all the time it took his robot copilot to consider anything. "I note that there was an anomaly where, for an instant, it appeared that the *Audacia* was not in hyperspace and at the same time not in normal space. But as that's impossible, I cannot confirm it."

Jay looked back at the starlines of hyperspace out the viewport, then said, "So, you didn't quantifiably experience anything unusual, then?"

"Apart from you questioning me about an unusual experience that I have no recorded recollection of? No," Quinn responded.

Jay knew that while Quinn was able to sometimes apply a degree of sarcasm and skepticism to his statements, the robot couldn't lie. "Okay," Jay said.

He arose from his seat and departed from *Audacia*'s bridge. He made his way down the corridor back to the galley.

Char was there, still cooking. She was exactly where Jay thought she'd last been and was where he'd expected her to be.

"Char?" Jay questioned. "Do you have a sense that something weird happened? Something momentous?"

"Weird? Momentous?" Char asked. "No, not that I can think of. I might have blipped out for a second while I was doing meal prep, but nothing odd about that; meal prep tends to get pretty routine. Why?"

Jay shook his head again. "I can't explain it. Like, I feel as if I experienced something super improbable. But maybe I've just not been getting enough sleep."

"Or maybe it's a manifestation of your feelings about your family and having them aboard the ship for a meal," remarked Char. "Even when she sees *Audacia* up close and personal, your mom can't help herself but to comment about the fact that it's a ship, not a home."

Jay sighed. "Yeah, there is that. Another holiday meal with my family."

"Who knows," Char started. "I do get a strange, inexplicable sense that this particular meal we're making them is extra momentous and important."

Jay looked at his wife for a moment, then asked, "Are you just teasing me?"

"Maybe," Char replied with a mischievous grin.

Jay smiled, and his sense of wrongness with things evaporated. He moved further into the galley. With a sigh, he checked if he did indeed have all the other ingredients for the latkes, other than the potatoes.

For a moment, Jay again considered just skipping the latkes. He paused, realizing he'd seriously considered not making them only a few moments ago, but now felt that they were, for this particular holiday, an important cornerstone of the meal.

"They're just latkes," Jay said aloud.

"What's that, love?" Char questioned.

"Just talking to myself," Jay said. "You do like 97 percent of the cooking, all I make for this meal are the latkes. But they're expected to be on the table by everyone, and I feel like if I don't make them, I'm letting the family down."

"And you wonder why you don't care?" asked Char.

"No," Jay remarked. "I wonder why I *do* care."

Char chuckled. "Maybe, over the past year, all the attention has rubbed off on you. Maybe you've acquired an overdeveloped sense of importance."

"Which I'm applying to making potato latkes?" Jay asked, raising an eyebrow.

Char chuckled. "Maybe. I mean, in the grand scheme of things, it's too bad that making latkes is so mundane. And, of course, it utterly pales in comparison to saving the galaxy."

"Jay and Char Maybe Save the Galaxy: The Latkes Episode" is a story in the Jay and Char Save the Galaxy series. If you enjoy sci-fi comedy, you can read the rest at mjblehart.com/jay-and-char-save-the-galaxy.

RECIPE: JAY'S FAMILY'S ANCIENT RECIPE FOR POTATO LATKES

from MJ Blehart's "Jay and Char Maybe Save The Galaxy: The Latkes Episode"

PUT EVERYTHING IN A BLENDER IN THE FOLLOWING order:

- ¼ cup milk
- 2 eggs
- 3 cups diced raw potatoes
- 1 small onion quartered
- 3 tablespoons flour
- 1 teaspoon salt
- ¼ teaspoon baking powder

Blend on high.

Heat oil (preferably olive oil) in a shallow pan. Spoon the mixture into the oil and fry until it starts to get solid and the bottom edge crisps. Flip and keep frying until golden brown.

Serve plain, with applesauce, or with sour cream. Eat. Enjoy. Double the recipe to serve more people. Maybe save the galaxy from a zombie apocalypse.

EXCELSIOR CHRISTMAS

by Audrey Sharpe

THE CLINK OF CUTLERY AND THE LOW MURMUR OF conversation flowed around Ensign Aurora Hawke as she wound her way through the bolted-down bench tables in *Excelsior*'s mess hall. Five days until Christmas, but you'd never know it from looking around the room. No decorations brightened the utilitarian bulkheads, no holiday music played over the speakers, no scents of pine or cinnamon filled the air.

After more than twenty years of over-the-top Christmas celebrations at Stoneycroft, Aurora's first Christmas onboard a Fleet ship was shaping up to be underwhelming.

Skirting around a group headed in the opposite direction, she spotted the broad back and muscled physique of Jonarel Clarek, seated at the end of one of the long rectangles. Altering her trajectory, she headed in his direction.

As the only Kraed on *Excelsior*'s crew — the only Kraed serving in the Fleet, period — Jonarel stood out in a crowd. The thick mahogany mane that flowed past his shoulders during his off hours was currently contained in a low knot, the dark green skin it exposed at his neck a strong contrast to his Fleet greys. Kraed coloring, which included non-linear brown tendrils that twined across their skin, allowed the Kraed to camouflage themselves in the vegetation of their home planet to avoid the large predators who hunted the unwary.

On *Excelsior*, the dark green made Jonarel easily recognizable amongst the human crew. He was seated with Dr. Mya Forrest, Aurora's best friend since birth and the person who'd woken her with an excited squeal on every one of those Christmases when they were growing up together. Now they shared a cabin on *Excelsior*.

"How are things in engineering?" she asked Jonarel as she claimed the seat next to Mya. It had been a few days since all three of their schedules had synced up so they could share a meal together. "I heard you had some excitement when one of the engine coils overheated."

"Excitement is not the term I would use." Jonarel sent her a chiding look. "I prefer maintenance over emergencies."

Mya gave an indelicate snort. "I'm not buying it. You grew up on a planet with big, scary predators. I don't believe for a second you prefer mundane predictability to a little excitement."

Jonarel lifted one dark brow, his golden-eyed gaze holding Mya's in a subtle challenge. "I believe you have a saying regarding a pot and kettle that applies here."

Mya's eyes narrowed playfully, the leg of her medical uniform brushing Aurora's as she tapped her boot against Jonarel's under the table. "You know why I do what I do."

Mya specialized in trauma treatment. To date, she'd never lost a patient. She'd been assigned to *Excelsior* with Aurora and several other recent Academy graduates seven months ago, but she already had a reputation as the best doctor onboard. Everyone who visited the med bay asked for her, whether they had a broken bone or a splinter. Only Aurora and Jonarel knew about the special abilities that made her brand of healing so effective.

Jonarel acknowledged the point with a nod. "Excitement in life is welcome. Excitement in engineering is not."

"Now *that* I believe." Aurora forked a bite of pasta, studying Jonarel as she chewed. Like all Kraed, he was a protector to the bone. Unless they were talking about systems upgrades or new technologies, excitement in engineering meant people were likely to get hurt. "Speaking of excitement in life, does the crew do anything for Christmas?" Jonarel had graduated a year ahead of her, so he'd already spent one Christmas on *Excelsior*.

He considered the question. "I recall a more varied meal selection on the day." He motioned to the cafeteria line across the room.

Mya's face scrunched up. "That's it? A few extra food options? No decorations? No music? No socializing?"

"Not that I recall."

"Hmm." Mya turned to Aurora. "Looks like we might have to lower our expectations."

"Just because the crew doesn't celebrate doesn't mean we can't. We don't have any decorations, but I've got plenty of music. I also checked the duty roster, and there's a three-hour window in the late afternoon where we're all off duty. We can snag some food and gather in our cabin." Which would just barely fit the three of them comfortably. Not that she minded. She and Mya had shared a room until her eighth birthday, and they'd been roommates for their first three years at the Academy. Sharing the tiny two-person ensigns cabin made *Excelsior* feel more like home.

Mya beamed at her. "I love this plan." She turned to Jonarel. "You with us?"

He inclined his head. "I would be honored to join you."

Aurora grinned. "Then it's settled. Celebration in our cabin on Christmas Day."

For the third time in her shift, Aurora caught herself singing a holiday tune under her breath as she processed the flurry of messages coming through the comms relay. The crew might not celebrate Christmas as a group, but the sharp increase in traffic in and out over the relay indicated a lot of them were sending and receiving holiday greetings today.

Her empathic senses were also picking up on the mood shift around the ship, an overall lightness that was likely prompting her recurring singing issue. Thankfully, the two officers seated closest to her on *Excelsior*'s bridge didn't seem to mind the subtle serenade.

Aurora glanced at her comband. Only twenty minutes left in her shift. Jonarel wasn't on duty for another four hours, and Mya's shift had ended two hours ago. She'd already sent Aurora a message highlighting the holiday food options in the mess hall that would suit their celebration plans.

Giddy anticipation bubbled—

What was that?

Her hand shot to her ear, pressing her headset closer. She'd heard something, an unexpected snippet of sound that called to her for a moment, then vanished. It had almost sounded like... a bell?

Her gaze swept over the data on the bridge comm console, where the background harmonics of interstellar space — the frequencies that she thought of as the music of the universe — populated the display. She searched through them, looking for something new, something she didn't usually see. What she'd heard had seemed intentional, but it had only let itself be known for a split second.

Ting-tong.

She straightened, studying the readouts on her display as the unexpected sound repeated.

"Ensign Hawke, is there a problem?"

She swiveled her chair, meeting Captain Warner's gaze. "Not a problem, sir. But I'm picking up an unusual sound."

He sat forward in the captain's chair, resting his elbows on his knees. "What kind of sound?"

"Somewhere between a chime and a ping. It almost sounds like..." She frowned. "Bells."

"Bells?" His brow furrowed. "Can you pinpoint the source?"

"That's also peculiar." She faced the bridge-screen, which gave a view of the super-Earth planet *Excelsior* was currently orbiting to port, and an unobstructed view of the starfield to starboard. "According to my data, it's a short-range VHF transmission coming from a distance of approximately a hundred kilometers." She pointed to the starfield. But there was nothing there.

The Captain pivoted to Lt. Acosta at the security console. "Anything on tactical?"

Acosta's gaze swept over the data on his display with the precision and thoroughness she'd come to expect from the seasoned officer. "Nothing."

The Captain stood, moving beside her. Curiosity overlaid with caution emanated from his emotional field as he studied the readings on her display. "The Doppler data shows the signal's matching our orbit, at least so far."

Ting-tong, ting-tong.

She sent the signal to the bridge speakers halfway through, the second set ringing merrily across the broad expanse of workstations. "Still matching orbit," she confirmed.

"Bells," Captain Warner murmured, turning to the bridgescreen. "Acosta, magnify that section."

The image leapt closer.

Still nothing there.

"Any heat signatures?"

"No heat signatures — infrared or ultraviolet,"

Acosta replied. "No anomalies, no dead zones, no concentrations of heavy metals. Whatever's transmitting that must be infinitesimal and very well shielded. Shall I raise our shields?"

Captain Warner folded his arms, the movement emphasizing his barrel chest and muscled arms under his Fleet greys. "Only if you detect a change." He turned to Aurora. "Have you ever heard something similar to this signal?"

The same question had been nagging her ever since she'd first detected it. "I have a feeling that I have."

Feeling. Her breath caught as the penny dropped.

She knew exactly where she'd heard that sound before. And as soon as she allowed her empathic senses to expand, she picked up on the familiar emotional resonances of the two people she should have expected the moment she heard the bell tone. "Captain, I believe we have Kraed visitors."

That captured the attention of the entire bridge crew.

The Captain's gaze swung from her to the bridgescreen and back. "Explain."

"I've heard this sound before, at the Academy. I believe Ambassador Clarek is paying us a visit in a camouflaged ship." Jonarel's father had a flair for the dramatic. It's why Siginal had used Kraed *emtop* bells to get her attention rather than a standard hail. He had intentionally contacted *her*, expecting her to recognize the musical sound. "Do I have your permission to hail them?"

He nodded, a slight creasing around his eyes the

only visible sign of a reaction, but she picked up on his underlying emotions. He was intrigued.

She opened the Fleet hailing frequency, looping the transmission into the bridge speakers. "This is Ensign Hawke of the Fleet ship *Excelsior*, sending greetings to Ambassador Clarek of Clan Clarek."

A beat later, a Kraed starship materialized out of the black, appearing with the flourish of the galaxy's most impressive magician pulling off a sleight of hand. The collective gasp from the bridge crew would be music to Siginal's ears.

In this case, the trick involved the use of Kraed hull camouflage, which made their ships invisible to Fleet sensors and cameras, as Siginal had just demonstrated with aplomb. She'd heard about the technology from Jonarel, but this was the first time she'd seen it in action.

But that wasn't the only reason the entire bridge crew was staring at the screen with rapt fascination. The Kraed ship before them was breathtakingly beautiful, its curved lines and flowing form nothing like the streamlined and largely utilitarian design of Fleet ships. The outline reminded her of a cascading waterfall frozen in time. The hull mimicked the surroundings, currently taking on the inky blackness of space dotted with millions of tiny diamonds.

Her console pinged, indicating Siginal had requested a video link with the bridge. "Captain?"

He nodded. "On screen."

The visage that filled half the screen was as familiar to her as Jonarel's. She'd spent a lot of time with Jonarel's father over the past six years. Siginal had been her faculty advisor at the Academy, and after she and Jonarel became friends, Siginal and his mate Daymar had practically adopted her.

Siginal and Jonarel shared a strong family resemblance — same broad shoulders, same full lips, same strong jaw and cheekbones, same high forehead. The brown tendrils that twined over Siginal's forest green skin created a different pattern than Jonarel's, but the golden eyes gazing at her with amusement were a near perfect match.

Siginal's gaze swept the bridge. "Captain Warner," he boomed in his deep baritone. "At last we meet."

"It's an honor, Ambassador." His cheek creased in a wry smile. "If we had known you were coming, we could have prepared an appropriate welcome."

Siginal's eyes gleamed. "It is I who bring the welcome to you, Captain. If you will permit me and my mate to board, we would like to share a gift with you. And visit with our checalas." His gaze shifted to Aurora and held.

Checala was a Kraed term of affection that Siginal and Daymar had been using with her for years now. The direct translation was *beloved one*, the connotation being that she was like family to them.

Captain Warner glanced at her out of the side of his eye. "We would be delighted to have you as our guests. We'll have shuttle bay four prepped for your arrival."

"Excellent." Siginal's image cut out.

Aurora suddenly found herself the object of intense scrutiny from the entire bridge crew. Seeing her interacting with Jonarel during off hours was quite different from watching her being personally singled out by the leader of the Kraed, the alien race that had helped humanity overcome the consequences of their self-destructive behavior. She could almost see the questions popping up like text bubbles above their heads.

"Lt. Acosta, you have the bridge." Captain Warner turned to her. "Ensign Hawke, alert Ensign Clarek to meet us at shuttle bay four. You're with me."

She quickly sent a message to Jonarel's comband, then fell into step behind Captain Warner as he headed for the lift. As the doors closed behind them, her heart thumped against her ribcage. She'd never been alone with the captain before. The prospect suddenly seemed daunting.

He turned to face her. "I was aware you and Ensign Clarek were friends, and that Ambassador Clarek was your faculty advisor at the Academy, but I didn't understand the depth of your connection with their family until now. That signal was meant for you, specifically."

"Yes." She resisted the urge to fidget. "Jonarel and I met under unusual circumstances, and became good friends very quickly. When Siginal and Daymar learned about my family situation, they took it upon themselves to act as surrogate parents while I was at the Academy. They mean a lot to me."

"And you clearly mean a lot to them." He folded his arms over his chest. "Is there an understanding between you and Ensign Clarek I should be aware of?"

A flush crept up her neck. He was making the wrong assumption, which might have been Siginal's intention with his dramatic appearance and emphasis on her. He'd made no secret of how thrilled he'd be if she and Jonarel became romantically involved with each other. "No, sir. We're friends. That's all." She said it with more vehemence than she'd intended.

His lips twitched, amusement flitting through his emotional field. "It's okay, Ensign. There's no regulation against having a relationship with someone who isn't in your direct chain of command."

"It's not that. It's..." Not something she could explain in the time it would take them to reach the shuttle bay. "Complicated," she finished lamely.

The twitch turned into an encouraging smile. "I have no doubt."

The lift doors parted on the shuttle deck. As Captain Warner exited, he greeted each person waiting outside the lift by name.

Impressive, considering the size of the crew. After six months onboard, she could only easily identify about ten percent of the crew on sight.

The crew's emotional response to him indicated how much they appreciated being acknowledged individually.

That gave her pause. Since arriving onboard, she'd been so focused on learning and performing her bridge duties to the best of her ability that she hadn't made getting to know the crew a priority. But sensing the crew's reaction to his greetings indicated she needed to make a change. The deep loyalty and affection she sensed was exactly how she'd like them to respond to her. If she wanted to earn that kind of devotion and respect from the crew, she'd be wise to follow his example.

"Any idea what type of gift the Ambassador might be bringing?" he asked her as she followed him down the corridor.

"Specifically, no, but I guarantee whatever it is will be exquisite and beautifully crafted. The Kraed don't give gifts lightly. Rejecting one is a grievous insult. Not that you'd do that," she added quickly.

"No, I wouldn't, but I appreciate the insight." He glanced at her. "You'd think after patrolling this quadrant for three years on *Excelsior* and ten years on the *Roddenberry* I'd have a solid understanding of the Kraed. But I can count the number of interactions I've had with their ships on both hands. Most of those have been since Ensign Clarek joined the crew. I've never seen their camouflage before. Honestly, they're a bit of an enigma to me."

And that was another reason she respected her captain. He had no problem asking his crew for input when he felt his own knowledge wasn't sufficient for a given situation. "That's partly by design. They're a private people." The Kraed weren't deceptive, but they guarded their secrets very closely. Jonarel had revealed things to her that she was fairly certain no other non-Kraed knew. He'd also uncovered the secrets she kept locked away. He'd sworn on the forfeit of his own life to keep them safe. She'd never once doubted that he meant it.

"Any insights you can give me regarding the Ambassador and his family?"

A smile flitted across her lips. "As you just saw, Siginal enjoys spectacle. His lectures at the Academy were never boring. Jonarel has that tendency for dramatic flair, too, but only in private. He doesn't enjoy the spotlight the way his father does. He's more like Daymar in that way, quietly observant."

"Good to know."

They turned a corner into the wide shuttle bay corridor. Jonarel was waiting for them in front of the closed doors to shuttle bay four. He was looking in her direction, and had probably heard her comments to Captain Warner. The Kraed had exceptional hearing and eyesight, another fact they'd kept under the radar.

His emotional field lit up when his gaze met hers, joy shining like rays from the rising sun. The eager anticipation in his field answered the question about whether he'd been expecting his parents' arrival. In her message to him she hadn't specified why the captain had requested his presence at the shuttle bay, but clearly he already knew.

He was dressed in an outfit she'd never seen before — a brown long-sleeved tunic and matching pants that defined his physique like they'd been tailored to fit him. He'd unbound his hair, allowing the thick waves to drape loosely around his shoulders.

Captain Warner's gaze took in Jonarel's off-duty attire. "Ensign Clarek, your parents have decided to pay us a visit." He glanced at the display that showed the bay's empty interior, the outer doors open to admit Siginal's shuttle.

Jonarel inclined his head. "Yes, sir."

"It's clear they would like to spend time with you and Ensign Hawke, which I'm happy to accommodate. As their host, I would also like to provide appropriate refreshments." He turned to her. "Can you pull up the galley's holiday menu?"

She called it up on her comband and sent a copy to Jonarel.

"Mark whatever you think they'd like. Ensign Hawke can forward the request to the chef."

She was composing the message when movement on the bay's camera feed drew her attention. Siginal's shuttle — a baby version of the Kraed ship he'd arrived in — glided into the bay and touched down with the grace and precision of a hummingbird.

A small sigh escaped her lips. Kraed vessels were so *beautiful*, even their shuttles. In fact, everything the Kraed created was a work of art. She'd discovered that the first time she'd visited Siginal's and Daymar's quarters at the Academy. From the plates they served meals on, to the décor on the walls, every item was crafted with a passionate love of aesthetics combined with precision functionality.

The opportunity to be close to Drakar had been part of her decision-making process when she'd accepted a post on *Excelsior*. She'd been dreaming of seeing Jonarel's homeworld since shortly after they'd met, but she'd never asked him to invite her. He had feelings for her she didn't reciprocate, and she'd never wanted him to mistake interest in his planet and culture for romantic interest in him. It was why she was studiously ignoring the fact that he was watching her right now, apparently enjoying her reaction to the shuttle's arrival.

She'd hoped the crush he'd had on her at the Academy would have faded during their separation.

With a crew of more than a thousand, she'd expected him to hook up with somebody while she finished her studies. But if he had, he'd kept it casual. Ever since she and Mya had joined *Excelsior*'s crew, he'd seemed more focused on her than ever.

She loved him deeply, but like the brother she'd never had. She didn't feel the slightest romantic inclination toward him. That made their relationship complicated whenever he allowed his interest in her to show.

Turning her focus back to her comband, she finished and sent the message to the chef before following Captain Warner into the bay.

The shuttle was even more enchanting in person, reminding her of an expansive ice sculpture rather than a vessel designed to handle the rigors of spaceflight. She'd studied images in her history classes of Kraed ships, both those that had brought the first Kraed to Earth and the ships that had helped humans establish their first interstellar colonies. But those pictures, including the vids, completely failed to convey the sense of power and artistry the shuttle exuded. In the confines of the bay, the shuttle's hull had taken on a metallic sheen that mimicked the bay's bulkheads, but in an ethereal way.

An opening appeared in the shuttle's hull, a ramp extending with fluid grace, like water diverted from a stream to create a new branch. Siginal's broad shoulders filled the opening, his arms spreading wide. "My checalas!"

He strode toward Jonarel first, wrapping him in a fierce hug. The Kraed gave new meaning to the term *bear hug*. She'd once compared Siginal to a Grizzly, and the description fit. Only a fool would get on the wrong side of a Kraed.

Daymar followed Siginal down the ramp, her lithe athleticism a counterpoint to his bulk. She reached for Aurora, pulling her close. "I have missed you, checala," she whispered in Aurora's ear, her arms squeezing tight enough Aurora had trouble drawing breath. Jonarel's family took their hugs very seriously.

A lump rose in her throat. "I've missed you, too." She hadn't realized how much until that moment.

Siginal's hug made her spine pop, his cheek pressing against her temple. "You are well, checala?" he asked her as he finally released her.

"Very well. How about you?"

"Better now." He stroked his fingers down her cheek, his gaze sweeping to include Jonarel.

She bit the inside of her cheek, suppressing the twinge of discomfort his and Jonarel's emotions generated. Now wasn't the time to dwell on it.

Siginal and Daymar greeted Captain Warner with handshakes rather than hugs.

Daymar's golden gaze swept the bay. "Where is Mya?"

"Dr. Forrest?" Captain Warner asked, once again showing how well he knew the members of his crew.

Daymar nodded. "We had hoped to see her as well."

His gaze shifted to Aurora. "Is she on duty?" The growing amusement in his emotional field indicated he already suspected the answer.

"She went off duty two hours ago."

"And you just went off duty, correct?"

She glanced at the time on her comband and nodded.

The *aha* look in his eyes proved he'd figured out Signal had set this gathering up with the strategy of a chess match. But he didn't seem bothered by it. "Please ask Dr. Forrest to join us in the reception room."

As she sent the message, Signal turned back to the shuttle, summoning a cargo glider to his side, laden with two crates. "Lead on, Captain."

Their group drew curious glances from the crewmembers they passed as they made their way through *Excelsior*'s corridors to the reception room on the command deck.

Mya was waiting outside the doors, dressed for the holiday in a red sweater with a white snowflake pattern woven through it. The delighted smile that spread over her face when she spotted Daymar made her look like a teenager. Daymar pulled her into a hug just as bone-crushing as the one she'd given Aurora. Then Signal took his turn, his large body enveloping Mya.

"Glad you could join us, Doctor." Captain Warner nodded to Mya, motioning everyone through the doorway to the reception room.

Aurora had only been in the room once before, the day Captain Warner had held a meet and greet for her, Mya, and the other Academy graduates newly assigned to *Excelsior*. The décor was understated but welcoming, reflecting the personality of the ship's captain, with couches and chairs arranged to encourage relaxation and conversation.

The platters of food from the galley were already

in place, along with a stack of plates, a tureen of coffee, and a row of mugs.

Signal surveyed the offerings with a nod of approval. "Thank you for welcoming us so graciously, Captain."

"It's my pleasure, Ambassador. Please, help yourselves to refreshments."

"A moment." Signal held up a hand. "We would be poor guests if we did not bring a gift to this gathering. My mate's clan produces a drink called *tenrebac* that is renowned on our world. We would like to share it with you."

Aurora's gaze darted to the crates on the cargo glider. Jonarel had introduced her and Mya to the alcoholic beverage after Captain Warner's meet and greet, pouring generous glasses and toasting their posting to *Excelsior*.

The drink was delicious, but also sneakily potent, with twice the alcohol content of wine. Much to her shock — and Mya's — she'd gotten drunk. That had been a startling revelation. Based on her physiology, she'd assumed the alcohol wouldn't affect her. It certainly hadn't affected Mya. But the light-headed, giggly feeling had taken hold rapidly.

Since she'd never experienced anything like it before, she hadn't realized she had an issue until she'd started singing — loudly. Mya had stepped in, reminding her of the late hour and how thin the bulkheads between cabins were. That had brought her temporarily under control, at least until she'd fallen into a fit of laughter over some innocuous thing Jonarel said — she didn't even remember what

— ending up on her back on the deck, gasping for air as tears streamed down her face.

Not one of her finer moments.

Mya had quickly cleared the alcohol from her system, pulling her out of her fit before anyone reported a disturbance, but Aurora viewed the Kraed beverage with a wary eye.

Siginal hefted one of the crates off the cargo glider like it weighed no more than a pillow, but the solid *thunk* when he set it on the deck next to the wraparound counter proved otherwise. "For you to enjoy at your leisure, Captain." His golden eyes danced with mischief. "As your people say, a little goes a long way."

Captain Warner's dark brows lifted toward his receding hairline. "I'll keep that in mind." His gaze flicked to her, the burst of humor in his emotional field matching the sparkle in his light-brown eyes.

No doubt he was thinking about her comments regarding Siginal's love of spectacle.

Siginal lifted the second crate, setting it on the island countertop. "Tell me, Captain, are you aware of Aurora's and Mya's enthusiasm for the celebration of Christmas?"

"I can't say I am."

"During our time together, they regaled us with many tales of the Christmas festivities at their home. It was clear they looked forward to it all year." Siginal spread his arms to encompass the room. "As they were unable to join their families this year, we wished to bring the celebration to them."

Aurora's heart went a little squishy.

Siginal's gaze shifted to her. "I understand music is part of the celebration?"

"It is." But this was Captain Warner's space, not hers.

The Captain motioned to her comband. "By all means. I'm guessing you have a holiday playlist you can loop into the speakers?"

She had several. She selected one of the instrumental options, sending it to the room's speaker system. The cheerful orchestral music instantly added a burst of color to the room.

Daymar opened the crate Siginal had set on the counter, removing a large earthenware container. "For our celebration, I wished to create something new to honor the occasion." She set the container on the counter and lifted the lid.

An earthy aroma with a hint of spice tantalized Aurora's nose. She stepped closer. "It smells wonderful. What is it?"

A teasing light flared in Daymar's golden gaze. "The base is tenrebac."

Aurora bit back a groan. Clearly Jonarel had told his mother about her reaction to the Kraed drink. She wouldn't be on duty again until tomorrow morning, but that didn't mean she wanted to get sauced.

"However, the heating process decreases the alcohol content. The herbs and fruit essence also lower the potency. I crafted it so that it would not cause impairment." Daymar directed the last at Captain Warner, but Aurora knew the message was meant for her.

She could drink Daymar's creation without ending up flat on her back on the deck.

Daymar filled mugs with the spicy brew while the rest of them gathered plates of food. As Aurora accepted the mug of ruby liquid Daymar handed her, Jonarel's mother leaned in. "Do not be embarrassed, checala. Tenrebac affects all strongly when first imbibed."

She scrunched up her nose. "I had a feeling he'd told you."

"Only after we shared our plans for this celebration. It gave me a reason to create something new. Please, tell me what you think."

Aurora lifted the warm mug to her lips. Her first sip spread the remembered earthy sweetness of the tenrebac across her tongue, but this time it was mellowed by a honey-like smoothness, a citrusy note, a spicy tang, and a robust flavor that made her think of the redwood forests of her childhood. "Wow."

Daymar beamed at her. "You approve of my creation?"

"It's amazing." She took another sip. Her body wasn't reacting the way it had last time. That was a good sign. "What are you going to call it?"

"*Tenrebac dellum.*"

"What's in it besides tenrebac?"

"Fruits and herbs from our world." Daymar reached out, stroking the tips of her fingers along the side of Aurora's face in a loving caress. "One day I hope you will visit so I may show you in person."

Aurora swallowed. "I'd like that." Although making it a reality wouldn't be easy. Fleet regulations didn't permit personnel to take shore leave outside of Fleet space. The policy hadn't ever been questioned, since neither the Kraed nor the Teeli invited ships to cross their borders except on official Union business.

When Jonarel joined the Fleet, he'd been given a special dispensation by Admiral Schreiber, the Fleet Director, because Drakar was his homeworld. But that argument wouldn't work for her.

Mya sidled up next to her. "I see you found the chocolate." She nodded to the two chocolate chip cookies on Aurora's plate.

Mya knew better than anyone how devoted she was to dark chocolate, although her favorite was brownies. "It wouldn't be Christmas without chocolate." Every Christmas Day as far back as she could remember had ended with the two of them curled up in front of Stoneycroft's fireplace with warm mugs of hot chocolate or tea and a plate of delicious homemade brownies courtesy of Mya's dad, Gryphon.

"No, it wouldn't," Mya agreed, a bittersweet pang vibrating in her emotional field.

The same feeling echoed in Aurora's chest, but she quelled it. This was a celebration. She didn't want a touch of homesickness to make her maudlin.

Conversation flowed as easily as the tenrebac dellum. True to her word, Daymar's creation did not cause intoxication. Aurora was able to go back for seconds, and while her muscles felt a little looser, that was the only change. No spontaneous songs or hysterical laughter.

As the celebration began winding down, Signal stood. "Captain, you have been a most gracious host, but it is time we take our leave."

A quick glance at her comband confirmed Jonarel was due to report for his shift in half an hour.

Captain Warner rose as well. "I'll escort you to your shuttle."

When their group reached the shuttle bay, Siginal held out his hand to Captain Warner. "I look forward to our next encounter."

"As do I." The Captain stepped back, giving them privacy for their goodbyes.

Siginal and Daymar started with Mya, then moved on to her.

Moisture gathered behind Aurora's eyes as Daymar pulled her into a hug. "Thank you for making this day so special."

"You are special," Daymar murmured, holding Aurora close. "We will always be here for you, whenever you need us."

The unconditional acceptance and support in that statement almost triggered waterworks. Her own mother had never offered her such assurances. Since she was a teenager, she'd been forced to forge a path on her own against her mother's wishes. The scars of those emotional wounds were still tender, especially this year.

She held onto Daymar until she wrangled her wayward emotions back under control. When she trusted herself to keep it together, she stepped back.

Daymar cupped Aurora's face in her palms, her gaze tender. "Be well, checala."

"You, too."

Siginal's goodbye was just as heartfelt. "I am grateful every day that the stars brought you to us."

Much more of this and she was going to start bawling like an infant. She leaned back in his embrace to meet his gaze. "You and Daymar are family to me."

Fierce joy filled his emotional field, something flickering behind his eyes she couldn't quite quantify. "And you are clan." He pressed a kiss to her forehead before releasing her.

She joined Mya as Daymar and Siginal said goodbye to Jonarel, the length of the hugs making it clear how difficult it was for them to let him go.

How hard must it be for them, to have their only child serving on a non-Kraed ship? Unlike most humans, adult Kraed remained with their families all their lives, living together in one of the compounds on Drakar, or on a Clan ship. Jonarel was an outlier in so many ways, choosing a life with the Fleet rather than with his clan. She still wasn't entirely certain why he'd made that decision, but he'd always seemed happy with it. She'd also never heard his parents criticize his choice.

Unlike her mother. When Aurora had been accepted to the Academy, her mother had thrown a fit, then launched a cold war that had yet to thaw. The passive-aggressive attack was no less painful than a frontal assault.

Once Siginal and Daymar had returned to the shuttle, Captain Warner led their group into the corridor, then turned to Jonarel. "How likely are we to have another unexpected visit from your parents in the future?"

Jonarel's gaze flicked briefly to her before he answered. "Very likely."

She narrowed her eyes, a sixth sense alerting her to... something.

Captain Warner nodded like he'd anticipated that answer. "Second question. I have an entire case of tenrebac in my reception room. Define *a little goes a long way*."

Again, Jonarel glanced at her, but this time with amusement. "The alcohol content is roughly twice that of the most potent human-made wines. A quarter of a glass can cause inebriation."

That rocked Captain Warner back on his heels. "Understood." He held each of their gazes in turn. "I can see having the three of you onboard is going to keep me on my toes." He inclined his head. "Merry Christmas."

"Merry Christmas," they replied in unison.

As he strode down the corridor, Aurora turned to Jonarel. "That was a much bigger celebration than I'd anticipated we'd have. How long have you known they were coming?"

"I contacted them weeks ago."

Weeks. And she'd had no idea. Jonarel was better at concealing his emotions than she gave him credit for. "Thank you. It was a lovely surprise."

"It certainly was," Mya agreed.

"You are welcome." Jonarel checked the time on his comband. "I must go."

Aurora made a shooing motion. "Go, go. Merry Christmas."

The smile that stole over his face would make a Renaissance master proud. "Merry Christmas." Turning, he loped off down the hall with the grace of a panther.

"Whew." Mya fanned her face with both hands. "He really should warn us before he does that."

Aurora laughed at Mya's theatrics. Jonarel's smiles were as rare as a blue moon, and definitely showstoppers.

"I saw you hadn't opened the package from home yet," Mya commented, looping her arm through Aurora's and tugging her in the direction of their cabin.

"I was waiting for you."

"Then let's go see what they sent us."

The package had arrived the previous day through Fleet courier. Aurora unfastened the web netting securing it in place in the small storage cubby in their cabin and carried it the two steps to her bed. Mya settled in next to her, pulling open the flaps to reveal the colorful boxes inside.

"This one's to me from your mom." Mya's brown eyes sparkled with excitement as she pulled the first box out and set it on the bed. Four others followed.

Aurora picked up the one with evergreen trees on a red background that was to her from Gryphon and Marina. "If they believed us when we told them we had no space to store or display anything non-essential in this room, then my bet is on something consumable." And she knew exactly what she was hoping for.

"Let's find out."

A delectable, decadent scent rose from the box as Aurora opened it. "*Brownies.*" She inhaled deeply, the rich chocolate aroma filling her senses. "Stars, I've missed that smell." Gryphon had spoiled her, packing in three layers of his famous dark chocolate brownies, nine to a layer, in an airtight cooling storage box.

She glanced at the box with Mya's name on it that was exactly the same dimensions. "I have an idea of what they sent you."

Mya opened the box and lifted out the parchment paper, laughing as she tipped the box slightly sideways. Three petite Yule logs nestled inside, the dark chocolate icing ridged to resemble bark, with edible cinnamon-flavored faux holly sprigs. "They're clearly expecting us to share with each other."

Aurora grinned. "Oh, we will definitely be sharing. What did my mom send you?"

Mya picked up the tall rectangular box and popped off the lid. "She's continuing the theme." Her gaze met Aurora's. "Take a guess."

They had brownies and Yule logs. But no beverages, yet. She had a fifty-fifty chance of getting it right. "Tea?"

"Yep. Her lemongrass ginger blend."

Aurora's mom handmade that special tea blend each autumn, the ingredients sourced from the plants she grew at Stoneycroft.

Aurora snagged the matching box and pulled off the lid. Sure enough, it contained the hot chocolate mix her mom also made from scratch. A handwritten note sat on top. It was short and to the point.

Wish you were here. Merry Christmas. Love, Mom

Such a simple, innocuous message. It hit her like a gut punch.

"Sahzade, are you okay?"

Aurora gave her a strained smile. Mya only used her childhood nickname when they were alone, and then mostly when she was concerned about her. "Fine." She held up the note.

Mya read it, then sighed. She knew better than anyone how challenging Aurora's relationship was with her mother, and how pointed the first four words of that brief message were. "There's one box left. It's to both of us."

Aurora picked up the remaining package, which was far smaller than the others. "I don't think this is consumable." Pulling off the lid, she stared at the slim object inside. "It's a data card."

"Huh. I wonder what's on it."

Aurora plucked the card from the box. "Let's find out." She inserted it into the reader for their shared desk display. A moment later cheerful Christmas music flowed out of the speakers. An image of a gigantic, decorated evergreen filled the display, covered in white sparkling lights and bright red bows. The holiday tree had always been the focal point of their celebrations at Stoneycroft, especially on Christmas morning.

Three figures stepped in front of the tree. Gryphon had a Santa hat pulled down over his brown hair, his warm smile drawing an answering smile from Aurora's lips. Marina stood between him and Aurora's mother, her thick dark hair pulled away from her face with holiday-themed clips that matched the red holiday sweater she was wearing — the twin to the one Mya had on.

Mya chuckled. "Even when we're lightyears apart, we still manage to match our clothes."

Aurora's smile widened. Since Mya and Marina were close to the same height and build, and shared a similar taste in clothing, they'd often purchase matching outfits when they shopped together.

Aurora and her mom did not.

In the vid, her mom was putting on a show of holiday cheer, but the tightness around her blue-grey eyes and the brittle quality to her smile gave lie to the performance.

"Greetings to our two favorite star travelers!" Gryphon called out, lifting a mug to toast them. "We didn't want the holiday to pass you by without your favorite treats. Hopefully they all arrived safely."

"As you can see," Marina swept a hand behind her to indicate the tree, "the holiday spirit is alive and well here. And if I know the two of you..." She lowered her voice to a conspiratorial whisper. "You've found a way to have your own celebration on *Excelsior*."

Mya bumped Aurora's shoulder with hers. "Wait until they hear what Signal and Daymar did."

Aurora nodded absently, but her focus was on her mom.

The bright smile her mom turned on the camera didn't warm her expression, it made it harsh. The flat look in her eyes didn't help, either. "I hope you're doing well." The corners of her mouth pinched. "It's not the same here without you."

Direct hit. Aurora's stomach hollowed out for the second time in as many minutes. Guilt, frustration, and anger warred for dominance. Her mom knew just how to get under her skin.

"Merry Christmas," her mom continued, raising her mug in a mockery of Gryphon's enthusiastic toast. "My Christmas wish is that you'll come home soon."

A scraping sound filled her ears as Aurora ground her molars together. Even now, when she'd graduated top of her class at the Academy, earning a coveted post on one of the newest ships in the Fleet, her mother still hadn't given up trying to sabotage her. She seemed to think if she kept firing emotional missiles at every opportunity, eventually she'd wear Aurora down and she'd give up her dreams.

In reality, the continual attacks were making her emotional walls stronger.

Marina and Gryphon tried to conceal their winces before they turned back to the camera. "Merry Christmas!" they called out with effusive enthusiasm that tried to block out her mother's displeasure.

"And now for the grand finale." Gryphon stepped forward, turning the camera away from the tree. "One more holiday tradition." He walked the camera toward the huge stone fireplace on the Hawke side of the central room, where a crackling fire created a cheerful glow on the cushions of the couch facing it. "Enjoy." The audio changed, the crackling of the fire replaced with an instrumental version of *Feliz Navidad*.

"Awww." Mya leaned her shoulder against Aurora's. "We get our holiday fire, too."

"Yeah." She knew Mya was trying to distract her, to take the sting out of her mom's bad behavior. Which left her with a choice. She could hold onto her resentment, or she could enjoy the remainder of the holiday.

Reaching behind her, she snagged the box of brownies and held it out. "Brownie?"

Mya grinned. "As if I'd say no."

Aurora plucked one from the box and held it aloft. "Merry Christmas, Mya."

Mya tapped her brownie against Aurora's. "Merry Christmas, Sahzade."

Her first bite sent her taste buds into the stratosphere. "Oh, my goodness. It's official. Gryphon is the best baker in the galaxy." She took another bite, savoring the rich flavors.

Mya chuckled. "Which we can assert with authority, now that we've expanded our horizons beyond Earth."

"Mm-hmm. And I plan to keep expanding them." Her mother's fear wouldn't get in her way. She wanted to see everything Fleet space had to offer her. And if she was very lucky, she'd get that visit to Drakar someday, too.

Excelsior Christmas is a prequel story in the Starhawke Rising series. Delve into the Starhawke

Universe and discover a future of possibilities at Audrey-Sharpe.com.

RECIPE: TENREBAC DELLUM

from Audrey Sharpe's "Excelsior Christmas"

INGREDIENTS:

- 2 tenrebac
- 1 daybrembran
- 4 rugnod tegmun
- 5 brak of camninon
- 3 hedel of gonyon
- 6 arogen

Instructions:

1. Pour the tenrebac into a large cooking pot. Add the daybrembran.

2. Combine the rugnod tegmun and camninon in a small container. Add the mixture to the pot.

3. Add the gonyon and stir until blended.

4. Cut the arogen into thick slices and add to the pot.

5. Warm slowly to desired temperature, but do not boil.

6. Ladle and serve.

As many people will not have access to the ingredients from Drakar, Daymar has graciously provided more accessible substitutions to achieve a similar flavor.

Please note - using the Earth-based substitutions will render the drink intoxicating. Imbibe with caution.

- Tenrebac – 3 bottles of red wine, preferably cabernet
- Daybrembran - 1 ½ cups brandy
- Rugnod Tegmun – a pinch of ground nutmeg
- Camninon – ½ tsp ground cinnamon
- Gonyon - 3 spoonfuls honey
- Arogen – 3 oranges, sliced into rounds

THE EGG ROLL FESTIVAL

by Tami Veldura

LISSIE, THE EATER OF ALL, CROUCHED OUTSIDE the doorway to the mess in her shipden as her stomach rumbled and gurgled. She was hungry and there was something interesting happening in the mess that smelled like it might become food. She flicked her forked tongue into the air and settled her wings along her back.

Lissie was the size of a small dog. She had never seen a dog, but Maj had mentioned them once, and Lissie had decided that if dogs were her size, they must be excellent creatures indeed. Clearly, dogs were modeled after dragons like Lissie.

She did not have fur like a dog. Instead, her scales shimmered under the soft shipden lights, shifting colors as she moved: green as fresh leaves, purple like station dusk, pink and blue like candy wrappers she had once stolen, pale cream like the center of a boiled egg.

Maj, who was very small for a human but quite

large for a friend, called Lissie's color *opal*. This was a good word. A word with a smooth, cool taste, like the shell of an egg before she crunched it between her teeth.

Lissie's wings weren't very large, just broad enough that she could stretch them and touch both walls of the Trinordia Dragon's narrow hallway. She liked to do this when she was feeling especially grand.

Her tail was long and clever, and she was practicing wrapping its tip around important things: like spoons. Or dirty socks. The smellier the better. Her claws were black as the starless dark between systems, and Maj helped her keep them sharp and tidy. This was important. A dragon's claws must always be at their best.

The Trinordia Dragon was a small shuttle of a ship, which made it perfect. It had tunnels—Lissie called them tunnels, though Maj and Oriana called them hallways—and nooks and cargo corners that smelled of metal, old grease, and the spice of human skin. The shipden had a hum to it, a soft purring sound that Lissie liked to match with her own purr, deep in her throat.

It wasn't just a ship. It was her home. She had hatched here, back when the ship had been tucked into a cave on a planet. Now it traveled the stars and she along with it.

The mess was Lissie's second-favorite part of the shipden. (The best part was *all* of it, of course.) But the mess had smells, and smells were very important.

It was a small room, barely wider than Lissie's wingspan, and cozy the way a den should be. The counter was built right into the wall, with cabinets above and below that clinked and rattled softly whenever the Trinordia Dragon stretched her metal skin. The table was a flat circle of cool metal, bolted tight to the floor so it couldn't wander off in zero-G. Around it were fold-up chairs, thin and practical, with little magnets in their feet so they'd stay where they were supposed to. Lissie had tried chewing on the magnets once. They tasted sharp, like lightning. Not her favorite.

Oriana stood at the counter, her long brown hair tied back in a braid that swayed like a rope toy every time she moved. She was tall, tallest of the shipden family, and cheerful—always smelling of warm bread and clean soap, with a bright sparkle of something sweet on the air that Lissie liked very much.

Today, Oriana wore her holly day clothes. Lissie knew these well: a fluttery red shirt, soft like flower petals, and white-and-red pants printed with little red blossoms. The pattern tasted gentle, like soft fruit.

Holly day, Lissie thought with delight, her tongue flicking again to sample the mess-room air.

Maj crouched near the table, inspecting a loose bolt in the floor with their usual squint. They were small, half Oriana's height, and fast. Lissie liked how they moved—sometimes upright like humans were supposed to, but often on all fours like Lissie herself. Maj's teeth were sharp and pleasing to look at; they filed them that way, and Lissie approved. Their clothes never changed. Cargo pants with too many pockets and a t-shirt that always smelled faintly of oil and adventure. Even on holly days.

Lissie tasted the air again, catching the mood that shimmered between the sisters: warm, bright, a little fizzy like the bubbles in station cola. A good flavor. A *safe* flavor.

She padded forward, nose high, wanting to see what the holly day would bring.

Oriana hummed a little tune—one of those soft, ripple-sweet ones that tasted like honey on the air— as she unpacked the bag she'd brought from the station market.

Lissie's head shot up, her forked tongue flickering with eager interest. Groceries. Groceries meant food. And food meant tasting. And tasting was Lissie's *most important job*.

Lissie leapt onto the cool metal table, claws clicking as she landed, and crouched low, tail twitching behind her. Her bright eyes fixed on Oriana's hands as she pulled things out of the bag, one after another. She settled her wings—left then right—with impatience.

Lissie flicked her tongue at each treasure as it appeared.

There were long, thin, pale sticks that smelled sharp and wet and green. There were crinkly leaves that tasted of cold air and the faint bitterness of station water.

A bottle that glugged when Oriana set it down, its scent tangy and dark like fermented fruit. A little jar that smelled of fire and heat and made Lissie sneeze—a small, surprised chirp of sound that made Maj glance over and grin.

There were thin sheets of something soft and floury that Oriana handled carefully, laying them flat on the counter. Lissie didn't know these, but they smelled of dust and starch and station kitchens.

And then—then came the best part.

Eggs.

Round. Smooth. A dozen of them in a paper tray that Oriana set reverently on the counter like treasure.

Lissie's whole body hummed with delight. The eggs smelled warm and full, like the promise of a meal and the promise of play at the same time. She craned forward, tongue darting out, tasting the faint dusty shell, the hint of yolky yellow sealed inside. Perfect.

Oriana started sorting the ingredients, her braid swinging behind her as she moved. She spoke over her shoulder to Maj. "Did we get enough wrappers? I'm not sure if one pack will do."

Maj straightened from the floor, where they'd been checking that stubborn bolt, and loped over on all fours, peering at the counter. "We'll make it work. We've got enough eggs for the three of us. That's the important part—can't have an Egg Roll Festival without eggs."

Egg Roll Festival.

The words sparkled in Lissie's mind, bright and certain. That was it. The name of the holly day. The purpose of the celebration.

The Egg Roll Festival...

Her tail lashed with joy. The Festival wasn't just about *eggs*. It was about *rolling* them. The eggs were meant to roll! And surely, surely it was the duty of a dragon—*the* dragon of the Trinordia Dragon—to become the best egg roller on the ship.

Lissie approved of this holly day with all her heart.

She would roll the eggs. She would roll them well.

She would become a master egg roller.

Oriana shuttled the green veggies to the counter and began preparation, but Lissie's eyes were fixed on the tray of eggs. Shortly, Oriana and Maj were busy, heads bent together, talking softly about wrappers and sauces and other things that didn't matter at all.

Only the eggs mattered.

Egg rolling started with an egg. Obviously.

Carefully—so carefully—Lissie stretched her neck out and opened her jaws. She plucked one of the perfect, round treasures from its cozy little nest of paper. The egg fit neatly between her teeth. She held it gently, gently, so as not to crack the delicate shell.

The eggshell tasted cool and chalky against her tongue. A soft dust flavor, with the faintest tang of the station air where it had been packed. Lissie purred deep in her throat, pleased with her prize.

She hopped off the table and trotted proudly out of the mess, tail high, wings tucked tight to keep from scraping the doorframe. The egg was hers, and the Egg Roll Festival was about to begin in earnest.

The tunnel stretched before her, narrow and

familiar, with soft lights along the floor and the faint scent of engine oil and recycled air. It was perfect. Long, straight, just the right size for egg rolling.

Lissie lowered her head and set the egg down with the utmost care. It made a tiny click as it touched the floor, a good sound. A ready sound.

She stepped back, crouched low, and nudged the egg with her nose.

It wobbled. It rolled—sort of. It started straight, but almost at once the egg turned, curved to the side, as if it had its own ideas about where it wanted to go.

Lissie blinked, surprised. She trotted after it, gave it another nudge. The egg curved again, stubborn and playful.

This was going to take practice.

And Lissie, Eater of All, Master of Holly Days, was ready for the challenge.

Lissie sat back on her haunches, tongue flicking thoughtfully at the air. She eyed the egg where it had come to a stop, tipped slightly against the wall of the hallway.

The egg was not like a ball. Lissie had rolled balls before—Oriana's crumpled paper, a dropped apple, once a loose engine bolt that went in circles (that had been a fun game until Maj found out). Balls went where you pushed them. Balls were loyal.

But eggs...

Lissie padded over and sniffed at her prize. The smooth shell smelled faintly of dust and air and the soft promise of food. But it was the *shape* that was the trouble. Long and round all at once, pointy at one end, fat at the other.

She crouched, angled her nose, and gave it a gentle nudge. The egg rolled in a slow, lazy curve, like it was enjoying itself far too much to go straight.

Lissie huffed, sending a puff of warm air over the egg. She tried again, pushing harder this time. The egg rolled faster, but it curved sooner, bumping into the wall with a little *tock* that made Lissie's claws twitch in frustration.

Too hard, she decided.

She circled the egg, thinking. The flavors of thought were rich on her tongue—curiosity tasted like warm bread, determination like a pinch of salt. She liked both.

This time, Lissie crouched very low, lined up her snout, and nudged the egg just so. Not too hard, not too soft. A perfect nudge.

The egg rolled.

It rolled straight.

One, two, three, four turns before it started to wobble, before its own strange shape made it veer gently toward the side.

Lissie froze, delighted. That had been *perfect*.

Her tail lashed with excitement. She trotted after the egg, nose close, ready to try again. Now she knew the secret: a sweet spot of pressure, a perfect nudge.

She just had to practice her newfound technique, and the Egg Roll Festival would be glorious.

Lissie lined up again, nose just so, and gave the egg a measured nudge.

It rolled beautifully—oh, *beautifully*—straight down the middle of the hallway, clicking softly as it turned, just like the perfect sweet spot she'd discovered. Lissie trotted after it, eyes bright, tongue flicking in excitement.

The egg rolled right past the open doorway of the mess.

Lissie paused, nostrils flaring. The warm air from inside tickled her nose, full of scents she couldn't name but liked anyway—rich, savory smells, sharp things, sweet things, crackling oil. But more than that, the air was flavored with conversation.

She tasted it, the way only Lissie could.

Light. Joy. The warm fizz of happiness on her tongue.

She crouched low, peering into the mess with one eye, and sent a curious thought down the bond that connected her to Oriana.

Roll?

Oriana's voice floated back, gentle and cheerful, tasting like honeyed tea.

"Yes, Lissie! I'm making rolls now!"

Lissie blinked. She glanced at her egg, sitting patiently where it had come to rest against the wall.

Making rolls?

She tilted her head, confusion sparking in her chest. Oriana was making rolls, but Lissie already had one. Was there more to it?

She nosed her egg thoughtfully. Maybe Oriana was so good at egg rolling that she could *make* them. Clearly Lissie needed to practice more if she was going to win at the Egg Roll Festival.

Tail high with determination, Lissie nudged her egg back into position. The hallway was hers, and she had rolling to perfect. It didn't take long.

The egg rolled with satisfying rhythm. Lissie had

found the right pressure—the sweet spot between too soft and too hard—and she chased her prize down the hallway with growing pride. The egg clicked and turned, its funny shape trying to wobble, but Lissie was ready for it. A quick nudge of her nose kept it mostly straight.

The hallway ended at the big door of the airlock.

Lissie stopped, panting happily, tongue flicking out to savor the cool metal taste of the air. She eyed the door. Beyond it was the cargo hold, and Lissie *knew* the cargo hold. It always brought new smells: the tang of machinery, the sweetness of fruits Oriana had bought, the sharp bite of cleaning supplies Maj liked to stash there.

Today would be no different.

The light above the airlock glowed green. Safe. The pressure on the other side matched the shipden.

Lissie, clever with claws and tail, reached up and pulled the handle with practiced ease. The door slid aside with a soft hiss, and a wash of new smells flooded over her.

Oh, *delicious*.

The cargo hold smelled like metal warmed by engines, like old oil in forgotten corners. There was the dry, papery scent of crates stacked near the wall— empty now, but once full of something Lissie decided must have been tasty, because the memory of it clung to the plasteel. A faint trace of ozone tickled her nose, leftover from some tool Maj had left behind. The ramps, folded neatly along one side, smelled of dust and space station air from the last time they'd been used.

It was perfect.

Lissie gathered up her egg carefully between her teeth, feeling the smooth, cool shell on her tongue, and trotted through the door.

Here, in this wide, empty space, she would master the art of egg rolling.

The Egg Roll Festival would see her victorious.

Lissie set the egg at the top of the cargo steps, her claws clicking softly on the metal. She peered down the narrow stairs, tongue flicking at the air, tasting dust and old oil and the faintest trace of space. The egg gleamed in the shipden light, pale and smooth.

This was going to be *glorious*.

She gave it a gentle nudge with her nose.

The egg wobbled, hesitated, then began its descent with a soft tap... tap...

Crack!

On the very first step, the shell gave way. A thin golden thread of yolk oozed from the break, and the egg bumped down to the next step, leaving behind a sticky smear.

Lissie froze, eyes wide. She sniffed the air eagerly.

Oh, *oh*. The smell was *heaven*. Rich and warm and savory, with a hint of sweetness like the words Oriana liked to say when she was happy.

Still, Lissie tried. She nosed the egg gently, hopeful. It rolled a little, but the crack made it lurch oddly, spilling more of its treasure. The shell was no good for rolling now. It didn't sing under her tongue the way it had before.

But it *did* smell like the best thing in the universe.

Without another thought, Lissie crouched low and licked up the yolk, quick little swipes of her tongue against the metal. She slurped up the egg white, too, and crunched the broken shell between her teeth. The bits of calcium crumbled like sweet grit, and she swallowed it all down, satisfied.

The stairs gleamed clean behind her, no trace left of the egg's short, noble journey.

Lissie lifted her head proudly. That egg had served its purpose, and she had honored it in the best way a dragon could.

Time for another.

Lissie trotted back down the hallway, belly pleasantly warm from her snack, nose twitching with purpose. Her stomach grumbled for more and Lissie was happy to fill it. The mess door stood open, letting out a swirl of good smells—steam, oil, something tangy and sweet that clung to the air like sticky words.

Without hesitation, she leapt onto the cool metal table, claws clicking, tail swishing behind her. Oriana stood at the counter, humming a tune that tasted like sunshine and cinnamon. Her long braid swayed as she worked, pulling and folding and pressing things Lissie couldn't quite make sense of.

Lissie crept closer, tongue flicking to sample the air.

Oriana turned just in time. "Lissie! No, no, not yet—they're not cooked!"

The cheerful words made Lissie's wings perk, but she still eyed the plate curiously. The oblong shapes on it smelled warm, but *not right*. They weren't eggs. They weren't even shiny or round. No, these were something else entirely. Therefore, *unimportant*.

Her gaze shifted, sharp and clever, and she spotted the prize: the tray of eggs, sitting on the edge of the counter.

Maj was nowhere to be seen. Oriana was busy at the stove.

Perfect.

Lissie, swift as a comet, snatched another egg between her teeth and hopped lightly down from the table. The smooth shell felt cool and promising on her tongue.

She trotted proudly from the mess, head high, already imagining the graceful arcs this egg would roll down the cargo ramp. This time, she would master it. She would become the best egg roller the shipden had ever seen.

Lissie padded into the cargo hold, the egg secure between her teeth. The air still tasted of metal and old grease, of boxes and straps and the faintest memory of planetside dust. She flicked her tongue, savoring the mingling flavors.

Down the stairs, the loading ramps waited— wide, sturdy metal slopes that stretched from the floor of the hold to where cargo could roll in or out. She knew these well. She'd watched Maj shove the ramps out with practiced grunts, hooks clanging into place at the ship's edge so crates could glide aboard or down to some waiting dock.

But today, the ramps had a nobler purpose.

Today, they would serve the Eater of All and her egg.

Lissie climbed to the top of the tallest ramp, claws clinking softly. She set the egg down carefully, admiring its roundness, its soft cool shell against her nose.

The egg had barely kissed the metal before it betrayed her.

It took off, spinning, wobbling, *racing* down the ramp faster than any proper egg should.

Lissie's eyes went wide. She launched after it, claws skittering, wings flaring for balance. The egg threatened to veer off the side, to smash its precious self at the bottom—*not yet!*

In a swift snap, Lissie caught the egg back between her teeth just before disaster. She skidded to a halt, heart thudding with excitement, wings fluttering. Her breath tumbled in her throat.

The egg was still whole. She rolled it gently against her tongue, tasting the smoothness of the shell, checking for cracks.

No cracks. No leaks.

Lissie breathed out a small puff of relief, warm as a steam vent.

She wasn't ready. Not yet.

She climbed back to the top of the ramp, this time determined to *plan* the perfect roll.

Lissie crouched low, her bright eyes locked on the egg resting delicately in one of the narrow metal tracks. The ramp stretched wide and steep before her, a smooth decline of cool steel, gleaming faintly under the dim cargo bay lights. The small ridges — narrow lips of metal running straight down the length — caught her attention like secret guides waiting to be discovered.

With a careful nudge of her snout, Lissie sent the egg rolling. At first, it was smooth and steady, gliding along the track like a tiny comet racing on rails. But soon, the egg began to wobble, its round form leaning precariously, threatening to veer off course. Lissie's heart jumped—no! The egg couldn't fall! She darted forward, tongue flicking out, claws tapping against the metal as she raced after it.

The egg wobbled hard, teetering dangerously close to the edge, but just as Lissie lunged, the metal lip of the track caught the shell with a soft *click* and nudged it back in line. It was like magic—the ramp itself was helping, steering the egg safely along its path. Lissie's tongue flicked out again, barely grazing the egg, but she didn't need to catch it. The track held it true.

She padded faster, eyes wide with excitement and relief. The egg slid smoothly now, racing toward the bottom of the ramp, following the straight, shining guide. When it finally slipped off the ramp onto the cargo bay floor, it spun in a tiny joyous twirl, like a dancer finishing a perfect pirouette.

Lissie arrived, her chest heaving with the thrill of the chase. She lifted her head and flicked her tongue around the egg, tasting the cool smoothness of its shell. The track had saved the roll — had made it better, more certain.

Lissie's chest puffed up, and her wings fluttered with excitement—tiny gusts ruffled the air like whispered applause. Her bright eyes sparkled, gleaming with the purest delight she had ever tasted. This was it. This was the Egg Roll Festival. This—the perfect, gliding, wobble-and-correct roll—was what it was all about.

Her tail curled tight with happiness. She could feel it bubbling up inside her, a joyful warmth that tasted like honey and fireworks on her tongue. *Egg roll!* she thought, over and over, the words as sweet as the shell's crisp crunch.

Without hesitation, she sprinted—no, *bounded*—back toward the mess, claws clicking rhythmically on the floor, her little body a blur of gleaming scales and eager energy. Her wings flicked excitedly as she moved, nearly lifting her off the ground as she raced up the stairs.

She was going to declare herself the egg roll master. Anyone who would listen would know. She was going to *roll* that egg right into the mess and show everyone her new skill.

She passed through the airlock, her breath catching as she reached the slim tunnel outside the mess door.

Lissie carefully set the egg down on the smooth floor. Her nose twitched as she gave it a gentle prod. The egg wobbled, then rolled forward—just a little too quickly. Lissie flicked out her tongue, lightly tapping the shell to nudge it back on course. Like magic, the egg steadied, following a straight path.

Rolling down the hallway was child's play now. She grinned, her sharp teeth glinting in the soft ship lights. Her wings fluttered proudly, and she puffed up her chest, feeling like the true master of egg rolling.

Suddenly, a familiar voice caressed her bubble of joy.

"What're you up to?"

Maj stood at the doorway to the mess, hands on her hips, watching Lissie with amused eyes. Lissie blinked at Maj, then glanced down at the egg. With a careful nudge of her nose, she sent it rolling a short distance.

Maj barked a sudden laugh. "You've been rolling eggs, haven't you?"

Just then, Oriana appeared behind Maj, carrying a plate steaming with something fragrant. The scent was warm, rich, and yes—a little eggy.

"What's going on here?" Oriana asked with a smile.

Maj grinned, "Lissie's taken the Egg Roll Festival very seriously. She's been rolling eggs all over the ship."

Lissie spread her wings wide and puffed up her chest even more, her eyes shining bright. She was very good at rolling now.

Oriana giggled softly and held out the plate. "Well, come on, you two. Time to join me at the table. I made something special for the festival."

Lissie's tail flicked happily as she grabbed her egg and followed them inside. She carried it proudly to the table, hopping up onto the cool metal surface with a soft *thump*. She placed the egg beside her, the most important seat at the table.

Maj settled into one of the folding chairs, the little magnets in the feet clicking softly as the chair locked into place. Oriana followed, carrying a warm plate she set gently in the center of the table.

Curious, Lissie flicked her tongue toward the plate, tasting the mingling scents that rose from the food: a warm, savory blend with hints of something crispy and fresh. Her nose twitched with excitement — this was definitely food, and new food was always an adventure. After all, she was the Eater of All.

Oriana smiled at Lissie's eager expression and said, "These are eggrolls. They're stuffed with veggies and sealed with egg so they stay rolled up when they're cooked." She reached for a small bowl beside the plate and added, "And here's the dipping sauce I made to go with them."

Lissie took in the rich, tangy aroma of the sauce, then swirled her tongue in the air, tasting all the layers of flavor. Eggrolls, she decided thoughtfully, might just have a place in the Egg Roll Festival — but only if they tasted as good as they smelled.

Lissie reached out with her dark claws, careful and precise, and plucked one of the eggrolls from the plate. The crispy shell crackled under her grip, and the moment it touched her teeth, it broke with a most delightful *crunch* — like biting through the thinnest layer of ice, or the brittle crust of a sugar glaze. The eggroll was hot, steam swirling up into her nose, but Lissie was a dragon; heat was a flavor to her, and it tasted like sunshine and warmth and good things cooking.

She chewed, savoring the textures and tastes that burst across her tongue. The crisp outer shell was golden and flaky, tasting of toasted flour and just a hint of oil — not unpleasant at all, like the smooth richness of roasted nuts. Inside, the vegetables were soft and bright, with sweet notes from slivers of carrot, a grassy freshness from cabbage, and a curious earthiness she decided must be sprouts or shoots of some kind.

And there — hiding just beneath the crispy shell — she found it: the egg. It clung to the inside of the wrapper, sealing it closed, and tasted like the smooth, creamy edge of a hard-boiled yolk, like warm, rich silk on her tongue. The egg's flavor blended with everything else, binding it all together. Yes, Lissie agreed, a proper egg to eat must be part of the Egg Roll Festival.

Curious, she flicked her tongue and the last bite into the bowl of sauce Oriana had made. The sauce hit her senses like a sharp tang — citrusy and sweet, with a flicker of heat that danced like tiny sparks along her tongue. It made the crispy shell taste brighter, the vegetables sweeter, the hidden egg even richer.

Lissie licked her teeth clean, savoring the last wisps of flavor, and without hesitation, reached for another eggroll. These, she decided firmly, were a fine addition to the Egg Roll Festival indeed.

It wasn't until every last eggroll had vanished—their crispy shells crunched to crumbs, their delicious insides savored, and the dipping sauce cup licked so clean it gleamed—that Oriana leaned back with a contented sigh. She rested her elbows on the table and grinned at Lissie. "So tell me, Lissie," she asked, warm and curious, "where exactly were you rolling all these eggs to?"

Lissie's wings fluttered, and she lifted her precious round egg between her teeth. *Roll!* she declared in her bright, chiming thoughts, the word bursting with joy and pride. She looked at Oriana with shining eyes, inviting her to witness the grand art of egg rolling herself.

Oriana laughed, standing, brushing crumbs from her fluttery red shirt. "Ok, ok. Show us how you celebrate the egg roll festival, Master Roller."

Yes! Lissie thought, thrilled beyond measure. They would see. They would see the best egg roller ever.

With great ceremony, she bounded from the table. Her claws clicked smartly on the floor as she trotted from the mess, tail high, wings spread in her excitement. Maj followed, curious and grinning, while Oriana trailed behind, still laughing softly, the sound filled with affection.

Lissie reached the cargo bay and set her egg down at the top of the ramp with utmost care. She positioned it just so, lining it up with the metal track. She gave a delicate nudge with her nose, and the egg rolled—smooth, true, and perfect—right down the ramp. Lissie chased alongside, ready, as always, to catch it if it strayed, though it did not. The egg was a champion now, just like her.

And as it reached the bottom and did its little celebratory spin, Lissie puffed up with delight. Yes. The Egg Roll Festival was the best holly day. And Lissie was the best—the *Master* Egg Roller of the whole shipden.

Maj laughed and it tasted like sparkling soda. "I think Lissie has invented a new Egg Roll tradition," they said. Maj picked up the egg and climbed up the ramp. "Let me give it a try!"

Lissie readied herself at the bottom of the ramp, wings and tail up with delight and anticipation. She wiggled her body into a crouch and chirped at Oriana, *Roll!*

Oriana laughed. "Maj, Lissie thinks she can roll eggs better than you can."

"Is that so?" Maj crouched and lined up their egg. "We'll just see about that."

The adventure continues! Pick up a free Maj and the Outlaws scifi short story and join Tami's newsletter to read more at BookHip.com/BWWQQJF.

RECIPE: NAPA CABBAGE SHRIMP ROLLS

From Tami Veldura's "The Egg Roll Festival"

I GREW UP EATING EGG ROLLS, SPRING ROLLS, dumplings—all kinds of delightful things. But around 15 years ago, I developed a string of food allergies that suddenly limited my diet. No flour, no eggs: no more crispy egg rolls for me. Determined to find a workaround, I've started making these Napa Cabbage rolls whenever I celebrate a holly day. Enjoy!

serves 2, prep 5 minutes, cook 20 minutes

veg/vegan alternative – replace shrimp with tofu or simply leave it out

Filling:

- ½ of 1 nappa cabbage
- 1 whole carrot

- 3 green onions
- 2 cloves garlic
- ½ inch ginger root
- 1 lb shrimp, raw
- 2 tsp sesame oil
- 1 tsp coconut aminos (or soy sauce)
- ½ tsp salt
- 1/8 tsp pepper
- grapeseed or avocado oil for frying

Dipping:

- 2 tbsp coconut aminos
- 2 tbs water
- 1 tbs kombucha vinegar (rice vinegar or apple cider vinegar also work)
- 1 tbsp agave (or your sugar of choice)

Prep Leaves:

- Chop the bottom off the nappa cabbage and fill a pot with as many leaves as it will hold (try not to break them!) If the pot is small, you can fold leaves in as they boil to prevent breaking.
- Top off with water and set on high heat
- When at a rolling boil, time 2 minutes, then remove from heat, drain, and set aside

- If leaves are too hot for assembly, fill the pot with cool water while prepping filling.

Prep Filling:

- Combine all other filling items in a food processor until smooth
- If you find yourself with leftovers, freeze the filling!

Assemble rolls:

- Roll 1 or 2 teaspoons of filling into each cabbage leaf. Start at the bottom of the leaf and roll upward, folding in the sides as you go.
- Heat your avocado oil on medium high until flicking a drop of water into it makes it jump
- Add rolls to the oil (use tongs!) with the end of the cabbage face down on the pan. Fill the pan with rolls and cover for 3 minutes.
- Flip rolls and continue to cook for another 3 minutes until leaves are browned.
- Resist the amazing smell, these come off the pan HOT!
- Serve with dipping sauce

. . .

Prep Dipping Sauce:

- Combine all ingredients and whisk vigorously for 20 seconds.
- I do this with a small jar, combine all ingredients and shake.
- Dip will keep in the fridge for up to a week

ABOUT THE AUTHORS

JEANNETTE BEDARD. Always writing, Jeannette has filled hard drives with ones and zeros that occasionally coalesce into books. Her non-linear career path has included working as both a soldier and a scientist (but not at the same time). Currently, she lives on a non-tropical island in the Pacific with her husband and daughter, and she loves a good math joke, especially if there is pi involved.

Website: jeannettebedard.substack.com

MJ BLEHART is a storyteller, dreamer, philosopher, geek, writer, editor, voice artist, medieval reenactor, and more. He's been writing fiction since he was 9 years old, and his first completed story was an illustrated, 50-page hand-written sci-fi adventure called *Wildfire*.

MJ is originally from the suburbs of Minneapolis, Minnesota, relocated to the East Coast for college and has lived in New York or New Jersey ever since. Currently, he lives in New Jersey, just east of Philadelphia, with his wife and three feline overlords (cats).

Website: mjblehart.com

PETER J. FOOTE got locked in a bookstore as a child and has been reading his way to freedom ever since.

As a blue-collar sci-fi author, Peter tells gritty and personal sci-fi and fantasy stories of ordinary people placed in extraordinary situations that resonate with readers and provide much-needed escapism.

Website: peterjfoote.com

K. GORMAN is a Science Fiction and Fantasy addict from Western Canada who dabbles in different genres. In addition to being a fiction lover, she is also a history and culture nerd with a focus on China, Taiwan, and Japan. When she's not writing, one can find her devouring other author's stories, marathoning various sci-fi and fantasy franchises, or appeasing her ancient cat's need for laptime.

Website: kgorman.ca

R.M. OLSON writes queer, feel-good space opera, featuring diverse casts, found families, and loads of action. R.M. has ridden the Trans Siberian railway, jumped off the highest bungee jump in the world, gone cage-diving with great white sharks, faced down a charging buffalo bull, and knows how to milk a goat. Currently they reside in Alberta, Canada with their four children, three cats, and a dog the size of a small bear. R.M. goes hiking and skiing more often than they probably have time for, eats more chocolate than is probably good for them, and reads more books than is probably prudent.

AUDREY SHARPE is a bestselling science fiction author who grew up believing in the Force and dreaming of becoming captain of the Enterprise. She's still working out the logistics of FTL travel and transporters but writing science fiction creates her own private holodeck. Her award-winning first novel, The Dark of Light, launched the Starhawke Universe, which has expanded to more than a dozen books, including two sci-fi romances. Her books feature strong female characters, swoonworthy aliens, and epic battles of good versus evil. When she's not off exploring the galaxy with Aurora and her crew, she lives in the Sonoran Desert, where she has an excellent view of the stars.

For more information about Audrey and the Starhawke Universe, visit her website and join the crew!

Website: audreysharpe.com

ANDREW SWEET explores the "why" of how societies work through the "what if" of science fiction—he loves science and possibility! He maintains a personal 5-year project on cellular automata that has evolved into a CLI and an "infinitely scalable" (hardware limited of course) CA platform as he continues his obsessive search for cellular automata that can perform simple math functions. Former lead guitarist for the grunge/punk band Permanent Ascent, Andrew has been involved in music as long as he's been writing. Now proud owner of a Takamine, Andrew has traded his rapid punk chops for chaotic jazz riffs. Finally, last but definitely not least, Andrew's reasons for living are his wife and two children in their home in Portland, OR.

Website: andrewsweet.net

HEATHER TEXLE is the award-winning author of the Reliance Sinclair science fiction series who finds inspiration in quirky, weird, and I-can't-believe-that's-true things. With a lifelong passion for learning, Heather is fascinated with the creativity and ingenuity of the human spirit. She also adores a good conspiracy theory.

After graduating college, Heather moved to Minnesota where she attained her law degree and continues to live with her husband and two cats, Mew and Spots. For more information about Heather and her work, sign up for her newsletter and receive a free *Reliance Sinclair* story on her website.

Website: heathertexle.com

TAMI VELDURA, Anna Morgan, London Kemaker, and S.T. Lynn are all pennames for one single writer who contains too many stories to count. Tami is an aro/ace, autistic, adhd, and nonbinary individual. Their pronouns are they/them.

Tami has been published in a number of places,

including Galaxy's Edge and Boundary Shock Quarterly; numerous anthologies by such lovely editors as Jamie Ferguson, Leah Cutter, and Lyn Worthen; and has indie published over 100 titles.

Website: tamiveldura.com

A. WEBSTER is a screenwriter, novelist and short story writer whose edgy and often satirical style strives to push audiences out of their comfort zones so they can connect with their deepest emotions. In addition to writing, she is a pharmacist and documentary filmmaker. She lives in Oregon with her husband, daughters, two cats and dog.

Instagram: @anaiswebmen

ABOUT THE EDITOR

Jessie Kwak has always lived in imaginary lands, from Arrakis and Ankh-Morpork to Earthsea, Tatooine, and now Portland, Oregon. As a writer, she sends readers on their own journeys to immersive worlds filled with fascinating characters, gunfights, explosions, and dinner parties. As an editor, she's trying to make Sci-Fi Crime a thing.

When she's not raving about her latest favorite sci-fi series to her friends, she can be found sewing, mountain biking, or out exploring new worlds both at home and abroad.

Learn more at jessiekwak.com.

(Author photo by Meghan Paddock Farrell.)

MORE SCI-FI SHENANIGANS

Thank you so much for reading!

If you enjoyed this anthology, please let others know by leaving a review or telling a friend. As a scrappy crew of authors, we depend on word of mouth to connect with new readers.

Looking for more great sci-fi crime reads?

Don't miss the stories in CROOKED V.1, CROOKED V.2., and CROOKED V.3

Head to jessiekwak.com/crooked